PAINLESS

STEEL DEMONS MC BOOK FOUR

CRYSTAL ASH

To the nurses and medical staff who risk their lives and mental health to save others.

You matter.

You're everything.

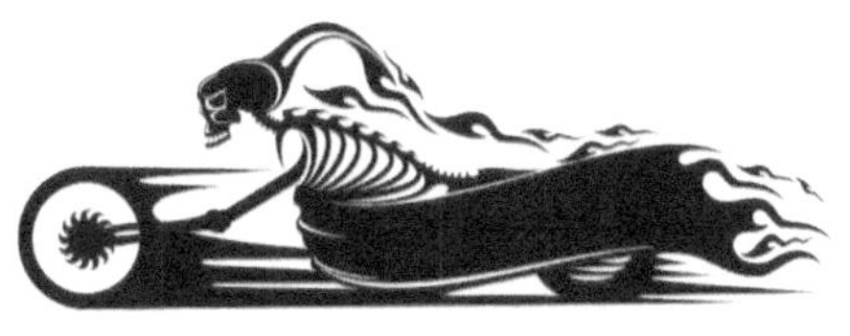

Prologue

SHADOW

SIX YEARS EARLIER

The woman flipped her skirt back down over her hips and stood from her kneeling position without a glance at me. She left my room, closing the door behind her, before I even discarded the condom.

Well, that was...fine. I guess.

I took my time cleaning myself off and re-fastened my pants. My fingers trembled slightly, either from needing a drink or nerves at what just happened, I wasn't sure.

The heat and numbness of alcohol called to me, more alluring than any woman. I didn't have any left in my room, so I'd have to go out to the dining area of this service center. Where more women walked around, serving food and drinks.

That wasn't so bad anymore, as long as they came and went quickly. But Jandro would be out there too. After how much he begged, goaded, and pleaded for me to do this, my biggest fear right then was his inability to keep his mouth shut.

I steeled myself with a breath in front of my door. With any luck, he'd be too drunk to remember, or preoccupied with his own woman for the night. I was fine with either option, as long as he didn't draw attention to me.

After a few more breaths, I left my room and squeezed down a staircase that was much too small for someone of my size. At least I remembered to duck under the beams this time.

"Yoooo, there he is!"

Fuck. No luck for me tonight.

I glowered all the way across the dining room, but it did nothing to deter Jandro's clapping and hollering. As I got closer, I noticed the six empty beer pitchers on his table, his flushed complexion, and how he was nearly sliding off the picnic bench seat.

"Are you done?" I grunted, grabbing his cut to pull him upright before he slid down to the floor.

"Bro, I'm jus' gettin' started." He leaned over the table, propped up on his forearms as he smiled woozily at me. "So how was it?"

"Can I get you anything, sir?"

The feminine voice sent my fists and jaw clenching. I stared hard at the table surface as I forced myself to breathe normally. My eyes lifted to Jandro's in a silent plea. His mouth tightened and he gave a small shake of his head.

Fuck. He was making me do this myself today.

"...Sir?"

"Whiskey," I ground out. "Your largest bottle. The whole thing."

She gathered up the empty beer pitchers and headed off without another word. I unclenched my hands while Jandro shot me a disappointed look.

"It won't kill you to say please," he lectured. "And to look at a server when they're talking to you."

"I forgot."

"Well, start remembering. I'm gettin' a little tired of reminding a grown-ass man to have manners."

The server flew by our table with another beer pitcher for Jandro and a handle of Jack Daniels for me.

"Thanks," I forced myself to mutter, but she was already several feet away tending to other tables.

"Doesn't count if they don't hear you." Jandro brought the beer to his lips with two hands.

"You know this doesn't come naturally to me," I told him, after taking a deep swallow from the bottle.

"It won't come at all if you don't practice. I'm not even asking you to say full sentences. But as my *tia* used to say, please and thank you is something every human being should know." He set the pitcher down and the giddy smile returned. "Now *please* tell me you were more successful at losing your virginity than speaking words."

I sighed before taking another deep drink. And I almost thought he'd be distracted enough to forget it. "It happened. So I guess it was successful."

"Did you come?"

"Yes."

"Did she?"

"I don't know."

"My man," Jandro shook his head, "You would know if she did. That's okay, though. Not everyone hits a home run their first time. Did you do what I told you?"

"No."

"No?" His jaw dropped, eyes narrowing at me. "Why the hell not?"

"I didn't really have the opportunity."

"You were alone with a naked woman in your room. Her *job* is to fuck. How is that not an opportunity? It's a two-way street, man, you gotta make it good for her, too. The clit is the center of a woman's pleasure, you can't just--"

"She made it pretty clear she didn't want me to touch her aside from...what was necessary."

"Did you at least kiss her some? Play with her nipples, maybe?"

"No and no."

"Shadow," Jandro groaned, lowering his forehead to the table. "You're killing me, dude."

"This was your idea," I reminded him. "The whole sex thing has never mattered to me."

"Because you don't know what you're missing!"

I shrugged with a grunt, then took another long drink to a memory I would be all too happy to erase. The small, hesitant knock at my door. The curious glance at my face before jerking away with a soft gasp. Then the petite, red-haired woman climbed on all fours onto the bed, facing the wall. She pulled her underwear down, her dress up, and waited. Waited for me to take what she'd been paid for, and nothing else.

After Jandro and I left the prison, I started to figure

out that most women weren't capable, nor had any motivation to treat me in the same manner as I'd been raised. Even so, women in general made me uncomfortable. Frightened women made me scared of myself.

I was capable of awful things. I killed men that rivaled my own size without breaking a sweat. But my brain was convinced the true enemies were half my size, coming at me with sharp blades, and taking joy in making my blood spill on the floor.

None of these women here wanted to hurt me, but my basic instincts seemed to keep missing the message. I'd never been able to fight back before. Now, every time someone came near me, I felt the need to defend myself.

What if I fucked up? What would happen if I was too rough with a woman much smaller than me? I used to fantasize about making my torturers suffer. Now I was afraid to find out what my strength was capable of.

I had seen the terror in women's eyes, the way they screamed and tried to flee as men began to violate them —before a Steel Demon put a bullet through their attackers' heads. The women out here avoided my eyes and made themselves smaller, as though hoping I wouldn't see them. It didn't take a genius to figure out that they expected me to hurt them in the exact same way other men did.

I should have just locked my door and jerked off.

"Bro, listen." Jandro flattened his palms on the table. "I hope this doesn't sound weird coming from me, but you're not a bad-lookin' dude."

"What?" I snarled at him, but it had little bite. The whiskey was finally making its way into my system, lulling me into delicious numbness. However, that didn't make his statement any less confusing.

"Every woman in this service center has checked you out at least once. But once they're in your line of sight, they scatter like mice."

"Because of my face," I told him. "Because of all this." I ran a hand up my forearm to indicate the extensive scarring under my sleeve.

"Nah, man. That ain't it." At least the loudmouth VP was talking quieter now. "It's because you look at everything as a threat. Like you've already fantasized about the most efficient way to kill something, and are just waiting for the chance to do it."

"That's not *always* true."

"I know, dude, because I know you. But that's the vibe you give off to people who *don't* know you. No one wants to get in your way because they want to keep their heads attached to their necks."

"Okay. So what do I do?"

"Well." Jandro rubbed the five o'clock shadow on his jaw, a side-effect from three straight days of riding. "You can carry on as you are and just not give a fuck. It might hurt you in the long-run, though. *Or* you can work to start changing how you come across to people. That would entail letting your guard down around women a bit. Pushing yourself out of your comfort zone, little by little, until you're comfortable with human interaction. Then, you never know. You might meet someone special."

I killed the bottle of Jack while listening to him, too

embedded in my alcohol-soaked bubble to really consider his advice.

"I've never cared about, or needed, human interaction," I grumbled out with a shake of my head. "I just don't see the point."

"It probably didn't matter while you were some cunty bitches' endless blood sacrifice, but it does now," he insisted. "You're a person, dude. We're social animals. Not only that, you're part of an MC, the MC that brings true justice when the world has given up. I'm sorry, but you're gonna have to interact with people in ways that don't involve killing." He began gesticulating wildly with his hands. "And the longer you go without some kind of...affectionate human contact, the harder it'll be to connect with others."

Before I could retort, Daren stumbled out of the hallway into the dining room. His shirt was unbuttoned, and he was trying to get his pants zipped up as he walked.

"Hey guys, turn the radio on!" he yelled. "Something big is going down in DC. There's a journalist reporting it right now."

A half-dressed blonde woman followed Daren out from the hallway. She jumped on his back, giggling and kissing his neck as she wrapped her legs around his waist. Yeah, women definitely didn't respond to me that way.

"What station, *burro*?" Jandro was already fiddling with knobs on the radio at our table.

"Don't matter. It's on all the stations."

"That can't be good," Jandro muttered as he settled on a frequency.

A quietness settled over the dining room as static from the speakers filled the air. Even the servers paused in their work to listen.

Only indistinguishable mumbling came through for the first minute, like people were having a conversation just out of range of the microphone. Then a voice charged with emotion addressed everyone listening, which, at this point, was probably the whole country.

"My fellow Americans, this is Emery Jones reporting with Freedom of Speech News," the reporter paused, their voice already cracking. "I've received multiple reports, and gotten eyewitness confirmation that...that..."

A long pause followed. Everyone in the dining room seemed to be holding their breath.

"Washington D.C. has fallen," the reporter finally continued in a harrowed tone. "All nine Supreme Court justices have been assassinated, gunned down right in...in the building. The Senate has been barricaded, with at least forty senators inside. They've set fire to the building and rescue teams are being blocked from getting in. A mob has...has stormed the White House and is vandalizing the building as we speak. We don't know if all these incidents were coordinated attacks. There's still been no word on the president, since he fled the country two weeks ago..."

The journalist continued reporting on the carnage all around them in a flat, emotionless voice, clearly in shock. Some of the servers began to cry. The rest of us just listened, in various stages of shock ourselves.

No one, however, looked surprised. I didn't care for politics, having been isolated most of my life, and even I knew this tension had been brewing for years.

"I don't know how we'll come back from this," the reporter went on, now sounding like they were trying not to cry. "The United States as we know it has… collapsed."

ONE

MARIPOSA

PRESENT DAY

"Your rodent is trying to kill me again."

"Freyja is not a rodent, *Rory!*" I scooped up the kitten who, in that moment, had just started vigorously grooming Reaper's stubble with her tongue. "She'll be hunting rodents soon, won't you, little girl?"

My black kitten squeaked out a meow followed by an enthusiastic purr. I laughed at my…companion? Familiar? There was no word to describe my bond with this animal.

"She's a rodent compared to Hades," Reaper chuckled, folding his hands behind his head. "And I don't understand why she curls up over my mouth and nose, if not to suffocate me."

"Probably because your breath is warm." I placed Freyja on the mattress and tickled her belly, earning needle-like teeth in my finger for my endeavors. "Or she likes how you smell, as much as I do."

Hades jumped up right then, placing his paws carefully on either side of the kitten as he bent down to sniff her. I realized Freyja's head wasn't much bigger than his nose as she batted at him with her tiny paws.

"You're goin' soft on me, Hades," Reaper groaned as the Doberman licked and nuzzled the kitten amidst her fierce assault on his nose.

Freyja zoomed across the mattress and down to the floor. Hades chased her while still taking care where he placed his paws and teeth. With them no longer smothering either of us, I scooted closer to lay my head on Reaper's chest. His arm slid around my back as he brushed a kiss across my forehead.

"Has she said anything to you yet?" he murmured, lips moving on my forehead.

"No, nothing." I drummed my fingers on his ribs in contemplation. "Maybe she's too young? When did Hades start talking to you?"

"About six months after I found him. I don't know if it has to do with age, or because that was the first time I had to kill someone after finding him."

Their lives are yours to take. Reap what has been sown.

Those words echoed like a drum in my head ever since the Steel Demons came to my and Gunner's rescue from skin traffickers, two weeks ago. Reaper had hinted about it before, but told me the full extent after we all made it back home.

Ever since he found Hades as a puppy, that voice told him who to kill or not kill. It could only come from the dog, who had bonded deeply with Reaper, and was clearly more intelligent than any normal animal. Reaper was certain that only he could hear the voice of Hades, until I confessed that he had spoken to me too.

He came to me in the rough, hazy form of a man and told me who he was. I wrote it off as a dream, until I saw that same vision while Hades the dog tore through the ankles of those holding Gunner and I captive.

Interestingly, Reaper never had any dreams or other interpretations of Hades, other than hearing his voice.

Gunner had a bond with his falcon, Horus, though theirs seemed entirely different. Gunner could see through Horus, as though he were in the falcon's body. But he never mentioned hearing voices or seeing him in another form either.

And now I had Freyja. Some kind of invisible pull brought me to the junk pile in Jandro's backyard where she had been stuck. Getting her out felt infinitely more important than just rescuing a kitten. I felt like I would lose a limb, part of myself, if I didn't rescue her. The only word that popped into my head was her name, and somehow I just knew she was meant to be with me.

As far as *what* she was or *why* I had to find her? That remained to be seen. But three of us in the SDMC now had these animals with strange, unique abilities. I had more questions than answers, and it made my head spin the more I thought about it. But I found comfort in knowing these creatures were here to help us, to guide us with their abilities and heightened intelligence. I just didn't know for what purpose.

Before finding myself with the Steel Demons, I would have driven myself insane looking for answers. As someone who owed their medical training to research and science, my little head would have exploded at the implication that something magical or paranormal was at play.

Strangely enough, it was using Reaper's approach that kept me from freaking out. He simply accepted that some things couldn't be explained. These animals had proved themselves to be trustworthy, protective of us in many cases. He wasn't going to pick apart theories and go hunting for answers when we lived in a time where survival was our number one priority. After Reaper and Gunner saved their animals, their own lives were saved in return. And that was all that mattered.

I could only wonder what the silly kitten flopping all over the floor would save me from one day.

Reaper and I watched them from bed like adoring parents for a few more minutes before I kissed his chest and reluctantly rolled away.

"I have to go to Tessa's," I said to his pouting expression.

"You just checked on her three days ago." He rolled toward me, pulling me back into his warmth.

"She's at least thirty-six weeks now. The baby's almost here." Briefly giving in to his hold, I peppered kisses underneath his jaw. "And she's stressed. She needs to be among friends. She and Big G are…kind of on the rocks, it seems."

"I know he's a dog," Reaper sighed into my hair. "She's a good woman. She deserves better."

I paused with my nose against his throat, the wheels turning in my head. Tessa seemed convinced that Reaper would never let her separate from Big G, that the club would see it as breaking up their family. But the Steel Demons president grew up in a matriarchal society, where women had multiple partners as a sign of devotion and trust from their men. Surely Reaper wouldn't force Tessa to stay in a situation where she was unhappy.

"What if Tessa and Big G had been part of your parents' community?" I asked him. "How would they handle a man's cheating?"

"Oh, he'd be kicked out within a week," Reaper grunted. "He's not the sharpest tool in the shed when it comes to social graces. They'd give him a few chances for making some remark, or being inappropriate with a taken woman, but he's too slow to adapt to such a different paradigm. He'd be gone long before he could actually stick his dick where it didn't belong."

"Hmm." I swirled a finger through the hair dusting his chest. If I brought it up *gently* to Tessa again and indicated Reaper did not approve of his behavior, she might be more receptive to moving out.

"That being said," Reaper continued. "The situation here is different."

"How so?"

"We're an MC, sugar, not a 'peace and love' hippie commune." He squeezed my waist. "I need men that can ride, fight, and follow orders. Unfortunately, that includes some men with unsavory habits when it comes to women."

"But that doesn't mean she has to stay *with* him, right?"

Reaper's eyes narrowed to slits. "What are you saying?"

"What if they both stayed in Sheol, but lived separately? He could be free to do whoever and she could find another man if she wanted."

"A divorce?" He propped his head up on his hand. "That's illegal," he said with a smirk that made it clear he was joking.

I dragged a finger down his abdomen, teasing at where the sheet covered him just below his waist. "Since when do you care about breaking the law?"

"Oh, I care *immensely*," he played along, breath hitching at my touch. "Do you know about the law of mandatory morning blowjobs?"

"Who came up with that bullshit?" I laughed.

"A very wise lawmaker." He pulled me back to him when I tried to roll away, tickling my sides until I was breathless.

"Really, though," I panted. "Did they get married before or after the Collapse?"

Divorce *was* made illegal in some jurisdictions before the Collapse. But afterward, because no recognized government bodies remained, marriages weren't legally binding. A couple couldn't get divorced if they weren't married in the first place.

"After," Reaper admitted. I knew he was following my logic. "I'll think about what you're saying, sugar, but I'm not sure separating them is the best option. You have to realize being with him protects her, too. No one here will hurt her, but if some of the guys see that she's free, they'll try what they can with her. It'll be harmless, but may be more trouble than she needs."

"That's true," I sighed. "Plus, there's no guarantee she'll actually want to leave him if it comes down to it."

He stroked a finger down my cheek before kissing me there. "If she or the boys were in danger, there would be no question of stepping in and getting them away from him. I mean that."

"I know you do." My palm cupped his handsome face. I never got tired of looking at him. "Thank you for telling me that."

A few more kisses and protests later, I finally rolled out of bed and started getting dressed. Freyja stopped playing with Hades and darted over to me to rub my ankles. Much like the other two animals with their humans, she followed me everywhere. Right after finding her, I tried locking her in the bedroom to no avail. Eventually I just gave up.

She was like a furry potato, with legs she could barely use, yet she still figured out how to turn doorknobs and squeeze through tiny gaps. No matter what, she wanted to be at my side. At first I could fit her in the pocket of my scrubs, but she was getting too big for them already. Balancing on my shoulders was a work in progress. She was daring and adventurous, but *damn* those little claws were sharp, and she was still getting the hang of balancing.

So, for the most part, she was happy to follow me down the street.

"What do you have going on today?" I asked Reaper as I pulled a brush through my hair.

"Besides admiring your ass from right here?" he

grinned. "The scouting team is coming back today. I hope we get some good fuckin' news."

"Has Gunner seen anything about the drone?"

"No," he bit out, his jaw working with annoyance. "Even with Horus's eyes, he hasn't seen a damn thing."

While most of the club was at the traveling market, Shadow and a skeleton crew stayed back to guard Sheol. Their day was far less eventful than ours, except for Shadow shooting down a drone with a camera that flew dangerously close to the club.

The drone had to be controlled from a relatively close location, so Reaper sent teams out to comb the surrounding desert in search of whoever sent it out. Gunner also used his ability to see through Horus to scout high cliffs, mountains, and any other places motorcycles couldn't reach. The fact that he didn't find anything after two weeks didn't bode well.

I leaned over the bed to kiss Reaper again for reassurance. "Your guys are the best. They'll find something. And if they don't, it means there wasn't anything to find."

"God, I hope you're right, sugar," he sighed. "I hate feeling like I've got Tash's fucking eyeballs looming over my home."

"I know." I kissed his forehead. "I also know what kind of president you are. You'll find who's out there and make them regret ever playing with stupid toy planes."

He laughed and leaned his forehead against mine. "Damn, I fuckin' love you." His voice grew low and growly. His hands reached for me, and I stopped them with mine.

"I love you too, but I really have to go." Our lips collided for one final *final* time. "I'll come back here tonight so you can tell me how it went."

"Bring Jandro with you." He finally released me and delivered a walloping smack on my ass. Freyja arched and hissed at the loud noise. "Oh, you calm down, rodent," he scolded her. "Your human likes it. You'll see."

"Hm, some times more than others," I muttered, rubbing the sting on my right cheek. "Okay, I'll see you tonight."

"Ah, sugar."

"Yeah?" I spun around in the doorway to find Reaper sitting at the edge of the bed.

He looked thoughtful. Maybe even nervous, as his gaze slid to the walk-in closet.

"Uh, nothing." He shot me a sheepish grin. "I'll tell you later. I hope everything goes well with Tessa."

I hesitated. "You sure?"

"Yes, woman. Get out of here before I drag you back to bed and tear into you like my last meal."

Freyja was already pawing at the door, so I took my leave and wondered what that was about as we headed out for the day.

MARIPOSA

It wasn't Tessa, Big G, or even one of their boys, who greeted me at their front door, but Noelle.

"You came at the perfect time," she muttered, pulling me in and closing the door just as Freyja slipped through. "And also the worst time."

"What do you mean?"

The answer came in the form of a child's scream echoing through the house, like the call of a banshee. Toys and laundry littered the floor, creating quite the obstacle course as I followed Noelle through the house.

We passed by the kitchen where Tessa's youngest son squirmed in his high chair, his face red as a tomato. He was the source of the banshee cries and I quickly saw why. An upside down cereal bowl was on the floor, milk spreading out into a puddle, and soggy frosted flakes turning to mush.

The toddler's anguish was exacerbated by his older brother, who sat on the counter as he tore open the cereal box to rain the rest of the contents down like confetti. Big G emerged from the next room and rushed over to lift his youngest out of the high chair.

"Aw man, you're all wet," he groaned, holding the boy out away from him. Just then he noticed Noelle and I heading up the stairs. "What the hell am I supposed to do about all this?"

"I dunno, be a fucking parent to your kids," Noelle snapped back, stomping her feet louder.

"Hahaha, she said *fuck!*" the oldest boy cackled from the counter.

I wanted to simultaneously disappear and rush down to help clean up. But there was no steering Noelle, who led me back to the master bedroom. Tessa sat there, propped up against the headboard with piles of pillows. And she was crying.

"Oh my God, Tess!" I ran to her, throwing my arms around her shoulders. "What's wrong?"

"It's nothing," she sniffed, lifting her red eyes to me and forcing a smile. "Just pregnancy hormones. I'll be fine."

"That's not all it is," Noelle muttered, handing her a tissue box.

"Something to do with the war zone downstairs?" I ventured a guess.

"Please, you guys. I don't want to get into it." Tessa wiped her eyes and sniffed. "I just needed a break. Five fucking minutes to myself and he acts like the house is gonna fall in on him without me there to do everything."

"Yeah, God forbid he actually step up and act like a

father," Noelle sneered. "My mom would have any one of my dads' balls if they didn't pull their weight."

"Nellie, please. I said not now."

I rubbed Tessa's arm. "You take as much time as you need. The three of them will live for the next few minutes."

Before she could reply, Tessa hissed in pain. Her hands flew to the lower side of her baby bump. "On top of everything else, I've been dealing with this little shit-kicker all day."

"He's been moving non-stop," Noelle added, with a tone of concern. "That's probably why you're so worn out lately."

"Moving is good," I said, pulling my stethoscope out of my case. "That means the baby's healthy. You ready for me, mama?"

Tessa nodded through winces of pain. "Do you think he'll come early if he's so active?"

"Not necessarily." I lifted her shirt and warmed the end of the stethoscope against my palm. "The other two were full-term, right?"

She nodded. "My oldest took almost 42 weeks, the little shit-head."

"It's normal for first births to be a bit late," I explained. "Now that your body is used to the process, your labor should be quicker, and this one's likely to come right on time."

"Big G's already begging me for another one," she groaned. "But I am fucking done."

"Fuck what that big man-child wants," Noelle growled.

"I'll get you on birth control right after this one arrives," I promised.

"He won't like that," Tessa frowned.

"Noelle's right, though." I moved the stethoscope over her belly in search of the little shit-kicker's heartbeat. "It's your body. He doesn't get a say."

"Thank you," Noelle huffed. "Finally someone is making sense."

I finally found the heartbeat, and frowned to myself. It seemed high.

"Is something wrong?" Tessa's eyes widened with worry.

"No, just…" I pulled the eartips out and let them hang around my neck. "He's in a weird position. I'm going to put some pressure on you, okay?"

The moment I pressed on her with my hands, I felt, and saw, the kicks and movements going on inside her.

"Oh fuck, here he goes again," Tessa moaned.

Noelle moved in to sit on her other side, rubbing her back. "Breathe, honey."

I gently pressed lower, down near Tessa's pubic bone, and felt the unmistakable shape of a foot. It was just as I feared.

"Tess." I tried not to sound grave. "The baby is in a breech position. His feet are down here and his head's up in your ribs."

"That's not good, is it?" She flinched at another kick.

"It's not ideal," I said carefully. "Breech deliveries are a bit riskier, but they can still be done. I think we should try to turn him around before you're due, to be safest."

"He's moving so much, though," she groaned, pressing a hand to her side.

"I know. It's possible he'll get into the right position on his own. Or if we are able to turn him, he'll flip right back around to a breech position."

"Stubborn ass." Noelle rubbed Tess's belly affectionately. "Why you gotta make it so hard for your mama, huh?"

"I say we give it another week." I placed the stethoscope eartips back in my ears and took out my blood pressure cuff. "If he doesn't flip back around, we'll start trying to turn him."

Tessa eyed me hard. "And if that doesn't work?"

"Then he's coming into the world feet first." I patted the hand on her side before wrapping my cuff around her bicep. "You've had a healthy pregnancy, so I'm not too concerned. I won't let anything happen to you, mama."

"Ugh, I want a fucking drink so bad," Tessa groaned. "Just a shot so this kid can mellow the fuck down."

Freyja jumped up right then and walked over the mattress toward Tessa. The black kitten sniffed at her swollen belly before rubbing her head against one of the feet pressing on her lower abdomen.

Tessa chuckled. "Well, aren't you a nice kitty."

"Aren't black cats supposed to be bad luck?" Noelle joked.

"I hope this one's not," I murmured, watching the

blood pressure dial. "She's been my little shadow ever since I found her."

Tessa sighed, this time in relaxation as I finished taking her blood pressure and started putting my supplies away. Freyja purred up a storm as she rubbed her face and side against Tessa's belly.

"Well, your little kitty seems to have calmed the kid down finally," Tessa breathed. "Even my fucking cramps are hurting less. I'd call that a good luck charm."

"Good girl, Freyja." I scratched the kitten's ears and got a headbutt in return. "I wish I had a treat to give you."

The black cat stared at me, her green eyes holding an uncanny amount of wisdom. It almost felt humbling, and I knew I just got the first taste of what this animal was capable of.

"Did you train her to do that?" Noelle reached over to give some head scratches of her own.

"Nope." I stared at the little ball of fur, now grooming one of her front paws. "She did that all on her own."

THREE

MARIPOSA

The deep, thumping bass of rap music floated down the street as I headed toward Jandro's shop. Having lunch together became our routine and was one of the highlights of my day. I touched the butterfly pendant at my throat, smiling when I saw him stretched out on a creeper, doing some kind of repair under a motorcycle.

His knees were bent, jeans worn down thin, beat-up work boots on the concrete floor. The white undershirt tank tops he wore while working looked so hot on him, even as they got covered in dirt and grease throughout the day.

As I got closer, I heard him rapping along to the song playing on the boombox. The music was loud enough that he didn't hear me walk up. He didn't even notice me there until I stepped one leg over his torso and sat down to straddle him.

"I really hope that's you, *Mariposita*, or someone's about to get a socket wrench up his ass."

"Damn. I really hope it's me too, then."

I lifted my feet so he could roll the creeper out from under the bike. If I wasn't already laughing, his smile would have done it for me. Seeing my sexy grease monkey always lifted my mood.

"Hi, *bonita*." He lifted up to plant a kiss on me, careful to avoid touching me with his hands.

"Hi, *guapito*. You hungry?"

"Always," he purred, kissing me again, deeper. His hips shifted underneath me, lighting heat in my core like a match.

I smiled against his lips before opening up to let our tongues meld together like they did so well. I had sat on him on a whim just to be silly, but quickly realized I might've gotten more than I bargained for.

He kissed my nose sweetly when our erotic tongue-fucking ended. "Let me up so I can wash my hands."

"Hmm." I ground into his lap instead, finding his bulge with the space between my legs. "I like you right here, actually."

"Mari," he groaned. "You can't complain about getting dirty when that mind of yours is so filthy."

"I think it'd be fun," I teased, tugging down the front of his tank top. "You can't get my scrubs all greasy, but I can touch you anywhere I want."

"Reaper!" Jandro yelled in mock despair, tossing his head back. "Help me, we've created a monster."

I kissed his throat, laughing as I finally stood up. "You love that I can't get enough of you both."

"My dick hasn't fallen off yet, so yes, that remains

true." Grinning, he stood and headed off to the restroom to wash up.

I set up our lunch in the tiny kitchen, finding comfort in the small, domestic routine. Jandro kissed my cheek and thanked me for lunch when he returned, then flicked water droplets from his wet hands in my face. I aimed a punch at his bicep, but he batted my fist away and kissed me again. Ah, domestic bliss.

Freyja circled the small table as we ate. The humbling wisdom I'd seen in her eyes earlier was gone, replaced by eagerness to catch a piece of the steamed fish we had with our rice and beans today. In other words, she was just being a cat.

Gunner had recently set up a deal with a guy who stocked local ponds and lakes from a fish hatchery way up in the northern territories. It wasn't chicken or steak, but at least we had a regular source of protein and denser calories to eat.

"Reaper wants you over tonight," I told Jandro, once we stopped messing with each other. "Doesn't sound like he's expecting good news from the scouting team."

"He's always expecting the worst," Jandro said dismissively. "The way I see it, the first drone was destroyed and we haven't seen any more flying overhead. Tash, or whoever it was, tried something and it didn't work. That in itself is good for us."

"Makes sense. I just hope you can make Reaper see it that way."

"I try, but you know how he is." Jandro shrugged. "He sees it as his personal responsibility to expect the worst and prepare for it. After what happened to his mom's community, he's not even willing to risk cautious optimism. To him, it's the same as letting your guard down. And that's not something he's ever willing to do when it comes to protecting his people." He nudged my shoulder playfully. "Until you came along, he never let his guard down at all. Now he's only crotchety when it comes to running the club, and that's a huge improvement."

I smiled at him. "I do love seeing both of you happy. Like actually happy, and not just celebrating being alive for another day. It makes me hopeful for the future."

"I feel the same way, *Mariposita*." He leaned in for a kiss, but I pulled back, making a face at him because he'd just taken a big bite of fish.

We finished lunch with more lighthearted banter, then he made a big show of sticking a piece of gum in his mouth while I cleaned up the table.

"I'll see you tonight," I said, finally tilting my head up for a kiss. "Have a good da—"

"Oh no, *diablita*." Jandro grabbed my hips with a devilish grin and pulled me flush against him. "You don't get to sit on me and tease me like that without answering for it."

"I have patients waiting." But none of them were emergencies and I wasn't really concerned. My core ignited, like embers roaring to a flame from the perfect gust of wind. Only it was Jandro's hands on me that ignited the fire.

"Let them wait." He guided me backward until the freshly-cleaned table hit the back of my thighs. With an effortless lift, Jandro sat me on the table top and nudged his way between my legs. "You belong to both members of Steel Demons leadership. No one's gonna raise a stink if you're five minutes late."

"Five minutes? That's all you got in you?" I teased.

"Just warming you up for tonight," he groaned, taking a nibble at the edge of my jaw. "And the prospects are coming back from their lunch soon," he added apologetically. "So as much as I'd like to take my time with you on this table, I probably shouldn't."

"Hmm, I'll accept that." My teeth grazed his earlobe, earning another hot groan from him. "For now."

He stepped away, only to slide my pants and underwear down my legs. When he returned, his hand came between us, caressing me into an aching, hollow need for him.

"Fuck, I wish I could eat you for dessert," he moaned, slicking his fingers through my folds.

"Tonight," I reminded him, as I unclasped his jeans and freed his hot, heavy length from his boxers. I barely had time to stroke him before he nudged against my entrance.

"Why does tonight have to be like, *six* hours away?" he said in a choked whisper as he pressed in, his thumb still on my clit as his length slowly disappeared inside me.

"Because *you* decided you wanted me at lunch time." I locked my ankles behind his back, drawing him in, with my thighs glued to his hips.

"*You* snuck up on me and trapped me under that bike," he argued back, now fully sheathed inside me.

"Caught me in a vulnerable position…coulda had your way with me and I wouldn't have been able to escape."

His breaths grew ragged as he rocked in and out of me, filling me up so deliciously, before leaving me empty and wanting more. He held me secure on the table with one strong hand on my waist, the other still working my clit into a rapid build up of sparks that lit up my whole body.

"Maybe I really will trap you under there one day," I panted, my fingers digging into the back of his broad shoulders. "When you least expect it."

"Baby, I'm going to be dreaming about it every day until it happens." His hips crashed against my thighs. "Trapped under a bike and in the best pussy I ever had. My two favorite places."

"Wouldn't that be a dream come true?" My laughter choked off as I felt him swell inside me, hitting spots that made me see stars.

"You know it," he grunted through gritted teeth, fighting to hold himself back.

"I'm right there," I whimpered, my body so tightly coiled on the edge of release. "Come with me, Jandro."

"Fuck, Mari…"

He held me so tightly as he climaxed, like I would break apart. I did, milking and draining all of him into me, but the love of this man kept me whole.

"Fuck…Damn." He shuddered as another convulsion of my orgasm squeezed around him. "You feel too good to be real." His forehead leaned against mine, eyes hooded and sated. "Sometimes I can't believe you're really mine. I love you, Mari."

"*Te amo, Alejandro,*" I murmured over the heavy thud of my pulse in my ears, running a finger over his gorgeous jaw.

My skin still buzzed with pleasure even as we separated and got dressed. I just got my pants back on as Larkan and Stephan's voices floated through the garage.

"You still eatin', boss?" Stephan poked his head into the kitchen.

"Nah." Jandro grinned as he hooked an arm around my waist and pulled me to him, pressing a slow, open kiss to the side of my face. "We're all done. For now."

FOUR

REAPER

I almost did it. I was close. But I wasn't ready yet.

Quit kidding yourself, Rory. You chickened the fuck out.

The conversation in my head on the way to the clubhouse was an odd mix of tearing into myself for being a little bitch and psyching myself up for my next chance.

I almost gave Mari the ring this morning. Seeing Jandro's butterfly pendant around her neck reminded me of it every time. He was coming over tonight, so I couldn't do it then. I wanted the moment private, between just us.

I couldn't pinpoint why I was taking so fucking long to give it to her. I had the thing made at the market two weeks ago. Sure, scouting around for whoever was spying on us kept me busy, but that was just an excuse. I knew she'd probably like it, even love it. Not just the ring itself, but what it symbolized.

Years before the Collapse, men gave rings to their women as a sign of commitment. A symbol of his devotion to her, his willingness to stay by her side through thick and thin. An engagement, it was called. And it was not something taken lightly. Along with offering the ring, the man would ask for marriage—the same commitment from his woman in return. By the time a relationship reached that point, a 'yes' was usually expected. But there was always a chance she could say no.

Marriage didn't exist anymore, not in the legal sense. But people still held ceremonies and gave each other tokens of commitment. Mariposa was already mine in body, heart, and soul. The chances were low, maybe even non-existent, that she'd refuse my ring.

But that tiny, minuscule chance that she could, was enough to hold me back.

"President."

The mumbled greetings of my men drew me out of my own head, for the time being, and back to the matter at hand.

"By all means." I dropped into my chair at the head of the table, Hades sitting at my right side. "Don't leave me in suspense."

"Horus saw footprints and evidence of a campfire in a little valley in this mountain range." Gunner unfolded a map on the table and pointed at a spot roughly three miles away. "However, we can't scale that elevation on our current rides. The terrain is far too steep and wild, even for dirt bikes. We need Jeeps, ATVs, or some shit, to get up there. I'm willing to buy them if you think it's necessary, but those kinds of vehicles are costly."

"Anything else?" I looked up, Gunner and Horus both meeting my gaze. It didn't matter that Horus was a bird, those eyes with binocular vision were unsettling.

"No other signs of people in the area for twenty miles in every direction, boss."

I steepled my fingers in front of me, taking in this information.

"Everyone out." I swept my arm over the table. "Except Gunner."

He wasted no time in elaborating the moment the door closed. Most people assumed Gunner trained his falcon. They didn't all need to know he literally *saw* through Horus. I needed to hear him speak freely, without anyone getting weirded out at how he was able to know these things.

"The campfire was old, just a circle of rocks with barely any ash left," he explained. "It could have been set up and abandoned that same day Shadow shot down the drone."

"And there's literally nothing else?" I repeated, not wanting to believe it.

He shook his head. "The footprints disappeared halfway down the mountain. Too much time has passed with all the wind and sand around here. Honestly, I saw all there was to see. It's not worth getting off-road vehicles just for this, in my opinion."

"No tire tracks? No personal belongings left at the campsite?"

"Reaper," Gunner sighed. "You know I'm nothing, if not thorough. There was nothing there."

"So what the fuck am I supposed to do now?" I brought a fist down on the table. "We never should have gone to that stupid fucking market, least of all because of what happened to you and Mari."

"A little too late for that now, Pres." Gunner stood from his seat and leaned against the table. "I'm working on building up our arsenal. We're decently armed now, but I'm making sure we build up to where we were when we were supplying Tash. I'm also keeping double guards posted on the perimeter. If some asshole so much as throws a rock at us, we'll know."

"I'm tired of fucking sitting around and waiting for him to come to us." My fists closed, causing my fingernails to bite into my palms. "I want to hit him where it hurts. Sitting around and getting too comfortable was how he was able to infiltrate us in the first place."

"We need intel and allies for that," he reminded me. "I'm working on that aspect too." He reached up to stroke one of Horus's wings. "It's just hard to know who we can trust."

Hades stuck his nose in my lap and licked my arm. I unclenched one fist to pet him, the rage already simmering down to a manageable level—for now. I just hated feeling like I always had to look over my shoulder, and expect to see Tash's smug grin looking back. This whole drone thing was even making me lose sleep.

"Anything else?" I sighed, eager for my woman, a fat cigar, and three fingers of whiskey, in that order.

"Uh, yeah. Kinda." Gunner suddenly looked nervous. "Nothing to do with this, though."

I peered at him curiously. "What, then?"

"I was thinking of taking Mari out to the coast. Since you showed her where you're from and all, I just..." He trailed off, lifting one shoulder into a shrug.

"I kinda wanted to do the same. Spend some time with her, get to know her a little better."

"You mean you're not fucking done testing the waters before diving in?" I demanded. "Fuck me with a rattlesnake, Gun. When are you gonna quit jerking her around and make up your mind?"

"I'm not jerking her around, I'm just going about it slow. Look, I take this shit seriously, alright?"

"What, like you think I don't?" I shot back. "Like Jandro doesn't? We knew what we wanted, so we went all in. You're the one acting like she's a side piece you can just drop and pick up when it suits you."

Now his fist came down on the table, and it made me glad to see. If he didn't care about her, he would have no reaction.

"That's not what she is to me," he hissed. "I *do* want her, just sharing her with you two kinda squicks me out, that's all."

"Then you don't want her. Not enough, anyway. Now tell her, so she can get the fuck over you."

"No, dude. Come on, I—" He brought a hand to his forehead with a sigh, then scrubbed his palm down his face. "I just want to be sure. I want to make absolutely sure this is the right choice, okay? None of us have known her for that long, if you think about it."

"The length of time doesn't matter," I argued. "We could die tomorrow, you know that. It's why Jandro and I love her so hard. If one of Tash's scouts picks you off with a sniper rifle tomorrow, are you going to feel good about *taking it slow?* Will you have lived without regrets? If you can look me in the eye and tell me *honestly* the answer is yes, then I'll never give you shit about this again."

He couldn't, as I expected.

"I just wanted your blessing to take her out for a day," he muttered, shoving his hands in his cut. "Guess the answer's no."

"My *blessing?* What am I, her father?" I scoffed. "She's my woman, but I'm not her keeper. You want to take her somewhere, you're asking the wrong person."

A tiny light bulb seemed to go off in his head as he shot me a skeptical glance. "Yeah?"

"Yeah, Gun. It's not all that complicated. If she tells you to fuck off, I trust you'll honor that answer."

He nodded to himself, the wheels turning in his blonde head. "Okay. Well, if that's all, president—"

"Look, if she says yes, the coast is romantic and all, but I need you here," I interrupted. "And we need to be pragmatic. Mari's getting her tattoo soon, but that's not always enough. She needs to learn how to defend herself."

He glanced at me, the question lighting up his eyes. "And you want me to…?"

"You're the best person for the job. I want her to learn weapons and hand-to-hand combat." I humored him with a smirk. "And if things don't develop between you two then, well, I got no hope for you."

FIVE

MARIPOSA

"How'd it go?" I asked Reaper, as he and Hades came through the door.

"They found a whole lotta nothin'," he grumbled, shrugging off his cut to drape it on the back of a chair. "Just as I thought."

"Which isn't a bad thing," Jandro piped up from his spot on the couch beside me. "Like I told you, it means whoever wanted to fuck with us is miles away from here."

Reaper muttered something unintelligible as he rummaged through the kitchen. "You want wine, sugar?"

"Yes, please!"

I stretched my legs out on the couch, so my feet would have their place in his lap while Jandro's chest made a nice pillow for my head.

Hades stood in the center of the room, looking torn. Jandro and I took up the length of the couch, while

Freyja's tiny black form was curled up in the center of his massive dog bed next to the fireplace.

"What a sucker," Jandro chuckled. "Just pick her up and move her, Hades."

"He got a nose full of claws last time he did that." Reaper returned from the kitchen and held my glass out to me. "The little rodent just walks all over him."

"Who does that remind you of?" Jandro poked me in the ribs as Reaper lifted my legs to take his spot on the couch.

"I do *not* walk all over you two!"

"Not in the bedroom, you don't." Reaper brought my feet into his lap, his hands sweeping over my ankles and calves in a way that turned me to jelly. "But we're yours, sugar. Utterly and completely. I hope you know that."

"I dunno," I joked, despite his words turning me to mush. "Rub my arches a little more and maybe you'll convince me."

He proceeded to lift my foot and close his teeth around my big toe, making me shriek and kick like a madwoman. The two of them found it totally hilarious. I barely noticed Jandro taking my wine so I wouldn't spill it.

By the time we settled down, Hades took up the love seat across from us. Reaper usually didn't want him on the furniture, but I noticed him growing more relaxed with his dog in recent weeks.

"Oh, Dallas said that Andrea finished the prospect's cut," Reaper said over me to Jandro, his hands now back to treating my feet properly. "We're all set for tomorrow."

"Good." I could hear the grin in the VP's voice. "I can't fucking wait to see what he thinks of his road name."

I tilted my head back on his chest to look up at him. "You didn't let him pick his own name?"

"All his ideas sucked." Jandro dropped a kiss on my forehead. "The one I picked for him is perfect."

"Can I have a hint?"

He caressed my jaw, grinning down at me. "Nope."

I pouted and he kissed my lower lip.

"He ain't sayin' shit. Not even I know what it is." Reaper's massage moved up to my calves and shins.

I slid down Jandro's torso, snuggling under his arm. "I'm just proud of Stephan, honestly." I refused to call him *prospect*. "After all you've put him through, he deserves some respect and recognition."

"He's a good kid," Reaper agreed. "Smart, and loyal down to his bones. He'll make a fine Demon."

Jandro's arm squeezed around my waist. "You're gonna be part of the ceremony, you know."

"Me? Why?"

"You're the president's old lady," Reaper grinned. "You're just gonna put the cut on him when I say to. Not much more to it than that."

"Then we're gonna fuckin' party!" Jandro raised a fist in the air. 'Cause fuck knows we all deserve one."

I rolled my eyes. "Like you guys ever need a reason to party."

———

STEPHAN'S PATCHING ceremony was held right after breakfast the next morning. Everyone gathered in front of the front gate where a crudely-assembled platform, similar to the one at Python's execution, was set up to provide a stage.

I stood off to the side where Stephan's cut draped over my arm. The Steel Demons skull grinned up at me from the back, freshly sewn on by Andrea, Dallas's wife. Jandro instructed me not to peek at the front, where Stephan's new road name was embroidered. I resisted, tempting as it was.

Reaper and Jandro stood on the rickety, wooden stage together, both trying to hide elated grins. They waited for everyone to gather and quiet down before Reaper addressed them.

"The Steel Demons recently lost a member," he began. "But we're about to gain one who is ten times the man Python was."

I stole a glance at Bones, who kept his eyes trained on the president with no change in expression. Reaper, and my guess, Hades, had determined Bones's innocence, and allowed him to stay in the club with no repercussions.

"Admittance into this club is *not* handed out lightly," Reaper continued. "We are demanding. We are harsh. We don't tolerate bullshit. And that's exactly why we've survived for this long, while other clubs have eaten dust."

A low murmur of agreements and nodding heads came back from the crowd.

"But once you've earned my trust and respect," he placed a hand over his heart, "Once you've proved your loyalty, the Demons will never turn their back on you. You become part of our family and we always take care of our own." His hand lowered again to his side. "Today we're making someone an official part of our family."

Reaper took a step back and allowed Jandro to step forward. "Stephan, come on up."

The young man, his face already pink from the warm morning sun, slid through the crowd to join his president and VP on the stage. Jandro directed him to face Reaper, who began asking him a series of questions.

"Stephan, do you swear to obey and uphold all laws of the Steel Demons MC, current and future?"

"I swear, president," the prospect answered solemnly.

"Will you obey orders from me, your VP, and any of your senior officers, to the fullest extent and without question?"

"I will, president."

The questions continued for another minute, before Reaper turned to me with a nod. I drew in a deep breath as I ascended the stage, my heart pounding with nerves and excitement for Stephan.

"Then with my full authority as president," Reaper said. "I declare you, from this day forward, a fully patched member of the SDMC." He nodded at me again, and I couldn't help but beam as I held out Stephan's cut.

The young man never looked so happy as he turned his back to me, arms extended behind him. I slid the leather over one arm and then the other before tugging it in place over his shoulders. He turned back to me as cheers and applause erupted from the club, his brothers, and I couldn't stop myself from planting a kiss on his cheek.

"Congratulations," I told him, a grin splitting my face.

"Thank you, Mari—ma'am." He turned beet red, much to the amusement of everyone watching.

I stepped back to stand at Reaper's side, while Jandro came up to throw an arm around Stephan's shoulders.

"Stephan the prospect is no more." Jandro slapped a hand on the young man's chest, right over his new name patch. "You're a Demon now, and your road name is Slick."

"Hm," Reaper mused quietly at my side.

"Before you all get any ideas," Jandro raised an index finger to the crowd, "like he's slick with the ladies or some shit, let me set the record straight. Here's how I came up with his name."

Stephan groaned and brought a palm to his face, but that just riled everyone up and earned an affectionate ruffling of his hair from Jandro.

"The first day this kid started working in my shop," Jandro declared. "I told him to hand me a tool that was in a box across the bay. This young fucker walks over there, gets it, but on his way back to me…" He could barely get the words out from trying so hard to contain his laughter. "This motherfucker…slips on an oil slick and eats shit!"

The laughter rippling through the crowd was contagious. Even Shadow appeared to crack a smile.

"Oh my God, that's awful." I covered my mouth to hold in my own giggles, but some escaped anyway.

"It's pretty fuckin' funny." Reaper chuckled, hooking an arm around my waist as he brushed a kiss along my forehead. "He's a good sport, though. And it fits him."

It was true. Stephan's joy was uncontrolled, like a kid on Christmas. Reaper and I stood watching him like proud parents, Jandro messing with him like a little brother. The happiness and feelings of celebration were intense now, but everyone seemed to understand it would be short-lived.

It dawned on me right then, why Reaper was so protective of his club, why the Steel Demons found every possible excuse to party and have a good time. This kind of life gave so few opportunities to laugh, smile, and feel good, so they took those moments and lived them to the fullest.

Especially with enemies still lurking.

SHADOW

F ive.

Five tries was how many it took before I worked up the nerve to actually step into Mariposa's office. The first time, I made it to the end of my street before the anxiety overtook me. The third time, I got inside the clubhouse door.

I had to. There was no more getting out of this. I had talked myself out of going to her office every day for the past two weeks. But this morning, I woke up on the floor with my face covered in blood from a cut on my head. My mattress had been flipped up and leaned against the wall. My ribs were fucking sore and I was tired of this. I needed some help.

Now on my fifth and final attempt, she looked up from the counter with surprise. Those greenish-brown eyes and her smile wiped my memory of what I was doing here.

"Shadow! I didn't expect to see you here. How are you today?"

"Fine," I mumbled, my heart feeling like it was going to crash out of my chest. "And you?"

"Good, thanks." She turned on her wheeled stool to face me. Her smile accentuated the apples of her cheeks, flushing a delicate pink. "What can I do for you?"

"I, uh..."

...fucking forgot what I was going to say. Again.

I wanted to slam my fist into my forehead at how stupid I was. Why was this so fucking hard for me? I even practiced what to say, which I was certain nobody else did. Just having a mundane fucking conversation came so naturally to everyone, except me.

"Did the sleep aids work for you?" Mariposa's eyes fell to the plastic orange pill bottle I'd started crushing in my fist.

Fucking idiot.

"Um, yes. Sorry about that." I placed the now-dented plastic container on the counter. "You said to come see you if they worked."

"Yes, I'm glad to hear they were successful." She paid no mind to the ruined bottle. "So would you like to continue taking them?"

"Yes, if you would, um, advise that."

"If they're helping you, then certainly." She flashed me another smile before turning to open a set of cabinets. "So, no nightmares, then?"

"No." An aching breath escaped my chest. I felt a bit less like an idiot when she wasn't looking at me. "None during the nights I took them."

She nodded, still examining the various medications in the cabinet. "How's the quality of your sleep? Are you sleeping solidly through the night, or are you waking up frequently?"

"Pretty solid through the night." Much like last time I was here, the anxiety began to subside as we talked more and I got used to her presence. "The last three nights I, um..."

She looked over at me and the tightness in my chest nearly choked off my breath. "Yes?"

I forced the words out through the fear gripping me. "I didn't drink before bed. I didn't use alcohol to pass out at all. I just...fell asleep naturally."

Her expression morphed into one that had never once been aimed at me.

"Shadow, that's great!" She moved toward me with her hands extended, and now the fear running through me was of her touching me.

"It is?" I stepped back to put more space between us.

Do not *let her touch you. Reaper and Jandro will never forgive you.*

"Yes!" She stopped abruptly, dropping her hands to her sides with a sheepish smile. "Sorry, I just got excited for you. The drinking concerns me, honestly. I wanted to tackle that as a separate issue when you were ready. But it looks like you're curbing it on your own, which is fantastic to hear."

"It concerns you?" I stared at her, bewildered. "Why?"

"Because at the rate you were going, it could kill you, Shadow."

"You're...*concerned* about me dying?"

"Of course I am!" She said it like she never considered an alternative. "I'm the club medic. I'm responsible for keeping all of the Steel Demons alive and healthy. Besides, who would I say good morning to if you died?"

"You can say good morning to anyone," I pointed out.

She smiled and my chest tightened again, but it didn't feel like anxiety this time.

"I like saying it to you, though."

Why?

The statement was so utterly confusing to me. She knew how much I struggled with the most basic interactions. What possible enjoyment could she get out of talking to *me*, of all people?

Before I could ask the question rattling around in my head, a small black blur zipped through the office door. It slid across the smooth tiled floor and crashed head first into the lower cabinets.

"Freyja!" Mariposa bent to pick the thing up and placed it on the countertop. "You crazy kitten."

It was indeed a small cat, covered in dense black fur with green eyes. The kitten didn't appear to be hurt, as it immediately bounced across the counter to where Mariposa was sorting medications.

"No, I don't need your fur getting into everything." She picked up the animal around the midsection and turned it to face the opposite direction. "Go bug Shadow while I do this."

"Um—"

Before I could protest, the animal flopped over its own legs and crashed into my hand resting on the counter.

"She's about twelve weeks old, by my estimate," Mari laughed. "Still working on her coordination."

"Is she like Hades and Horus?" I asked, watching the tiny, furry thing play with my hand. I didn't move a muscle, but she jumped over my palm, chewed on my fingers, and kicked at my hand with her back legs.

"I think so," Mariposa said in a quieter voice. "Her name came to me as soon as I found her in the scrap pile behind Jandro's shop. Before I even heard her meowing, I felt this pull to look and find her. Reaper knew exactly what it was." She looked up at me with a small smile, her face pinker than usual. "Sounds weird as hell, right?"

Nothing is as weird as me.

"Considering we have three of these animals now, I suppose it's not all that weird."

"Maybe not," she mused, watching the kitten continue to attack my hand. "You can pet her if you want."

Again, such a simple thing didn't occur to me. I curled a finger and allowed it to scratch over the kitten's head. Freyja's skull felt so fragile under the weight of my hand, I worried about hurting her.

But when I lifted my finger away, the kitten pressed up and headbutted it. She began rubbing her head against my knuckles so hard, she nearly fell over. A tiny rumbling sound came from her, like the smallest motorcycle engine. Confused, I looked up at Mariposa.

"What's that noise? Did I hurt her?"

"She's purring," the grinning medic answered. "It means she's happy."

"Why is she rubbing her head on me?"

"She likes you. She's marking you with her scent to claim you as hers." Mariposa laughed as the kitten flopped over on the counter, wrapping her tiny front paws around my finger as she continued to purr and rub her cheeks against my hand. "Scratch that. She's utterly in love with you."

"Huh." I extended a finger to run over the kitten's belly. "You're a funny little animal with strange taste in humans."

"So, for your sleep meds," Mari turned back to her array of pills after another minute of watching the kitten and me. "I'd like to put you on a two-week dose this time. Take one at night before bed, just like before. These do have a risk of dependency so if they stop becoming effective, or new symptoms come up, let me know, okay?"

"Okay. That sounds good." The kitten was distracting me so much, it was like I forgot to feel anxious. Was this what people meant by baby animals being "cute"?

I jerked my gaze back up to Mariposa, hoping I didn't offend her with my distracted response. "Thank you."

"You're welcome, Shadow." She tucked a strand of hair behind her ear, eyes darting around, looking everywhere but at me.

Fuck. She really was scared of me, no matter how much she tried not to treat me any differently. I pulled my hand away from the kitten, and turned to leave.

"I'll leave you to your work. Thank you again—"

"We should do this tattoo soon, right?" she asked the words in a jumbled rush. "The Steel Demons tattoo."

"Um, yes." I paused in the doorway, which Freyja took as an opportunity to scramble off of the counter and rub herself against my ankles. "If you are comfortable with me doing it. Reaper wanted you to have it done as soon as possible."

She nodded with a swallow, her nervous gaze continuing to bounce around the room. An ache squeezed my throat, all the way down to my stomach. It was probably for the best, but I felt some kind of internal discomfort with the confirmation that she didn't want me to touch her. At all.

I may not have known how to act around women, but I knew how to be a professional tattoo artist. When Jandro told me to just imagine her bare skin as a blank canvas, it helped. I did good work, and after some time to think about it, I felt confident I could work with her.

Plus, I wouldn't mind just seeing her and talking to her again. After a few minutes of conversation, she had a warm, calming effect on me that not even booze could replicate. She eased my nerves without numbing me. I could still feel, and while I wasn't used to feeling this way—whatever *this* was—she made me want to feel it often.

But the fear in her eyes hurt me, in a way I didn't even know was possible to experience pain.

"It doesn't have to be from me," I told her, ignoring the odd pain sensation. "I can recommend an artist in the next town over. He's probably booked out for months, though."

"No, Shadow." Her eyes refocused on me. "I want you to be the one doing it."

"Are you...sure?" I was so confused.

"Yeah, I'm just nervous," she laughed lightly. "It's my first tattoo. And it needs to be pretty big, from what I understand."

"Oh, right. The pain." I hadn't felt physical pain in so long, I had forgotten it was part of the tattooing process.

"Yeah." Her smile was nervous, but her gaze remained on me. "Just go easy on me in case I'm a total wuss, okay?"

"We can do it over multiple sessions if it becomes too much." I reached down to pick up Freyja, worried about trampling her. The kitten squirmed, her whole body fitting into the palm of my hand as I placed her back on the counter. She just ran back down to weave her little body between my boots again.

"Thanks, that makes me feel better." Mariposa laughed, watching the kitten's antics.

"You've taken good care of me in your field of expertise. I'll make sure to do the same."

Shit. Was that too much or okay to say? Fuck, how do I know? She's smiling, but looking away. What does that mean?

"That's sweet, Shadow. Thank you." Her voice grew soft, almost taking on the same breathy quality as when she was riding me.

Fuck! No, don't think about that. I was doing so well...

"I'll let you know what my schedule's like one of these days when I'm over with Jandro."

"Okay. Sure, yes. That sounds good."

"Hey, before you go." She pressed a cap down on a bottle of pills and held it out to me. "Don't forget these."

"Oh, right." Careful to step over Freyja and not on top of her, I crossed the room to take my medication from Mariposa. I forgot all about being careful not to touch her however, and her fingers brushed mine with a gentle heat. "Thank you."

"You're welcome, Shadow." She smiled with a small head tilt toward her shoulder. It made my chest squeeze with that odd, non-painful sensation again. "Are you coming to Stephan—I mean Slick's, patching-in party tonight?"

"Yes, I'll be tattooing him during the event."

"Great. I'll get to see you in action then."

Something about the words she used heated my body up a few degrees. "Yes," I agreed. "You'll see it's actually not a bad experience."

Truthfully, that depended on where Slick chose to have his tattoo done, but I wasn't about to spook her with those details.

"Sounds good." She gave a small wave, her eyes never wavering from me. "I'll see you there."

I suddenly didn't want to leave, but forced myself to turn toward the office door.

"See you then, Mariposa."

SEVEN

GUNNER

I broke the surface of the water, taking a deep breath as I slicked my hair back. The calm silence of being underwater shifted to the din of the party in full swing. Some EDM music from the mid-2000s played on an ancient set of speakers as people drank, laughed, and jumped into the pool.

In the background, I heard the buzz of Shadow's tattoo gun as he permanently sealed the Demon into Slick's body forever. It had been a good day, and I was never one to drag down a party, so I couldn't place why I preferred the quiet solitude of being underwater over celebrating with everyone else.

Maybe I just wasn't drunk enough yet.

Hoisting my upper body onto the pool deck, I fished a beer out of a nearby ice bucket, then slid back into the water as I opened it with my teeth.

I hadn't heard a peep from my uncle yet and that worried me. It had been weeks, nearly a month, since I hightailed it out of Colorado. Or Jerriton, rather.

General Tash was not one to sit around idly. If he was gonna make a move to fuck over Uncle Jerry, he would've done it by now.

Could the shifty general have actually given my uncle a part of his territory? Anything was possible, of course, but I could not wrap my head around that logic. Why steamroll entire towns all over the Southwest? Why snatch up territories so ruthlessly, only to give them up to your competitors? I couldn't see Tash doing it, not for any reason that would benefit him. For all the lies he told us, I knew for certain that he'd protect his own interests at all costs.

I took a long pull of my beer and set it down on the pool deck, releasing it to dunk my head back underwater. Too much noise, too much thinking. It was so much more peaceful under the surface.

I swam to the far edge and kicked off, cutting through the water with long strokes. Just before I hit the opposite wall, a pair of feet dipped into the water. Slender, feminine feet.

When I broke the surface to take a breath, Mari smiled at me from her perch on the pool's edge. Her navy-blue bikini hugged her beautiful form in ways I only wish I could.

You don't have to just wish, a small voice reminded me. It sounded like the devil whispering into my ear, urging me to give in to temptations, to partake of what would, surely, feel so good. The other voice, the one keeping me on the righteous path, had been oddly silent as of late.

"Hey, baby girl." I slicked my hair back and cleared the water from my nose. "Coming in?"

"That depends." She kicked her legs, making small splashes. "You gonna make sure I don't drown?"

"You don't need me for that," I laughed. "But is your cat gonna defy the rules of the animal kingdom and follow you in?"

A few feet away, Freyja leaned as far as she could over the edge without falling in. Green eyes dilated, her tiny black nose flexed as she sniffed the water. Then she gingerly extended one paw to bat at the wet, blue stuff.

"I have faith in her," Mari declared. "I don't think those two will let her drown anyway."

Hades reclined nearby at Reaper's side. The dog was relaxed, gnawing on a bone, but his eyes remained on his new furry sidekick. Horus was also close by, perched on the wrought-iron fence surrounding the pool. I didn't have to slip my consciousness into him to know he took note of every single one of the kitten's movements. Those talons would be ready to push off, wings ready to dive, if she ended up in the pool.

Immediately after Mari found her, the animals went into protective mode. They guarded and took to her like she was one of their own. Maybe their animal forms were all different species, but the three of us knew they were cut from the same cloth. We just didn't know what that cloth was made of.

I raised a hand from the water and hovered it over Freyja. The water droplets falling onto her may as well have been acid with how she hissed and ran back to Hades.

"You're so mean!" Mari cried, but she was laughing.

"Nah, *this* is mean."

I wrapped my arms around her bare waist in a hug, and dragged her into the water with me.

"Gunner!" she shrieked, but didn't fight me. "I wasn't ready!"

"Keep psyching yourself up and you'll never be ready," I grinned, loosening my hold on her. "At least I didn't jump in with you this time."

"Yeah, *so* considerate," she groaned. Her fingertips lingered on my abs and she made no move to pull them away.

"Aw, come on, your feet touch the bottom here. You're no damsel in distress." I pulled away from her to grab my beer. Her touch on me felt good. Too good.

A quietness settled between us. I took sips of my drink while she gradually lowered more of herself into the water, until only her face was uncovered.

"There you go," I encouraged her. "See, it's not all that scary."

"I think I'm more scared of getting my tattoo now than water," she admitted with a nervous laugh.

"Oh, no way. Drowning's a lot scarier. You can't die from a tattoo, not even a bad one."

"Unless the needle has Hepatitis," she retorted. "Or HIV. Or I get a bad bacterial infection—"

"I get Shadow disposable needles," I assured her. "And he is meticulous about keeping his area clean."

She lifted an eyebrow. "Really?" she said, and looked over her shoulder.

Slick was stretched out a table, Shadow bent over him and oblivious to his surroundings as he inked the Demon onto Slick's torso. A few people gathered around to watch and pour alcohol into Slick's mouth when he requested it.

"No one's got food around him," I pointed out. "And look, Shadow's wearing gloves, see?"

Mari's eyes narrowed but she didn't argue. "Does it have to be so…public?"

"I mean, if you want to throw a party in honor of *you* becoming official, no one's gonna say no. But if you want yours done privately, no one's gonna tell the president's old lady otherwise."

Her eyes lit up at the title and she gave a small smile. My heart squeezed in my chest. She really did love being his. Hell, she was a natural at the patching-in ceremony this morning. And I had to admit, Reaper and her looked good together. All three of them seemed to have an easy, natural dynamic. I was beginning to see it the more I looked. But trying to see where I fit in felt like sticking a square peg in a round hole. I adored Mari, and would've made her mine in a heartbeat if there had been no one else. But what could I possibly give her that she didn't already have from those two?

"Can I be honest with you about something?" She had drifted closer to me and asked the question in a hushed voice.

"Always, baby girl." Fuck, her eyes looked so pretty with the pool water reflecting in them.

"I don't want Reaper and Jandro there while I'm getting tattooed."

"Really?" I almost choked on my beer. "Why not?"

"You know how they are," she murmured. "If my finger even twitches like I'm in pain, Reaper will go all crazy over-protective. Jandro will keep trying to make me laugh to distract me, and that could mess up the tattoo."

"True enough," I agreed. "Want me to be there with you?"

The look on her face proved that was exactly what she hoped I would say.

"Could you, Gun? If you're not too busy? I feel like I can handle Shadow on my own, I'm just not sure how well *he'll* handle it."

"Consider it done," I grinned. "I'll make sure the whole thing is so painless, you'll end up taking a nap."

"Somehow I doubt that," she mused skeptically, but returned my grin. "Thank you, Gun. I—" Her lips slammed shut, a deep, rosy flush filling her skin.

"You what?" I prompted. "Tell me, or we're both going under." I snaked my non-beer hand around her waist in a tight hold. She knew I was kidding, though.

"When something scares me, I just—" her heart brushed against my chest, betraying its rapid beating. "I feel safer, calmer, whenever you're around." She tilted her face up to look at me, almost resting her head on my shoulder. "That's all."

She said it like it was a silly, childish confession, but it meant everything to me. Here it was, the place where I could fit. The calm in her storm, her anchor and her safety. As she leaned on me, looking so damn kissable and perfect and mine, I started to think that this really could work.

"I miss you," I confessed like a lovesick teenager. "It's been a hell of a couple of weeks since our time in that cave, but I swear I haven't been ignoring you, Mari."

"I know," she assured me, sliding an arm around my waist under the water. "Finding out who sent the drone took priority. I get it."

"You haven't been starved for attention, I'm sure." It was meant to be a joke, but the words slipped out coated in my insecurities and doubts. "Sorry. Fuck, I'm sorry."

All the smiles disappeared from her face. "I've missed you too, Gun. *You*, specifically. Yes, Reaper and Jandro are always there for me, and it feels nice. But that's what I'm trying to tell you with this tattoo thing— you're not all interchangeable to me. You're all people I care about, but the three of you drive me fucking crazy for different reasons too."

"You're totally right and that was a dick thing to say. I'm sorry, it's just—" I sucked in a tight breath. "Old habits, I guess. Which is no excuse, really. But it's like I'm trying to unlearn everything I was taught my whole life, you know?"

Her expression softened. "Yeah, I get it. Me too. Although I guess it's different for me, since I'm the one at the center of this whole thing. Sometimes it still hits me hard and I panic."

"About what?"

"About being fair to all of you. I have to keep two, potentially three, men happy while you all just have me. Once I start to relax, I get hit with this worry that someone might feel neglected or ignored. I don't want to hurt anyone like that, not ever."

"I never thought about it like that," I said, cocking

my head. "It is a pretty big responsibility to put on you, huh?"

"One I don't take lightly," she replied solemnly. Only after she said that did a light, blissful smile spread on her face. "But it's so worth it to me. I feel so loved, so cherished. Seeing how Reaper looks at me, how Jandro holds me—I feel like I'm made of sunlight and I just want to give that kind of love back to them, so they can feel it too."

I want that.

Those three words hovered on the tip of my tongue, but never left my mouth. I didn't just want that feeling she talked about, I wanted it from her, and her alone. I wanted to be a reason she smiled so big and glowed like a little ball of sunlight. Did it really matter that I wasn't the only one who made her feel like that? Was it really so bad that she had the capacity to love more than one man at a time?

I wanted to tell myself no, it didn't matter. But doing so felt like stepping off the edge of a cliff. It felt like putting my heart in a box without knowing if it would be thrown in a blender or looked after with care.

What the fuck did I even know what love was?

"I'm glad," was all I could tell her. "That they make you feel that way. You deserve nothing less, baby girl."

Mari's eyes seemed to search me, like she was trying to figure out what I really meant to say. "I wasn't trying to rub it in your face—"

"You weren't." I dropped a kiss to the top of her head, sliding an arm around her shoulders to hug her close. "I just kept turning it over in my head, trying to see it from all angles like I do with everything. You've cleared up a lot for me, really."

"I have?"

"Yeah." I held her close enough to feel her heart beat again. "Just seeing that look on your face, knowing for sure that they're good to you and make you feel like that... It's a big weight off my mind."

Warm fingertips slid up my back, making water trail down my skin.

"It doesn't mean I don't miss you, Gunner."

EIGHT

MARIPOSA

"I cannot believe this!" Jandro whined dramatically. "I'm getting kicked out of my own house."

"You were going to the shop anyway," I reminded him, watching Shadow wipe down a chair with bleach out of the corner of my eye.

"I was going to ditch and make the prospects do the work so I could watch you!"

"Prospect, singular," I reminded him. "Larkan is the only one now."

"Slick is still my little bitch," he grinned viciously, leaning into me.

"Stop." I tried in vain to dodge his attempts to tickle and kiss me. "This is why I didn't want you here! You'll make Shadow's work look like chicken scratch."

"You were one of my squirmiest clients," Shadow added. The large, quiet man seemed at ease as he set up his tattooing area. Every passing day in my company seemed to make him more and more comfortable with me. That moment in my office with Freyja seemed to break another one of the many barriers between us. He looked like he'd never pet a kitten before, and it was oddly wholesome to watch.

The kitten in question was curled up in Gunner's lap, who reclined on the couch with his feet on the coffee table. His long fingers dragged luxurious scratches over Freyja's head, if her halfway closed eyes were a sign of anything. On Gunner's shoulder, Horus kept staring at the cat, either protectively or like he wanted to eat her.

"That's 'cause it was my ribs, dude!" Jandro protested. "That shit hurts."

"You picked the placement. My job is the same no matter what spot you choose. So maybe think ahead next time."

My eyes bounced back and forth between the two of them. Watching them talk and banter like two normal friends was utterly surreal. Usually it was Shadow being silent while Jandro spoke close to his ear. Judging by Gunner craning his neck to look, he didn't see this often either.

"Fine, I'm a bad example. I can take a hint." Grabbing hold of my arms, Jandro gave me a deep, toe-tingling kiss. "But I wanna see it right after."

"We'll see you and Reap by the pool when we're done," I told him, almost wishing he wouldn't let go. My heart started to pound. It was almost time.

He cocked an eyebrow. "We?"

"Gunner's coming too."

Jandro clicked his tongue in surprise, his gaze sliding

over to the blonde man on the couch. "All right then. See you both there."

He stole another kiss and went out the door. The moment it shut behind him, I turned nervously to face Shadow. For the first time since I walked in, he looked just as stricken with nerves as I felt.

"Have you, ahem," he cleared his throat, "decided where you would like the tattoo?"

I nodded just as Gunner came up behind me, placing a kiss on the back of my head as he rubbed warmth into my arms. A small bit of tension immediately released from my shoulders.

"I would like it on my upper back, please."

Gunner hissed in a breath, then I felt his smile on my cheek and an affectionate squeeze around my shoulders. "We're gonna match, baby girl."

"Yeah," I grinned back at him. "It just seemed like the best place to be able to see it."

"Okay," Shadow said. His jaw clenched as his dark eye settled on Gunner's face above my head. Was he blushing too? "I'll need to, um—"

"Don't worry, Shadow." I couldn't resist shooting him a teasing smile. "I *did* think this through."

Both guys seemed to hold their breaths as I peeled off my scrub top. Underneath I wore a halter camisole over a strapless bra. Taking the rubber band around my wrist, I piled my hair on top of my head in a messy bun.

"Will this work?" I turned my back to Shadow. With the exception of the halter strap across the back of my neck, my upper back was completely bare.

"Yes," he grunted out. I didn't catch his expression,

and when I turned back around, he was rummaging through the supplies on his desk. "Let me get you a towel. Your arms will be resting on the back of the chair for a while."

He took off quickly into the house, and Gunner looked moments away from laughing his ass off.

"A towel, huh? I think your little strip tease made him jizz his pants."

"Don't be a dick." I swatted at him, only to be dodged and have my wrist grabbed.

"This reminds me," he smirked, playfully pinning my wrists to my sides. "Reaper wants me to teach you self-defense stuff. Weapons and hand-to-hand combat. You down for that, baby girl?"

"Sure." I tried to ignore the heat in my body that erupted, seemingly out of nowhere. It could only be from his gentle, playful restraint. "It'll probably be useful."

"Let's hope you won't ever have to use it 'cause you'll have one of us there." He released my wrists, trailing his fingertips up my forearms. "But it's better to know than not. In case that tattoo doesn't deter someone."

Someone like Corinne, only more evil and deranged. He didn't have to say it, but we both knew what he meant. She was going to make him a sex slave anyway, tattoo or not.

At the sound of Shadow's heavy footsteps returning, I turned to see him place a folded towel over the back of the chair. "There. That should be more comfortable for you."

I smiled at him. "Thank you, Shadow."

He nodded and turned back to his desk, pulling on a pair of gloves as he sat on a wheeled stool, a bigger version of the one I had in my office.

"If you don't mind," he muttered with a glance at me. "I'd like to draw the design directly on you first, to make sure I have the proportions correct and it fits the whole area."

"I'm fine with that. Just sit with my back to you?"

"Yes."

"Here, baby girl." Gunner pulled another chair over, placing it directly behind mine. "Just hop on, straddle that thing, and look into my eyes."

I chuckled at his innuendo as I took my seat, resting my forearms on the towel Shadow placed and stared into his gorgeous blue eyes.

"I'm, uh," Shadow stammered behind me. "I'm going to clean your skin with some rubbing alcohol, okay?"

"Okay."

"Relax, man," Gunner said over me to him. "It's nothing you've never done before."

Shadow muttered something under his breath in reply. I felt nothing for a few long moments, maybe almost a full minute. But then a damp, cotton pad gently wiped across my upper back, from my shoulders to my bra line. When my skin dried, the tip of a pen pressed gently as it moved across my flesh. I could tell Shadow was trying not to press too hard, but still felt the edge of his gloved hand, warm and heavy on my back.

"What was getting your tattoo like?" I asked Gunner,

resting my chin on my hands as Shadow drew on my back.

"Same as you, pretty much." He leaned back in his chair, raking his hair back to put it in a bun like mine. "Shadow likes to draw on the body first to make sure the tattoo fits and flows well. I didn't get no towel for my armrest, though!" He glared at Shadow over my shoulder, who only grunted in response.

I got the sense that Shadow didn't like to be bothered while he worked. The lightest breeze of air from his breaths hit my skin as he drew, and I wondered if he noticed my goosebumps.

Shadow rides in the rear because he's the last line of defense, Jandro had told me. *Nothing gets past him.*

The large man at my back felt like nothing short of a shield. Even though he was drawing so carefully on my skin, I felt completely protected. The house could collapse in on us and I wouldn't get a scratch on me, because of Shadow.

"There were some parts," Gunner continued his tattoo story, "that had me white-knuckle gripping my chair. And I'm no puss, but fuck."

"Oh no." I felt the blood drain away from my face. "Did I end up picking the most painful spot?"

"No, the spinal column will be the worst part," Shadow said. "Because of the bones and nerves in there. But we can stop at any time, like I told you before." He seemed to lean in closer and said in a low voice, hovering just over my skin, "And Gunner *was* being a puss."

"I heard that!"

A giggle burst out of me, and I tried not to let my shoulders shake too much. Shadow made a throaty sound that could have been a chuckle. I smiled behind my hand, feeling like we just shared a private joke.

"Okay," he said, the pressure of his hand moving away from my skin. "The sketch is done. Take a look in the mirror."

I stood from the chair and walked to the hallway mirror, turning around to look over my shoulder.

"Wow!"

My jaw dropped. Sketched in rough purple lines, the Steel Demons skull grinned at me from between my shoulder blades. Its horns swept up along the back of my shoulders toward the base of my neck. The words *Steel Demons* flowed in an elegant banner just beneath the skull. He made it look more feminine somehow, fitting the contours of my body while still representing the club where I had found my home.

"Oh my god, Shadow." I kept turning and twisting in the mirror to see it from different angles. All the fear melted away at the sight of it, and now I couldn't wait to make this symbol a permanent part of me.

"Do you like it?" He sounded apprehensive.

"I *love* it!" I shot a face-splitting grin at his shocked expression as I returned to my seat, propping my arms up on the back of the chair. "Can't wait to get started now."

"I'm glad you like it," Shadow mumbled from behind me. I heard him rip a plastic package open, which I assumed to be the needle.

"Aww, look at you." Gunner scooted forward, his

grin matching mine as he rested his fingertips on my knees that were splayed out on either side of the chair. "Baby girl's all excited about her first ink now. What do you need me for?"

"Don't go." I clasped one of his hands on my leg. "I'm excited now, but I'll probably start chickening out halfway through."

"I'm not going anywhere." His breath fanned over my face, gorgeous blue eyes falling to my lips as his forehead barely brushed mine. "I wouldn't miss this for the world."

A buzzing sound from behind me startled me out of the moment. Holy shit, this was really about to happen. I was tying myself to this club forever.

"Are you ready, Mariposa?" Shadow asked.

I sucked in a deep breath, my vision consumed with Gunner's face. His eyes lit up as he gave a comforting squeeze to my hand, and brushed a soft kiss along my forehead.

"Yes, I'm ready."

"Here we go. Tell me to stop any time you need it."

The buzzing filled my ears again and my heart felt ready to jump out of my chest. The warmth of Shadow's hand returned to my back, followed by a sharp, scratching sensation on my left shoulder blade.

"Oh." I released a breath. "That's not bad at all."

"You won't feel much of anything in a few minutes," Gunner assured me. "The adrenaline takes over and you'll be numbed to most of it."

He was right. Once I got over the initial shock, it felt like little more than scratching or even tickling in some areas. I rested my cheek on my hands, gazing at Gunner while Shadow worked.

"Tell me about you," I murmured to the beautiful man in front of me. "It feels like I know so little about you."

He huffed out a dark laugh through a lopsided smile. "There's not much to know, baby girl. I try to separate myself from my past as much as I can."

"Why?"

"Because my family's a bunch of rich assholes." He hesitated, rolling his lower lip between his teeth. "Except for my grandparents, who raised me. I mean, they were rich too, but not as asshole-ish as all the others."

"What happened to your parents?"

"Nothing. They were just too busy being rich assholes to take care of their kid." His tone made it clear he didn't want to talk about it, so I stopped with that line of questioning and tried another.

"How did you get to be so good with weapons?"

His crooked grin returned at that. "Military academy, if you can believe that."

I couldn't. "No way! You?" I reached out and twirled a lock of his golden hair in my fingers. "With this hair and your attitude? I'm gonna need proof."

"Reaper might have a picture somewhere," he laughed. "But yeah, I had the pressed uniform without a speck of lint on it, shiny black shoes, and an even shinier flag pole up my ass."

"What was that like?" I was still trying to reconcile the free-spirited, crafty Gunner I knew with growing up at some prestigious academy.

"In the early years, about what you would expect," he sighed. "Lots of rules, long days of classes. Cliques and petty drama. Girls trying to get away with the shortest skirts as possible. That part wasn't bad, but I hated it overall. I lived for the weekends and breaks away from that place."

"You didn't fit in?" I asked.

"Nah, it wasn't that," he smirked. "I was popular enough, just thought everyone else was stupid and fake. But on the weekends, I could take off my stuffy school uniform and trade it for leathers and a motorbike."

"Ah," I said, understanding. "After you met Reaper and Jandro."

"Yeah, bailed them out of jail with my parents' money during my sophomore year." He chuckled. "I'm certain they never noticed it missing."

"And after you were done with school?"

"More school," he grumbled with an eyeroll. "Only this time, the Collapse was looking more and more like a reality. So my parents enrolled me at the finest military college money could buy. I was expected to become a general, an adviser at the Pentagon or some shit, I dunno. They had connections and could pull strings."

"What was that place like?"

"Night and day difference from my high school," he said. "It was basically a boot camp. Drill sergeants yelling at me at four in the morning to get out of bed. Push-ups and running every day. I learned how to field strip an M4 rifle within seconds. I'm telling you, baby girl, it was so much harder than prep school, but…"

"You liked it," I completed for him.

"I fucking loved it," he admitted. "Could've done without dickwads breathing down my neck, but I loved handling firearms and learning how they worked. I got engrossed in military tactics and strategy. I just," he sucked in a deep breath. "I didn't want to follow orders for some politician, you know? Be part of a system that was driving this country into the shitter. When Reaper told me he was making a real MC, I had to make a decision."

I smiled at him. "And are you happy with the decision you made?"

He leaned forward, folding his arms on top of mine along the back of the chair, and rested his chin there with a smile.

"I used to wonder about the *what-ifs* a lot. I was offered a job in DC when I finished school. Great pay, benefits package, the whole nine. But lately?" He shook his head, his eyes locked onto mine. "I wouldn't want to be anywhere but here."

NINE

JANDRO

"You think she's done yet?"

"I swear to God, I'm gonna waterboard you if you don't shut up," Reaper grumbled.

Hades growled in agreement, taking a moment to look away from the street to narrow his black eyes at me.

I sighed and folded up the rag I was using to clean the bike parts strewn out on the patio coffee table. Reaper sat across from me, cleaning a few of the guns we kept stashed around in case of an attack.

"She's bringing Gunner with her," I said, watching carefully for his reaction.

The president barely batted an eye. "So is he hers, or not?"

"I dunno. They were all close in the pool the other day."

"I saw." Reaper stubbed out his cigarette in the ashtray. "She hasn't said much to me about him, so I'm not pushing it for now."

"Same here," I agreed. "But it's pretty telling that

she wanted him during her tattoo and not us, don'tcha think?"

"Gettin' jealous, 'Dro?" Reaper glanced at me with a wry grin as he reassembled two Glocks.

"Not exactly." I rubbed my chin, trying to explain it. "Like I know they're into each other. I'm not bothered by that. But it's a special moment for her. We're her men, not to mention the leaders of the club she's getting a tattoo of, and she doesn't want us there?"

"What she said makes sense," he shrugged. "I don't like seeing her in pain, and it would stress her out. You'd be bouncing off the walls and probably fuck up the tattoo."

"You don't think there's something else to it?"

"No." His voice was stern, and he eyed me squarely. "I take her at her word. That's what trust *is*. That's how this whole thing works." He drew a circle in the air between us. "If you think she's up to something and treat her like she is, that's a quick way to send your whole relationship crashing to the ground."

I leaned back, scratching both hands over my scalp as I tried to calm whatever the hell was going on inside me. "I just wanted to *be* there. Not because I don't want her alone with him, I just wanted to support her doing this. I took it like a man when she told me to leave, but—"

"Your ego was bruised." Reaper lit up another cigarette. "You wanted her to choose you for something, and she didn't. Get ready for a lot of that, especially if she adds him in."

"I guess," I frowned.

"This shit's not easy, 'Dro," Reaper exhaled a cloud of smoke. "You can't treat it like being with one person. This isn't like if your girl gives some lame-ass excuse to not see you, and you've got reason to be suspicious. Mari is just telling all of us what she needs while going through this, and that happens to be Gunner. It's nothing against you, bro."

"I s'pose you're right." I looked at him. "That shit never gets to you? If she wants someone else and not you?"

"Sure it does," he shrugged. "But I know what it means and how to handle it, because I saw how my dads did. And you know what, dude?"

"Huh?"

He pulled the cigarette from his mouth and grinned. "It makes it so much sweeter when she wants you, and you alone. Everything you worry about just goes away when she's right here," he brought a palm to his chest, "and you remember that she really *does* need you. She needs what only you can provide."

"Damn." I reached for the smokes to light one up myself. "Thanks, Dr. Rory."

"Shut up." His face morphing from blissed out to scowling was the funniest shit I'd ever seen. I'd have to tell Mari about it.

Hades suddenly lifted his head with a soft whine. With his nose pointed down the street and ears pricked forward, he was the first to notice someone coming our way. Gunner's laugh floating down the street made my heart leap. Finally, she was done!

Reaper and I jumped up from the patio furniture at

the same time, following Hades to the pool gate. Mari and Gunner were a block away, walking side-by-side toward us with Freyja a few feet away. Gun's hands were shoved in his jean pockets with Mari's arm linked around his.

The contact could have been either friendly or flirtatious, but seeing it caused something to tighten in my chest.

Reaper opened the gate to let Hades out, and Mari's arm pulled away from Gunner as the giant black dog ran toward her. He reared up and hugged around her waist with his front paws, his usual greeting to her lately, while she laughed and wrapped her arms around his neck.

"Hades, down!" Reaper bellowed, but the command was unneeded.

He dropped all four paws back to the ground and walked at Mari's side, looking up at her with all the love and adoration a dog could.

The tightness in my chest didn't let up as she entered the gate to join us.

"Hi *guapito.*" Mari grinned at me first and slid her hands around my waist.

My heart skipped a beat. "*Hi bonita.*" I leaned down to meet those plump red lips tilted up to me for a kiss. "How do you feel?"

"A little sore, but fine." She rested her cheek on my chest, and only then did the tightness begin to soften. "Watch out for my upper back, that's where it is."

"Can I see it?" I led her by the hands to the couches to sit down, Reaper and Hades following closely after.

Reap smirked at me knowingly over the top of her head. Smug bastard. He was right—she came to *me* first. She needed *me* now.

"Shadow just did the outline." Oblivious to our silent exchange, Mari plopped down on the couch and pulled her arms out of the sleeves of her top. "I'm getting the rest of it filled in in two weeks."

She lifted her shirt, turned her back to show me, and I couldn't hold back the awe I felt at the sight of it.

"Holy…shit." Holding the sides of her waist, I leaned in to examine Shadow's work more closely. "My boy really outdid himself. Reaper, look at this fucking work of art."

"Mm…" I didn't even notice he'd been lip-locked with Mari until I looked up. She turned on the couch to face me, giving her back to Reaper, and let out a content little sigh as she leaned on my shoulder.

Mine. All fucking mine.

"You like it?"

"It looks amazing on you." I stroked a hand down the side of her cheek. "After that's done, you should get my name right here." I dragged a finger just underneath her collarbone.

"You get my name first," she shot back, laughing.

"You joke, but I just might," I warned her. Name tattoos weren't really my thing, but I could get a butterfly as a symbol of her. Shadow could make it look badass and not girly.

"So, it wasn't too bad, sugar?" Reaper leaned in and dropped a kiss to the nape of her neck.

"No." She turned to kiss him over her shoulder, but

slid her legs over mine to remain solidly in my lap. "Some spots were more intense than others, but it was fine. I was good to keep going, but Shadow said we were at a good stopping point."

"How was *he?*"

I had to admit that part of my reluctance to leave was due to what happened the first time they were alone together. They ended up having sex because he mistakenly believed I sent her over for that reason. He knew better now, plus he'd seen her in her office since then. Mari was sympathetic to his trauma and his many issues with socializing, which was sweet. But a small part of me was still uneasy about them together in close proximity. I just wasn't sure what made me more nervous—his potential to misunderstand something and cause her harm, or her pushing too hard in trying to help, and triggering something dangerous in him.

Ninety-nine percent of the time, Shadow wouldn't hurt a fly. But that one percent usually meant no survivors. The man lived at two polar opposites and knew nothing of the spectrum in between.

"He was...really good." She sounded surprised herself. "I think he even cracked a joke with me."

I stared at her. "Really?"

"Yeah, he made fun of Gunner for being a pussy during his tattoo."

"Highly uncalled for." The blonde man in question draped his long arms and legs over the lounge chair across from us. He shook his head disappointedly, but his eyes were full of humor. "Totally unprofessional."

"Other than that," Mari chuckled, "he just did his

thing, didn't talk much, like usual. Except for checking in with me about pain and discomfort and stuff. It was really sweet, actually."

"He got her a towel so she could comfortably rest her arms on the back of the chair," Gunner scoffed. "What a princess."

Mari threw my soiled cleaning rag at him. "You used that armrest more than me!"

"I didn't say *you* were the princess." He batted his eyes at her dramatically.

"See what happens when we leave you alone?" Reaper chuckled, returning to cleaning his guns.

"I have such great taste in men, don't I?" Mari teased him.

"You do in one, at least." I pulled her more into my lap, stretching her legs over mine to the other side of the couch. Now that she was all mine for the moment, I was going to savor her.

"Hmm, the same one who cooks me fresh eggs and plies me with good tequila," she grinned, grabbing my chin. "I definitely hit a home run here."

"You want me to help wash you later?" I ran my fingers lightly over the center of her back, just under her tattoo. "You'll need to keep the new ink clean and mois-turized."

"Bath time is *my* domain," Reaper barked. "You can rub her down with lotion afterward, though."

"Shit, man. Who gave you the monopoly on bath time?"

"No one," he grinned. "I took it for myself."

"Hmm." Mari looked between us, amusement in her

eyes at how we bickered over caring for her. "Maybe you can wash my back, and Reap can do my front?"

"I'm fine with that idea." My fingers dragged across her sides. "As long as we get to switch."

"Works for me," Reaper muttered with a shrug.

"Okay, for real?" The exclamation came from Gunner, who stared at us from across the coffee table. "This is how y'all work shit out?"

Reaper cocked an eyebrow at him. "How else are we supposed to work shit out besides talking about it?"

"It's just…weird to listen to. Like you're a family splitting chores."

"That's basically what we're doing," I pointed out. "Only it's no chore to make our woman more comfortable after getting needles in her skin for two hours."

"Okay, tell me this." Gunner rested his chin in his hand. "How are you okay," he directed at Reaper, "with her being all up in *his* lap?"

"I had her to myself this morning," Reaper shrugged. "'Dro gets up early to go to the shop, so we get to lay in together."

"Then she has lunch with me." I wrapped around her tighter.

Gunner kept his bewildered eyes on Mari. "And what about after you're all done for the day?"

"We split time between both houses," Mari answered. "The evenings are usually all three of us. We have dinner, talk, and wind down for the evening together. But we make sure to have alone time, too. We've established a cozy little routine."

"We sure have." I dragged my lips from Mari's ear to

her temple, and felt her completely melt in my arms as a result. The insecurity in my gut melted away, as if it were never there.

Reaper was right, as usual. Sharing a woman was tricky to navigate, but she held the wheel and steered us true. One woman could only do so much to keep multiple men happy. I had to trust her, to believe she was genuine in her feelings, and had all of our best interests at heart.

"But what about..." Gunner's question trailed off, but he raised his eyebrows pointedly.

"Gun, if you never heard of a threesome, I regret ever letting you into my fucking club," Reaper growled.

"Of course I know about threesomes!" Gunner snapped. "But...all the time?"

"No, not all the time," Mari answered. "If I want to be alone with one of them, I'll say so. I try my best to keep it equal, but honestly?" A rosy blush filled her cheeks. "I love it best when all of us are together."

"You're getting spoiled." Reaper leaned over and kissed the back of her shoulder.

"And that doesn't bother you either?" Gunner asked him. "Seeing your best friend and your woman in bed together?"

"Not a damn bit." Reaper set his gun and cleaning supplies down, resting his forearms on his knees. "Bottom line, I want my woman happy, whether it's from me or another man. This way, I know it's from someone I trust. Someone who'll love and protect her if anything happens to me."

"Don't talk like that," Mari scolded, reaching over to smack his arm.

"I'm just saying it's another benefit to what we have, sugar. Especially if we take on General Tash in the near future. I'll be at ease knowing you'll be looked after, no matter the outcome."

I decided to steer the conversation back to a less ominous topic. "The sex thing isn't as weird as your mind makes it out to be, Gun. Yeah, I love this woman. Yeah, I watch my best friend nail her until she's creaming all over his cock. One does not invalidate the other."

"They try to make it all about me," Mari groaned like she was complaining, although nobody missed the smug grin on her lips. "But I make sure nobody gets neglected either."

I nuzzled her neck and kissed her there. "You're too good to us."

"That's why we put up with you," Reaper added, playfully swatting her hip.

"I just..." Gunner ran both hands through his hair, tilting his head up to the sky with a long breath. He stayed like that for a while before resuming his gaze on the woman at the center of all of us.

"I want to be with you, Mari," he said in a rush of breath. "I tried to fight it, but that only made me want you more. I love that you trust me when you're scared and I want to be someone that's there for you. I just," he paused, his eyes filled up with only her, "I just don't know if I can handle *this*."

A long, heavy silence fell over us. Reaper and I

exchanged a glance and a mutual shrug. We answered all his questions, said all there was to say. If none of that was enough, maybe Gunner wasn't cut out for this. That was fine, but he couldn't keep being Mari's emotional support person if that was the case. It would be too close, too intimate.

Our woman stared at him with a gaze that reflected his. They only saw each other in that moment, and I wondered what was going through her head.

"I guess there's one way left to find that out, Gunner." She stood, grabbed my hand and then Reaper's. "Let's go home."

"Oh...kay?" I stared at her, my ass still glued to the couch. "What's on your mind, *bonita*?"

"We're going to bed." She turned her head to look at Reaper, then the man sitting across from us. "And Gunner's going to watch."

TEN

MARIPOSA

All three of them snapped their heads in my direction, shocked at what I just said. But my eyes were only on the blonde man sitting across from me.

"Why?" Gunner's tone was quiet, curious. He looked calmer than the two men standing on either side of me, squeezing each of my palms in a death grip.

"Because I told you two weeks ago," I replied. "We could take this slowly. You could ask us whatever questions you had on your mind, and we've answered them honestly. But at some point, you have to make a decision."

"I know, Mari. But what's that got to do with watching you all have sex?"

"To see if you can *handle it*, as you put it. Because this is a regular part of our relationship. And until you're there to experience it for yourself, you'll have no idea how you'll react to it."

Jandro chuckled darkly at my side, leaning in to whisper, "Smart girl."

Reaper's face remained stony on my other side, his signature resting scowl revealing nothing about what his thoughts were.

"Um, okay." Gunner shifted uncomfortably in his seat. "You're right, I guess."

"After tonight," I swallowed thickly, trying to conceal my own nerves, "there's no more dancing around this, Gunner. You're either with me or not. I want to be with you too, but I—"

Each of my men squeezed my hands reassuringly as my throat tightened up. It didn't matter that Gunner was the third man I had feelings for. I was giving him an ultimatum, and it was just as difficult as if he was the only one I wanted. If I said my whole piece, I'd have to follow through, no matter the outcome. My heart had already cracked from him pushing me away before, and I had to risk that pain again if he said no. But having Reaper and Jandro's support made a world of difference in strengthening my spine.

"I can't keep waiting and hoping for you to say that you want this. *All* of this." I lifted my hands to show how Reaper and Jandro held me, clasped between them. "So after tonight, you're either telling me yes, or," I pulled in a shaky breath, "or any other answer is a no."

Gunner watched me speak the whole time with rapt attention. His jaw clenched just before he rose to his feet.

"Okay," he breathed. "I'm in."

"Hold up." Speaking for the first time, Reaper raised his index finger. "I have one rule."

Gunner's eyes shifted to him. We all waited with bated breath.

"You don't touch her." Reaper's voice had the sharp edge of a growl that heated my core. "You do nothing but watch. I don't care if you jerk off, but no one except *her* men touches her in the bedroom. Am I clear?"

"Crystal," Gunner nodded.

With that, Reaper led the way through the pool gate toward his house. He tugged me by the hand and Jandro followed after me, with Gunner bringing up the rear. Once out in the street, Reaper released my hand to wrap an arm around my shoulders. He pulled me in close and murmured close to my ear, "You sure about this, sugar?"

"Not really," I admitted. "I just didn't know what else to do."

"It's probably the only option left to get a straight answer out of him," he said. "But it could go badly. If he's not cut out for this, it could fuck with his head."

"Well, he's agreed to it. That must mean something, right? That his gut instinct wasn't to shoot it down."

"Maybe. We're about to find out." His hand slid down my back, gliding gently over my tattoo and following my curves until he grabbed a handful of my ass. "You ever been watched before?"

"No." I pinched his side to make him let go of my ass, wondering if Gunner saw. "Have you?"

"Nope." He shot me a lopsided, cocky smirk. "I think it's a first for everyone involved."

THE MOMENT all four of us walked into Reaper's house, Jandro insisted we all take a shot of whiskey before heading up to the bedroom.

"I'll have two," Gunner grinned, following him into the kitchen.

"Make yourselves at home, why dontcha?" Reaper grumbled, but he pulled my body flush to his, nuzzling my neck before kissing under my jaw.

"Can I get wine instead?" I scratched over his scalp, making him hum against my neck. The vibrations of his voice traveled all the way to my toes.

"Nope. Won't work quick enough." Jandro emerged from the kitchen, holding shot glasses for me and Reaper.

"This better be the cheap stuff." Reaper tossed his shot back and handed the glass back to Jandro. "And make sure Gunner's not draining my whole handle."

"I heard that!"

"Waiting on you, *Mariposita*." Jandro gave me a naughty look. "Don't make me pour it in your mouth."

With a sigh, I knocked the whiskey back while trying in vain not to taste it. "Ugh, blech."

The guys laughed at the faces I made as I thrust the glass back at Jandro. "You love *añejo*, but not this?"

"Ugh, yes. Can I please wash this taste out with some wine?"

"Here you go, baby girl." Gunner was already heading over with a half-full glass for me with a smile that made my heart skip a beat.

"Thank you, Gun." I smiled back appreciatively and covered his hand with mine as I accepted the glass.

What? I silently asked Jandro and Reaper's glares. *The no-touching rule is just for the bedroom.*

"Hurry it up, sugar." Reaper playfully tilted up the bottom of my glass.

"What're you in such a hurry for?"

"You really need to ask that question?" His green eyes were devilish as his hand snaked around to grab my ass again.

"You can have me whenever you want." I teased, playing with the henley buttons on his shirt. Okay, that whiskey shot might have been gross, but it definitely got me relaxed and loosened up fast.

"And I wanted you ten minutes ago," he growled.

I finished my wine while the three of them looked at me like a pack of hungry dogs. Two of the hungry stares, I was used to. And the third one spurred a new thrill of excitement up my spine. I only hoped he found enjoyment, not despair, at what we were about to do.

Reaper pulled me into a ravenous kiss the moment I set my empty glass down. Whiskey tasted so much better when it was on his tongue. He was already hard, his cock thick and rigid against my hip. What kind of dirty fantasies had he been thinking about while we were all trying to calm our nerves?

The world beyond Reaper's skilled lips and tongue melted away, until I felt the firm pull of Jandro's fist in my hair. With gentle guidance on the base of my skull, Jandro turned my face to his. His pillowy lips devoured mine, soothing the roughness of Reaper's kisses a moment earlier.

Not even a second later, the heat of Reaper's

mouth latched onto the exposed side of my neck. I whimpered against Jandro's lips as his best friend nibbled and sucked on my tender flesh, marking me as his. Both men started pressing in on me, caging me between two hard bodies and rapidly accelerating heartbeats.

"Fuck."

Neither of my men said that. Their mouths were occupied.

I cracked open my eyes, sliding my lips across Jandro's cheek to look over his shoulder. My gaze locked onto Gunner's stare as I teased the VP's earlobe with my teeth. Blue eyes watched my every move, not missing a single detail. Gunner's lips parted, and he wet them with his tongue as he watched.

"Bedroom," Reaper growled at the nape of my neck, his hand returning to mine to tug me up the stairs.

"Thought you'd never say that," Jandro purred, sneaking a fast kiss before Reaper pulled me away.

For a moment they seemed to forget all about Gunner, who trailed after us a few feet away up the staircase. But as the three of us stumbled, kissed, and groped our way into the bedroom, Jandro turned and told him, "Close the door behind you. No animals allowed."

Reaper seized that opportunity to wrench me out of Jandro's grip with a devilish grin. He picked me up from the back of my thighs, allowing me to wrap them around his waist as he carried me to bed.

"Careful with her back," Jandro scolded as Reaper dropped us both down to the mattress.

"I know, asshole." Reaper's voice was muffled by my

skin. He had already lifted my shirt up and was dragging his rough, delicious kisses across my belly.

My fingers dug through his dark, rich hair before sliding down his neck and over his wide, muscle-bound shoulders. I tugged up on his shirt until he had to pull his lips away to bring it over his head.

Jandro, already shirtless, sat next to us and gave Reaper a playful shove. "Don't be greedy. Me first this time."

Reaper grumbled a complaint, but pressed a kiss on my navel as he moved away to let Jandro take his place.

"Hi, gorgeous," Jandro grinned, placing a smoldering kiss on my hip as his fingers dug into the waistband of my pants.

"Hi, handsome," I returned, scratching over his much-shorter hair.

My eyes lifted to find Reaper and Gunner in the room, while Jandro dragged my pants and underwear down my legs, chasing every inch of exposed skin with a kiss.

Gunner sat in the armchair in the corner of the room, his foot propped up on the opposite knee. With his elbow on the armrest, his fingers rested on the side of his face as he watched us, eyes rapt with attention.

Reaper stood a few feet away from the bed, bottom lip sucked between his teeth as he unbuckled his belt and yanked down his zipper.

A pulse of heat flooded my core just as Jandro removed my pants and underwear. Reaper's hand slid down the firm planes of his stomach and disappeared into his boxers as Jandro kissed his way back up my body, holding my legs apart.

Reaper's arm and chest flexed as he stroked himself beneath the fabric, smirking at me as he hid himself from view. Jandro's kisses reached the inside of my thighs, lighting me up with shivers as I watched Reaper tease me.

"Look at you, *bonita*. So fucking soaked already." Jandro cupped between my legs, soothing the needy ache building inside me with the pressure of his palm. He glanced over his shoulder with an amused look. "Is Rory putting on a little show for you over there?"

"Shut up. Hearing you talk makes me soft." But Reaper's stance was relaxed, his smirk still present and cocky as he continued to stroke himself. "You want me, sugar?"

"Yes please, president," I whined, loving the soft groan from his throat when I addressed him by his title.

"Where?" he demanded in a husky growl.

"Down my throat. Now please."

His smirk widened into a delighted grin. He liked to ask me where, to give me the illusion of control. But we both knew he held me like putty in his hands. Whether he held me gently or with an iron grip, I knew he would never let me fall.

He shoved his jeans and boxers down his thighs, letting his cock bounce free, just as Jandro pulled his hand away from my pussy and replaced it with his mouth.

My hips lifted off the bed with a moan at the sudden onslaught of sensation. Jandro sucked my lips into his mouth, tongue gliding up and down my slit to drink from me. He clamped one hand on my waist, the other hurriedly making off with his pants.

Reaper, now gloriously nude, kneeled onto the mattress and made his way toward my head. Across the room, Gunner didn't appear fazed by either of my guys getting naked. His eyes only roamed over me as Reaper pulled both my shirt and halter top underneath over my head.

"Her back," Jandro murmured through a kiss on my clit.

"Shut the fuck up, and put your mouth to good use. I would've made her come twice by now."

"I'm fine," I laughed lightly, scratching down the back of Jandro's neck. "My back is still pretty numb. And what you're doing feels wonderful."

"Good." Jandro lifted his head to look at me as he slid one finger inside my slick channel. "I like to warm my girl up nice and slow."

"Mmm..." I squirmed when he slid a second finger in, his tongue returning to dance lazy circles around my clit.

Meanwhile, Reaper grabbed a pillow and positioned himself to kneel slightly next to and behind my head. He gently lifted my shoulders up and slid the pillow between the back of my head and his thigh.

"So considerate," I cooed, gazing up at the power-fully-built man towering over me.

"Mm-hm. Suck me, sugar."

I held in a laugh, wrapping my palm around the thick base to stroke his rigid length to the tip.

"So bossy," I said in a poutier tone, darting my tongue out to flick the sensitive underside of his crown.

"Sugar..." He growled it out like a warning, but I heard the edge of desperation in his voice. One of the rare moments the balance of control tipped in my favor before I gave it all back to him.

I drew his swollen head into my mouth, swirling my tongue around it as I continued pumping his length with my hand. His sexy moans amplified the effects of Jandro's mouth and fingers working me down below.

"Damn, our girl loves sucking cock. She's squeezing like crazy around my fingers."

"Fuck yeah she does," Reaper agreed, stroking down my neck and over my sternum to palm my breasts.

I couldn't see him, but I still felt Gunner's eyes on me, almost as heavy as a physical touch. What was he thinking? I hoped my body didn't look weird in this position and completely turn him off. My guys showered me with attention and bantered like no one else was in the room. They didn't seem to feel the prickle of self-consciousness from having an observer.

"Hurry up and make her come. I need to fuck her." Reaper pinched my nipples, eliciting a muffled squeal from me as Jandro's tongue lashed my clit at the same time.

"She's a squirmy little thing today," Jandro laughed.

"You're too fucking chatty today."

"Yeah?" Jandro's tone was playful. "Help me out."

Reaper's weight shifted under my head and I felt the pillow get removed as my head returned to the bed.

"Keep my dick between those pretty lips, sugar. I'm showing Jandro how it's done."

With his knees on either side of my head, he started leaning down over my body toward my legs. In doing so, his cock slid further and further down my throat. The next thing I felt were his rough hands on my inner thighs. He splayed them open, leaving me completely exposed, as he pinned my legs down to the mattress.

"There. Now eat her out like she's your last meal."

Jandro's mouth descended on me with ravenous hunger and I had nowhere to run. Each swipe of his tongue felt like a jolt of lightning, his fingers inside me beckoning me closer and closer to the final strike.

As if that wasn't enough, Reaper began thrusting into my mouth.

I could hardly breathe, both from having my mouth stuffed *and* chasing an orgasm at lightning speed. I needed to move, for one of them to ease up because everything was so, *so* fucking intense. But the intensity just built and built and built, until it was painful. Searing, blinding, and then an explosive release.

Reaper withdrew from my mouth and I gulped in a gasping breath of air. Convulsions and my pounding pulse wracked my body. I thought I heard him say, "You're okay, sugar," but he sounded so far away. But I felt him stroke my hair and neck so I knew he was near.

"Holy shit."

I turned my head as the room started coming into focus. The proclamation came from Gunner, leaning forward in his seat.

"Your face was turning so red, baby girl. I thought you were gonna pass out."

"We don't need your commentary." Reaper hauled me up and hugged me to his chest. "We'd never do anything to hurt her. She just loves tag-teaming stuff sometimes."

Gunner's eyes fell to me, as if he was waiting for confirmation of Reaper's statement.

Still panting, I leaned my head back on Reaper's shoulder, smiling as I kissed his neck. "That was probably the craziest orgasm I ever had."

"You're welcome." Jandro was now sitting up against the headboard, with one arm behind his head, the other gliding up and down his cock.

My mouth watered as I gently untangled myself from Reaper and crawled across the bed to him. "You look delicious enough to eat."

He grinned appreciatively. "*You* certainly were."

I angled my body next to him, some of my awareness back on Gunner's voyeurism and giving him something pleasing to look at. From the corner of my eye, I saw Gunner's hand move. I resisted the urge to look over, leaning over to kiss Jandro instead.

"So beautiful when you come." Jandro cupped my face and pulled me in closer, fingers skimming from my shoulder down my side.

I slid a hand over his thigh, teasing him like he did with me. His kisses grew hungrier, frenzied, as I massaged his balls, and all around the base of his dick, without touching him directly. I heard Reaper's dry chuckle behind me, the weight of his hand stroking my back just under my tattoo. He knew I was getting Jandro back for that slow, teasing buildup.

The man in question tried closing my hand around his cock and groaned when I smacked him away. Jandro loved to tease, but didn't bask in control like Reaper. He'd sit back and wait for me if I made him.

Making a slow trail of kisses down his chest, I did just that. And I loved every hitched breath from his lungs on the way down. He squirmed like I did when I reached the head of his cock resting on his belly, and kissed it too. I placed soft kisses all along the hard length of his shaft, enjoying the twitches and grunts from him.

"You're so evil," he moaned, his body wound up tight like a spring.

I giggled, finally ready to give him some relief, and flipped my hair out of my face. Jandro held my hair back for me, and with my unobstructed vision I saw Gunner stroking his palm down the front of his pants.

Our eyes stayed locked on each other as I slid my lips over Jandro's silky crown. Gunner bit back a moan, rubbing harder at the bulge tenting his pants.

Take it out, I begged him with my eyes. *I want to see you.*

He didn't though, and the need to see my beautiful, golden man naked became a deep, greedy ache.

Because he *was* mine. He became mine that day he got captured with me, just so I wouldn't be alone.

Hell, he was mine since that first moment at the service center in Old Phoenix.

Reaper slid into me then with one long, powerful thrust. My eyes slitted halfway closed from the sudden fullness, but I still watched Gunner through my lashes. Reaper's cock driving into me eased the ache deep in my body, but I still wanted more.

Tension knitted Gunner's brow, his blue eyes sharp with desire. His cheeks flushed pink, ragged breaths left his chest. I wanted to see ecstasy on his face. I wanted to watch his pleasure ascend and release, and to be the cause of it. I wanted him to know how much he was loved.

"Fuck," Reaper rumbled behind me, each thrust a crash of flesh and power. "So fucking good."

My moans echoed over Jandro's dick, my mouth wet and slurpy and sliding all over him.

"I'm not gonna last if you keep screaming on my cock like that," he choked out.

That only made Reaper laugh and fuck me harder.

With a few strategic swipes of my clit, I was done for. The orgasm crashed over me like a wave, nearly making my knees give out. Just as my pleasure crested, Jandro's salty warmth spilled into my mouth.

I lapped him up, licking and sucking him clean, as he shivered from the aftershocks.

"You're my fucking dream woman," he murmured woozily, hauling me up for a kiss. "I love you."

"*Te amo,*" I smiled, panting against his plush lips.

He excused himself to the shower, leaving me alone with Reaper and Gunner. Only then did Reaper take notice of our voyeur.

He turned me to face the man in the chair, and began slow, rocking thrusts into me from behind.

"Do you like Gunner in here, sugar?" His fingers curled into the hair at my scalp and pulled.

"Yes," I gasped, my body already quaking under his dominance.

"What do you want him to do?" Reaper's voice was calm, steady, just like his thrusts, rocking himself into my body. But there was no denying the simmering power just beneath the surface.

"I want to see him," I moaned, heat tightening in my belly at the thought. "I want to watch him come."

Gunner's mouth dropped open and the sexiest sound escaped his lips. I needed to hear that sound again. In my ear, against the most sensitive parts of my skin.

"Well?" Reaper mused. "You going to give our girl what she wants?"

Gunner stilled. He didn't move a muscle. Fear began creeping into my mind, killing my buzz. After staying through everything that just happened, was he still going to pull away?

He stood from the chair and my breath caught in my lungs.

Then a rush of air returned, my heart pounding, as he shrugged off his cut and peeled off his shirt. He licked his lips, hands going to the button on his jeans as he took long strides toward me.

Reaper's thrusts intensified, bringing soft whimpers to my lips as Gunner stopped at the edge of the bed and pulled his length from his pants.

Unsurprisingly, his cock was just as beautiful as the rest of him. Long, thick, and veiny. My tongue lolled out, aching for a taste, despite Reaper's no-touching rule.

Gunner sucked in a hissing breath as he squeezed his dick through his fist, eyes rapt with attention as Reaper fucked me. He looked so sexy, a golden god pleasing himself at the sight of me, a mere mortal.

Heat coiled between my legs, my limbs shaky with fatigue. Another orgasm was only a few thrusts away and then I'd be down for the count.

"Jandro was right," Gunner rasped, his whole body rigid.

"About what?" My head swam. I could barely get the words out, I was going to explode.

"You're so beautiful when you come."

Reaper's cock flexed hard within me, then the last few crashes of his body on mine sent me hurtling over the edge. He spilled inside me moments later, muttering curses and dirty nothings as his forehead touched my back.

My eyes found Gunner again just as his hand became a fast-moving blur, his moans so hot and unrestrained. The first spurt of come landed on his chest, the next on his stomach. He stroked and squeezed again and again, wringing himself out with hot grunts and breaths, until his pleasure slowly ebbed away. His eyelids fell to half-mast, blue eyes still fixated on me as his abs flexed with effort of his breathing.

"I'd get you a towel," Reaper panted, "if Jandro wasn't in the shower."

"Didn't really think this through," Gunner laughed

breathlessly, holding his jizz-covered hand away from his body.

"I'll get you one," I muttered, rolling off the bed.

"If you can still walk, I clearly didn't fuck you hard enough," Reaper snorted.

I wobbled a little, but managed to get my feet underneath me. Using the wall for support, I just made it past the bedroom door when a rapid pounding came from the other side.

"Who is it?" I called.

"Me!" Noelle screamed from the other side. "Your orgy better be done, 'cause I need you!"

"What's wrong?"

"It's Tessa," she answered. "Her water broke and she's going into labor!"

ELEVEN

MARIPOSA

I threw clothes on in a frenzy, explained to the guys what was happening in some rushed, nonsensical words, and ran out the door.

"I'll meet you there, I need to grab supplies from my office," I told Noelle, my breath whooshing out of me as I gripped the banister. All the sex still had me wobbly.

"Okay! What do I do while we wait?"

"Have Big G start a pot of boiling water. Keep track of the time between her contractions. Tell her to breathe and that I'll be right there."

We reached the street and split off into opposite directions. I did a double-take as I noticed Freyja's fuzzy black form running after her. I had no time to dwell on it, though, and sprinted to the medic's office.

After getting what I needed and pushing through Tessa's front door, chaos waited for me on the other side.

Tessa was up and walking around, pacing back and forth as she rubbed her belly and sucked in deep breaths. Noelle was further back, in the boys' playroom next to the kitchen. She had a hand on each boy's shoulder as they sat on the floor, listening to her intently. I heard, "Mommy's going to be okay..." but the anxiety in her own voice betrayed her.

A pot of water boiled on the stove, beginning to spill over the sides in sharp hisses.

Big G hovered over his wife, following her pacing and pleading with her to sit still, lay down, anything. When he grabbed her arm and she flinched, I stepped in.

"Okay, that's enough." I used my best medic's voice and set my bag down on the couch. "Big G, I'm gonna need you to take the boys upstairs to play. Maybe even go to someone else's house."

"Fuck that, I ain't leaving!" He turned on me, stopping right in front of my shoes and leaning down into my face. "You might be a medic, but you ain't my family. I'm not missing the birth of my son."

"You are doing nothing but stressing out your wife," I shot back. "For fuck's sake, you've done this twice already. Don't you know walking around is normal?"

His teeth gritted hard with a non-answer. Tessa pitched in for him.

"He wasn't here for the first two," she huffed. "He was off on rides, begging Reaper not to leave him out of all the pussy they were going to drown in."

"Well, I'm fuckin' here now and I'm not leaving! And for real, shouldn't you be lying in bed or something?"

Tessa slapped a hand to her forehead, then clutched at her side with a pained cry. Big G and I ran to her at the same time.

"Sit down for a minute, Tess. Try to get comfortable. When was your last contraction?"

"Um—"

"Baby, let me carry you upstairs. You really should be lying down, right?"

"Oh my god, just go away!" she screamed at him. "Mari's right, you're just stressing me the fuck out." She turned to me, her face in a grimace of pain. "About ten minutes ago, I think."

"No way! You're really gonna listen to this bitch?"

"Watch it," I growled under my breath. "You want the president, *and* the VP, knowing you're disrespecting me?"

His scowl was venomous. In truth, I felt bad for him. Despite coming up short in the father and husband categories, he didn't outright deserve to miss the birth of this child. It was unfortunate that he *thought* he knew best, and kept ruining it for himself as a result.

"Take the boys upstairs and I'll bring the baby to you when she's here," I relented.

She? Why did I say that? Tongue must've slipped.

He finally conceded, with a scathing look, and backed away. "Boys!" he hollered at his sons. "Grab some toys, let's go upstairs and give Mom some space."

"Is Mommy hurt?" the youngest asked with wide eyes and a wobbly lip. "Why's the baby hurting her?"

"She'll be fine." Noelle hugged him, turning him to look away from where Tessa groaned and huffed from the couch. "Nurse Mari is taking good care of her. We gotta let her do her job, okay?"

He nodded and accepted being swept up into his

father's arms. When the boys finally left the room, Tessa released a deep sigh.

"Thank you," she whispered. "Maybe I'll get to deliver this baby in peace."

Her relief was short-lived as another contraction ripped through her. My hand flew to my own stomach. I swore I felt the shooting pain in my own body, along with something else that seemed wrong.

"She's still breech, isn't she?" I pressed my fingers around Tessa's pelvis. "Your contractions are still far enough apart that we can try to turn her before she starts moving."

"Why do you keep saying *she*?" Noelle asked. "Know something we don't?"

"I don't know, sorry. Can you get that boiling water and bring it here with some clean towels?"

When Noelle scurried off to the kitchen, Tessa grabbed my hand and squeezed. "I thought I still had a few more weeks. Is something wrong for the baby to be coming early?" She stared at me worriedly.

"My estimation could have been off," I told her. "Plus, we were going off your previous experience and the expectation of a boy. If it is a girl, she's probably a bit smaller, which is why you'd be farther along than I thought."

Noelle returned with the water and towels. I grabbed a washcloth to dab at the sweat on Tessa's forehead.

"And even if the baby is early, she—it's active and healthy. We might take some extra precautions, but we're close to full-term, regardless. I got this, mama. I promise you."

"And the breech position?" she huffed. "What if we can't turn her?"

"Then I'm going to have to pull her out as fast as possible, so she'll be able to breathe. I may have to make an incision, but I *will* get her out, Tessa. I promise you."

She nodded sharply, eyes hard and determined. "Cut me wide open if you have to. Just make sure the baby's okay."

"Rowwr?"

All three of us looked around for the source of the tiny sound. Freyja jumped onto the couch, seemingly out of nowhere, and rubbed her head against Tessa's belly with a loud purr.

"Hey there, little friend," Tessa cooed, scratching between the two triangular ears. "Thanks for helping me out last time. Are you here to do it again?"

Freyja answered with a meow, running the full length of her body along Tessa's side.

I immediately noticed the ease and relaxation settling into Tessa's body. "How do you feel?"

"Good," she breathed. "Still, you know, feeling like a watermelon is splitting me in half from the inside, but the pain isn't too bad now." She glanced down at Freyja. "You're pretty damn magical, kitty."

"Okay, good." I shot her a reassuring smile. "I'm gonna try to turn the baby around now, okay?"

She nodded and I reached for Freyja to move her out of the way. The kitten yowled and twisted in my grip, slicing me with tiny razor-like claws.

"Ow, what the hell!"

I dropped the cat and she immediately returned to Tessa's side, rubbing hard against her hip and belly with a rumbling purr that seemed to fill the room.

This way, child. Follow me.

The voice reverberated in my head and all around me. I heard it clearly, as if a fourth person was sitting right there with us. It was a feminine voice, deep and rich. Comforting and motherly, authoritative and full of power.

"Oh, she's on the move," Tessa winced, clutching her side and resuming her labored breathing. She gave no indication that she heard the voice. "I think... I think she's turning!"

I swept my hands along her belly again while Noelle wiped her brow and muttered encouraging words. Freyja slid her body along Tessa's left side again, which I could now see was a repetitive, rhythmic motion. Those eyes were losing their wide, kitten innocence and turning the bright, sharp color of green with gold flecks. Endless wisdom stared back at me.

I grabbed my stethoscope to be sure, even though I knew I didn't need to be. Freyja had turned the baby right in the nick of time.

"She's in the right position," I announced, relief filling my lungs as I pulled the ear tips out. "We just gotta let mother nature do her thing."

"Oh, thank fuck," Tessa sighed. "Good thing this ain't my first rodeo, but holy shit am I gonna need a drink."

"I'll get one started for you," Noelle squeezed her

shoulder before getting up. Her green gaze caught mine just as she turned away, and that look made my heart stop. She didn't look anywhere as relieved as Tessa or me. What was that about?

Her smile returned however, as she came back to the living room with a round of tequila shots for us once the baby arrived. As we worked with Tessa through her labor, I forgot all about that look.

Roughly four hours later, Noelle supported Tessa in a squatting position as her daughter arrived, headfirst, into the world. It was a beautiful delivery, one that nearly brought tears to my eyes.

Thanks to experience and sheer female bravery, Tessa barely pushed at all and allowed her body and gravity to do the work. All I did was wait with a clean, warm towel to catch her daughter. I cleared her airways when her head popped out, and seconds later, I held a tiny, newborn human in my hands.

I did nothing but stare at her for a moment. It felt like a lifetime ago that this was all I wanted to do. To humbly assist in an event so beautiful and divine—the first meeting of mother and child.

After the Collapse happened, and then had my license to practice ripped away at the final moment, I never thought I'd have the chance to do this.

But the Steel Demons gave it back to me. Reaper gave it back to me.

I cleaned off the baby and wrapped her in a dry towel, before giving her to Tessa.

"Do you want Big G to cut the cord?" I asked when

the baby settled in at her breast. "It's tradition for the father to cut it, but it's up to you."

"Noelle can do it," Tessa whispered without a second thought, then snorted. "She's practically my sister-wife anyway."

I handed Noelle a clean scalpel and she did the honors with a big grin on her face. "Time for shots!"

Noelle held Tessa's shot since her arms were full of baby. We clinked glasses, then she poured the alcohol down the new mother's throat.

"Ugh, that burns so good," Tessa coughed softly. "I'm never getting knocked up again."

"If you want," I broached cautiously. "I can stick a birth control implant in your arm right now. Won't take but a minute."

"Do it," Tessa whispered, her eyelids lowering to half-mast. "I might pass the hell out first, but do it anyway."

When the baby finished eating, Noelle took her tenderly from Tessa's arms to meet the rest of her family upstairs.

"You know what you're gonna name her?" I extended Tessa's arm and marked the spot to insert the birth control implant on her bicep.

"I'll have to think about it," she laughed softly. "I was so convinced she was going to be another boy."

Her brow knitted when the implant stuck under her skin, but she otherwise didn't react. "You're good for three years," I told her.

"It's not safe out there for girls," she mumbled as if she hadn't heard me.

"Hey," I squeezed her shoulder. "But she *is* safe, because she's in here. And if she ever goes out there, she's got two big brothers and an army of men to protect her. No one will even get away with looking at her funny."

Tessa nodded, her eyes droopy and tired. Freyja purred loudly and kneaded at the blanket covering the exhausted mother's legs. I reached over to give those fluffy ears a scratch and got my hand headbutted in return.

"I think our work here is done, Freyja." I kissed Tessa's forehead and adjusted her pillows and blankets. "Congratulations, honey. I'll come check on you tomorrow."

With the little black cat at my feet, I walked back to Reaper's house in a daze. I barely remembered the walk at all.

"That you, sugar?" Reaper called from his study when I entered the house. "We're in here."

I paused at the open doorway, my pulse thrumming at seeing Gunner still here. He grinned at me, sitting in one of Reaper's leather armchairs with a cigar and a glass of whiskey. The room was hazy with smoke.

"How'd it go?" Jandro approached me, examining my soiled scrubs. "Everything okay with Tessa? The baby?"

My resolve shattered and I burst into tears. Three men rushed me at once, but it was Reaper who pulled me into his chest, arms creating a fortress of security around me as he soothed and shushed me.

"What is it, babe?" he murmured over my chest-wracking sobs. "What happened?"

"Nothing," I blubbered.

His palms pressed to the sides of my face, making me look at him while someone else rubbed my back.

"What do you mean, sugar? Why are you upset?"

"I'm n-n-not." I hiccuped, and a hysterical laugh bubbled out between my sobs. "I delivered a baby!"

He stared at me like I lost my mind.

"She's perfect, beautiful, healthy," I gasped. "Ten fingers, ten toes, all there. Such a strong cry, and she latched right on to eat. Freyja even turned her from a breech position."

I was rambling, crying, and laughing like a madwoman, but I didn't care. There was no putting a lid on this pure, unbridled joy coursing through me. I did it, I delivered a perfect, healthy baby!

"So you're okay?" Reaper asked me skeptically. "You're just...really happy?"

"Yes!" I cackled, wiping at my eyes. "It's been my dream since I went to school. I never thought I'd be able to do it, but now..." I circled my arms around his neck, sinking deep into those green eyes. "I did because of you."

He smirked then cupped my chin and kissed me deeply. "I can't take credit for making *this* dream come true. But I'm glad everything went well."

Jandro's plush lips pressed to the nape of my neck, his arms enveloping my waist. "Proud of you, *mi Mariposita*."

My heart swelled to the point of tears gathering in

my eyes again. How did I go from hanging by a thread to a life full of purpose and love?

Someone came up to the side of me and kissed my temple. Gunner looked down at me with his dazzling smile and sky-blue eyes.

"Congrats on a successful delivery, baby girl. And if it wasn't obvious," he pressed his lips to my ear, "I'm all in. I'm yours and you're mine."

MARIPOSA

"**I** need to talk to you."

Noelle's look was stern, similar to the one she gave me while Tessa was in labor. I'd forgotten about it until now, the morning after.

"What's up?"

Noelle jerked her head to her bedroom, indicating I should follow. Her lips pressed into a tense line at the sight of Freyja right on my ankles, but she didn't comment.

Larkan was just putting on a shirt, smelling shower-fresh as we entered her room. The mess of sheets and pillows all over her bed indicated either restless sleep, or a highly enjoyable night.

"Hey, Mari," Larkan greeted me with a friendly smile as he pulled the shirt down over his torso. I caught a flash of a hickey low on his abs before he covered up.

"Hey, Lark," I returned, trying to keep my smile hidden. *A fun night indeed, then.*

He grabbed Noelle possessively, pulled her close, and

pressed a deep kiss to her mouth. They murmured low, parting words to each other, then he released her with a swat to the ass, flashing me another smile as he passed me on the way out.

"I take it that's going well," I mused after his footsteps hit the bottom of the stairs.

"Yeah." Noelle's face was flushed, her green eyes shining. "He's great. Perfect, even. It's all coming true."

"What is?"

Her smile fell again. She wrung her hands as she watched Freyja jump on the bed and began kneading her paws into the mattress.

"Has Reaper told you anything about our brother?"

"A little. He told me about how he died. When he took me to see the place you all grew up, he told me he came back and found you while everyone else was gone because of...some feeling Daren had."

"Daren was different." Noelle chewed her lip, still watching my cat make herself comfortable on her bed. "He knew things before they happened. But it wasn't like a good thing. He got headaches, had seizures. Our parents worried about him a lot."

"Noelle, do you want to sit down?" I wasn't sure what she wanted to tell me, but I got the sense it was heavy and important.

She lowered herself onto the edge of her bed, a few feet away from Freyja, and hugged a pillow to her chest.

"This is going to sound completely fucking nuts, but..." she took a deep breath, "Daren still talks to me. In my dreams."

A beat of silence passed between us.

"You heard the voice yesterday, while Tessa was in labor," I said. "Didn't you?"

She nodded, relief etched in her features. "It was your cat that spoke, or rather, the god that inhabits her." She swallowed. "I've heard Hades and Horus too."

My heart pounded. Finally, someone who understood how downright freaky all of this was. Reaper and Gunner played it off like, *no big deal, weird shit happens sometimes.* And to some extent, I could get behind that too. But Noelle's confession added a different angle I never thought of before.

"You think this has to do with Daren?" I whispered.

She nodded, reaching for my hand. Her fingers shook in mine. "He talks to me from...wherever he is, because Reaper won't listen to him. He shuts it down every time Daren tries to reach out. Maybe because it's still painful for him, the guilt over how he died. So Daren talks to me, because I let him in."

"What does he tell you?"

A dreamy smile crossed her lips. "That he misses us, but he's happy. He's not in pain anymore, he's let go. He's free of the pain his human body gave him. He's...outside of the boundaries of time now, so he can see the future much more clearly than before."

"Noelle?" I gave a gentle squeeze of her hand, trying to bring her focus back. "What's that got to do with the animals, er, gods?"

"He hasn't said this straight out, but I think when he was alive...fuck, this is nuts. I think they were all *inside* him."

"Inside him?" I repeated.

"Like how they're inside the cat," she nodded at Freyja. "The dog, the falcon. Using them as vessels, somewhat. Like, one and the same, but also separate."

I gaped at her. "All of them? Like how many?"

"I don't know, but I'm almost certain that's why he was different. He always talked about how his body didn't *fit* right. That his head felt too crowded. He would scratch himself bloody in his sleep sometimes. And then when he died—"

"He was free." I began to understand. "And the gods were set free."

Noelle gave a sad smile, her eyes welling up with tears. "I'd never tell Reaper this, but I think Daren was ready to go. Either *they* told him it was time or he just couldn't take it anymore. He just sounds so much more at peace now."

"I'm glad." I squeezed her hand.

"The parts of the future he tells me, though," she shivered, "they're scary, Mari. I'm a bitch that can laugh in the face of death, but what he says makes me so worried. The club is about to change, Mari. As a whole, all the way down to the individual people within it. "

The air in the room went cold. Noelle's gaze hovered just over my shoulder, and I had no doubt she saw something, or *someone* that I couldn't.

"You're going to get your heart broken," she told me in a strained voice. "And not just by one man."

"What? No." The faces of my three men flashed through my mind. It wasn't possible.

"It will tear you apart," Noelle went on. "Make you question everything."

"No," I repeated.

They wouldn't hurt me, not to that degree. My guys made me want to burst from how happy they made me. Reaper was doing so much better. He talked to me when he was frustrated, instead of shutting me out. Jandro never wanted anything except to make me laugh. And Gunner, my sweet beautiful man. Our love story had only just begun.

"But," Noelle's eyes fell on Freyja, who lay stretched out on her bed like she owned it, "the goddess of love will guide you when you feel like you can't trust your own heart. That's what my brother told me." Noelle's green gaze returned to me. "And Daren has never been wrong."

My chest ached, like my heart was already bracing itself for irreparable damage.

"Who's going to do this to me?" I asked, my throat going dry. "And how, other women? Is someone going to..."

I couldn't bring myself to say the word, but my imagination took me there. In my head I saw the shadowy apparition, the figure who called himself Hades, leading a man in an SDMC cut down a hallway to a light at the opposite end.

No, I couldn't lose one of them, or any of them, like that.

"Tell me," I begged in a soft whisper when Noelle didn't answer.

"Hey, there you are."

My head snapped to the doorway, where Gunner's

smile shined like the sun. Horus puffed up in a ball of feathers on his shoulder.

"Guess how many supply runs I got today, baby girl?"

"Um," I blinked, trying to act normal. "I don't know."

"None." His grin went sideways in a cocky, adorable way. "Which means I'm taking you out."

"Out?"

"Yeah, for a ride." He glanced up at Noelle. "Unless you're busy."

"Nah, get gone!" Noelle plastered on a smile and flung her hands at me in a shooing motion. "We were just having some girl talk."

"By the look of those bedsheets, I'm sure you had *lots* to talk about," he teased her.

"Pft! I don't even want to know what my brother's bed looks like, now that you're roped in."

"I'm more of a headboard breaker, myself." Gunner's tongue slid along his lower lip as his gaze returned to me. *Lord have mercy.* I had a feeling he was going to be trouble, in the best way.

"Where are you taking me?" I added a flirtatious tone to my voice as I rose from Noelle's bed, trying to shove down the unsettling feeling from what she just told me. I waited so long to call this man mine. After everything we went through and overcame, would he really hurt me again?

"Somewhere fun and educational," he smirked.

"Meow!"

We both looked down, watching Freyja rub herself

between his ankles with a loud purr. "Don't worry, little one." He reached down and scooped her up. "You're coming too."

"She is?" I stared at him.

"We'll figure something out." He flipped her over belly-up, holding her like a baby. "For all we know, she can keep right up with the bikes like Horus and Hades."

"She's barely left my side, so I guess we'll find out."

He scratched the cat's head while Horus tilted his head to peer down at her from his shoulder.

"Get your gear on, baby girl." Gunner leaned in and kissed my forehead. "We'll take off when you're ready."

"Okay," I smiled at him, hoping the freedom of the open road would release my fears. "I should let Reaper know where I'll be."

"While you're at it," Gunner stepped closer, bringing his lips to my ear, "I'd love to bring you home tonight. Just you and me. I know you haven't seen my place properly yet, and," his eyes dropped shyly, "I just want some time with you. Naked or not."

My chest finally started to relax, the tension melting away to all the warmth and safety I felt with this man. It couldn't be him to hurt me. Never him.

"That sounds amazing."

His smile lit up the darkest depths of my soul as he set the cat back down on the floor, then touched a chaste kiss to my lips.

"I'll bring the bike around," he said. "Meet you out front, baby girl."

I found Reaper in the garage. He was dressed in full riding leathers with the engine idling on one of his bikes, and the garage door open. He had his back turned to me, fiddling with something in his saddlebags. When Hades looked at me, I pressed a finger to my lips and the dog stayed put, grinning slightly.

I snuck up on Reaper and hugged him from behind, feeling his body jerk in surprise.

"Shit, sugar. I didn't hear you." He lifted an arm and tucked me into his side. "Hades," he chastised.

The dog tilted his head, returning his look with wide, innocent eyes.

"Where you off to?" I asked, sliding my hand across his lower stomach.

"Paying a visit to some other MCs in the area. See if Tash's been busy cutting deals elsewhere." He gave a gentle squeeze of my nape. "We're gonna need allies."

"Really?" I looked up at him in surprise. "I thought it was every club for themselves. Two sharks in the same ocean are still enemies, I think was how you put it."

"I know what I said," he nodded. "And it worked for a time. But going up against a general? We're more than just us. And I'm tired of waiting around for Gunner's dickwad uncle."

"Who's going with you?" I asked.

"Slick, Dallas, Big G, maybe a couple other guys."

"Big G?" I raised an eyebrow. "His wife just gave birth yesterday."

"I know, sugar, but he was dying to ride. We're not going anywhere where pussy's on sale, so you don't have to worry about that."

"I'm not, but Tessa needs to rest, feed a newborn

every two hours, *and* take care of the boys! Jesus, I'm so pissed for her. I can't imagine how *she's* feeling."

"Dallas sent Andrea to help her," Reaper assured me. "I'm sure she'll be happy to have you and Noelle check in, too."

"I'll make sure Noelle does, but Gunner's taking me out for a ride today." I chewed my lip. "That's what I came down to tell you."

"Oh yeah, where?"

"Somewhere fun and educational, he said."

Reaper chuckled, his hand sliding down my back to cup my ass. "Will I see you tonight?" His voice lowered to that gravelly rumble that drove me wild.

"I told Gun I'd come home with him," I answered sheepishly. "I haven't actually been inside his place, or had any one-on-one time with—"

"You don't have to explain it." He released my ass, rubbing up my back as he kissed my temple. But I already felt the distance in his touch, heard the shift of emotion in his voice.

"I can tell him another time," I said. "If you really want me home, I—"

"Nah, it's fine, sugar." He cupped under my chin and pressed a lingering, sensual kiss to my mouth. "I get you every night. I'm just greedy," he smirked.

I frowned. He was being sweet, but his actions still felt forced. He was disappointed, but would never admit it at this point. Was *this* the first sign of Noelle's warning? Would he leave me over not making enough time for him?

Fucking hell. I started to wish she'd never told me.

"You're sure?"

"Do I have to throw you over my shoulder and carry you to Gun's place?" he laughed. "You *should* have alone time with him. He'll open up to you more than with us around. You'll know for sure if he's got any issues with the sharing aspect."

"You think he still does? After being there with all of us and saying he's all in?"

"I think he's being genuine about that," Reaper paused, scratching his jaw, "but he's going to have more lingering insecurities than me or Jandro. We love it when your attention is focused on us, but me and 'Dro are solid, babe. We trust you when you're not with us. Gunner will try, but this doesn't come naturally to him. He might need a little more reassurance."

I nodded my understanding, reaching on tip-toes as I wound my arms around his neck. "Tomorrow night," I murmured against his lips. "Just you and me."

His smile touched mine as his hands molded to the small of my back. "I'm gonna hold you to that," he said in a playful warning.

"Wouldn't miss it for a damn thing, Mr. President."

REAPER

Talk about getting a taste of my own fucking medicine.

As Hades and I took off out of the garage, I had to remember what I told Jandro only yesterday. So what if Mari was spending time with Gunner? It didn't mean she didn't have room for me.

He was part of us now, and a new, shiny fixture for Mari. It was normal for her to spend the day and night with him. And what I told her was true—he would need more assurance from her than me or Jandro.

In other words, I had to stop being a pussy. My woman would miss me and come back to me. She always did.

Slick, Big G, and Dallas fell in line behind me as we tore out of Sheol. I had to keep my focus, stay at least one step ahead of General Tash. Unfortunately for me, I was completely blind as to what step he was on. He could be plotting world domination for all I knew.

The dipshits of Razor Wire MC and us only had

one thing in common—the general used us like pawns in an elaborate chess game. We couldn't have been the only clubs, not for the grand scheme of things he was planning.

An alliance with Razor Wire was out of the question, considering they attacked us at the entrance to our own home. I gave every Steel Demon the authority to shoot a Razor Wire on sight, that's how fucking done I was with them. But not every MC was as slimy as those assholes. There had to be others like us, who lived by a code.

For years I'd heard rumors of just such a club, who called themselves the Sons of Odin. At first I'd written them off as white supremacist fuckheads parading around under a Norse flag, but apparently I was wrong. These guys guarded an area of the northern border, near where the Four Corners used to be—the spot where the old borders of Arizona, New Mexico, Utah, and Colorado all intersected at perfect ninety-degree angles.

That was definitely an area Tash would be interested in, especially if he was successful in stampeding over Gunner's uncle in Jerriton. I'd never heard whispers of the Sons of Odin making trouble for anyone else, so I figured they were worth a visit. I respected any club that handled their shit and kept a tight lid on any drama.

My boys and I went hard on our bikes, kicking up clouds of pale dust as we raced across the landscape. Hades stayed just ahead of me, his running pace leisurely despite our speeds.

Lately it was getting harder for me to obey him

without question. Now, especially with Freyja in the mix, I felt the burning need for answers. What was he, and why was he sticking with me? What Mari said about Freyja helping with Tessa's delivery couldn't be a coincidence. Horus being able to hold my two-hundred pound ass from falling off a cliff couldn't be a coincidence. I wasn't ready to believe Noelle's dreams about Daren, but Hades especially had some kind of link with the dead.

That voice he spoke to me with sounded more than ancient. It sounded eternal. And nothing else had scared the living shit out of me more.

Two hours into the ride, Hades threw his head back in a howl as he ran. A chill ran over my skin. No, it went deeper than my skin. I felt an eerie coldness in my bones.

We're too late.

Somehow I already knew, even before the remains of the clubhouse became visible on the horizon.

I signaled my guys to ready their weapons as we approached the burned-out husk of the building. There wasn't even a smell of smoke or charred anything in the air. We were days, maybe even weeks, too late.

Hades stayed alert and guarded as we parked and dismounted the bikes. My hand drifted over my holster, eyes and ears alert to any movement or sound. But it quickly became clear that no one was around.

"Someone fucked these guys up," Big G astutely remarked.

Only a pile of ashes and a few structures, like a stone

fireplace and a fireproof safe, remained. The safe door swung open, the inside already looted and empty.

"Tash?" Dallas tilted his head at me, an eyebrow lifted.

"Most likely," I muttered, relaxing my weapon hand. "These boys didn't play ball with whatever Tash had planned. No one else would waste resources on torching the whole place like this. He did it to make an example of them."

"What about the club itself?" Slick asked, his face pale. "Did they get out? D'you think…"

Hades' sniffing through the rubble answered that question soon enough. He dug out a human skull, half-buried in a pile of ash.

"Damn," Dallas breathed, his forehead creasing at the sight. "Poor bastards."

"Fuckin' shame," I agreed, walking through the ashes with care. "Whatever they did, they get all my respect for standing up to Tash. It's too fucking bad they lost their lives in the process."

A dark pit of dread filled my gut. Sheol could be the next ashy ruin if we weren't careful. That didn't mean we'd roll over and give into the general's demands, we just had to think long-term and be smarter, craftier. Tash used MCs because he didn't think like us. He saw us all as lawless road pirates, who'd turn over their favorite child for the right price.

Sure, we played dirty. We fought in ways no uppity general would ever consider. He thought we didn't have the same tactics and strategy as he did, but we had Gunner. With his falcon eyes and military school background, we had the means to meet Tash at every corner. I knew we could play at his level and not be doomed to meet the same fate as the Sons of Odin.

"Pack it in, boys." I turned back toward the bikes, having seen enough. "There's nothing left for us to do here."

"Shouldn't we bury them or something?" Dallas ran a hand over his shaved head. "I dunno if you feel that, man, but this place feels…bad. Not just because they died, but it's ninety fucking degrees out and I'm fucking shivering."

I knew exactly what he was referring to, and couldn't explain it myself. These men were murdered in their home, their safe haven. Probably with their old ladies and children, too. Their deaths were sudden, painful, and unjust. I didn't know if it was their spirits, souls, or anything else hanging around, but this place was drenched in a cold, creepy atmosphere.

"Let's just go, this place is freaky," Big G declared.

"I agree with Dallas. We should pay our respects, somehow," Slick piped up.

"All of you shut up." I was busy watching Hades.

The Doberman was sniffing through the ash-covered foundation and appeared to be collecting remains. He picked up the human skull and placed it next to a cactus just to the side of the ruin. Then he went back and picked up another bone fragment, part of a hand from the looks of it, and placed it next to a nearby aloe plant.

Hades went back and forth several times, finding pieces of the former club members and gently laying them next to their own plants. He didn't just find bones either. One item looked like a charred piece of leather from a cut. Another was a silver ring with a skull on it.

If my guys said anything to me, none of it registered as I watched my dog approach the skull—the first artifact he found, and lay a paw on it.

Rest, he said.

I nearly fell to my knees as Hades walked to the aloe plant and placed his paw on the bone fragment there.

Rest, he said again.

The same voice that boomed at me with the command to reap, now spoke gently to the restless souls taken without warning from this world. One by one, he approached the remnants of their earthly belongings and ordered them to rest. To move beyond the plane of the living.

Slowly, the heaviness and the cold in the air lifted. My guys didn't hear Hades speak, but they noticed the difference in the atmosphere immediately.

Rest, he commanded the final object, a metal picture frame with two men hugging and smiling behind the warped glass.

The last chill down my spine faded away, and nothing was left but a pile of ashes in the desert.

"All right, boys." I held my hand out to Hades, who trotted over and let me scratch his ears. "Now we can go home." With a final glance at the simple memorials over my shoulder, I muttered, "Rest in peace, Sons."

Flying somewhere over our heads, a raven cawed ominously.

FOURTEEN

MARIPOSA

Ten minutes after seeing Reaper off, I stood next to Gunner and his bike with no clue on how to bring Freyja along. Naturally, she was sitting in my spot right behind Gunner.

"I dunno how you expect to hold on with just your claws." I scratched the base of her tail. "The bike goes pretty fast."

"Maybe she's got like, Wolverine claws," Gunner laughed. "But then she'll slice my seat to ribbons, which would suck."

"Can we stick her in your saddle bags?"

"Don't think she'll fit. They're filled with stuff we need." He still wouldn't breathe a word of what we were doing. "It'll be bumpy and loud in there, anyway. She won't like it."

I picked up the black kitten, turning her belly-up in my arms like Gunner had earlier. "What are we gonna do with you, huh?"

She squirmed, twisting and batting at the zipper on

my jacket. When I lowered my arm to put her down, she twisted onto her feet and jumped *up*. Her claw snagged at my zipper pull and yanked it halfway down my chest. Then she jumped again, into my jacket.

"Freyja, what are you doing?" I laughed.

Gunner turned around just in time to see the kitten-sized bump wriggling under my jacket. Freyja finally oriented herself and stuck her head out just above where the zipper opened.

"Well, that's an idea," Gunner grinned with a scratch between her ears. There was no ignoring how close his fingers were to my breasts. "She's secure, protected from all the rattling. The noise probably won't bother her too much."

"You gonna stay put in there?" I looked down to ask her. She licked my chin, but was otherwise completely still. "I guess we're good," I relented, looking back up at Gunner.

He held my gaze as he leaned toward my chest ever so slowly. His lips curved in a tiny, wicked smile as he placed a soft kiss on Freyja's head, his nose barely brushing my cleavage.

Sensation rushed to my nipples, aching for a touch, *his* touch. But he pulled away and returned to face forward on the bike.

"Hold on, girls!" He hit the accelerator, bringing the machine to life with a roar. With a roll of his right shoulder, Horus took off flying.

I slid my arms around his waist, leaving some space between his back and my chest so as to not squish the cat. "Don't I get a kiss?" I teased, my lips touching the side of his neck.

He grinned at me over his shoulder. "If you're good."

———

THE FIRST PORTION of the ride was short. Gunner pulled up to what looked like abandoned horse stables, just a few miles outside of Sheol. Freyja popped out of my jacket and shook her fur out as we came to a stop.

"Grab the case in there for me, will you, baby girl?" Gunner nodded to the left saddle bag as he popped out the kickstand and swung a leg over the bike.

I unbuckled the top flap and pulled it open. A plain, plastic box sat conspicuously on top, but when I went to pull it out, the box felt like it weighed fifty pounds.

"Holy shit, what's in here?" I huffed, cradling the box against my body.

"Ammo." Gunner opened another case on the bike seat, and held up a matte-black handgun. "We're target practicing."

I shouldn't have been surprised. He did mention teaching me how to defend myself.

"So this is the educational portion of our outing?"

"Might be the fun part too," he smirked, slamming a magazine up into the pistol grip. Sure enough, the horse stalls had been converted into a makeshift shooting range. Metal casings littered the dirt floor. The frames of the stalls stayed intact to designate each range. Walls on the sides and far end had been knocked out, with targets placed in the field behind them at various lengths. Gunner led me to one with a closer target.

He laid the gun on the stall door and patiently explained its parts and their functions. After I successfully repeated everything back to him, he showed me how to load it, then had me do it myself.

I'd always hated the sound of gunfire. It meant there was a chance I couldn't save someone, no matter how fast or efficiently I worked. Invented hundreds of years ago, guns were still one of the most effective ways of killing people, or injuring beyond repair.

But when Gunner aimed the gun at the target and fired two shots through the center ring, none of my old feelings resurfaced. When he handed the weapon to me with an encouraging smile, something else surged through me when I held the weight of it in my hand.

The script had flipped. Now I had just as much power as the next piece of shit who wanted to enslave me.

I lifted the gun, aimed through the sights, and fired two shots.

"Nice, baby girl," Gunner praised. "You're a little jumpy on the pull, but that's all right. It'll go away as you get used to it." He moved behind me, fingertips caressing my arms. "Relax," he whispered. "Put a little bend in your elbows." His touch ran from my shoulders, down the sides of my body, to rest at my hips. "Widen your legs a little more," he added, his voice growing husky.

I shot through several more magazines until my hands started cramping. Gunner adjusted and praised my technique with each reload. After the last one, he massaged my sore palm between his thumbs and told me that was a good stopping point.

"You feeling alert and full of adrenaline yet?" The gleam in his blue eyes hinted at more surprises.

"What are you scheming next?" With all of the flirty touches and innuendo, I was fired up in more ways than one. If his plan was to take me against one of the stable doors, I certainly wouldn't be disappointed.

He placed a kiss on my fingertips, then released my hand. "Wait here."

Instead of heading back out toward the bike, he headed down to the opposite end of the stables. I watched him spin a combination lock on what looked like a supply closet, and pulled out a set of gymnastics mats.

"Little dusty," he muttered, then went back to the closet and retrieved a broom.

"We gonna be wrasslin'?" I asked, unfolding the mats from their stacked position as he swept them.

"Kinda." The naughty gleam never left his eyes. "If you don't have a gun, you might have to fight close up. We'll have to repeat this a lot so it becomes instinct, but I'll just give you a basic overview today." He put the broom aside and handed me a slender piece of wood carved in the rough shape of a knife. "You're going to use that like an actual weapon."

"Okay." I held it a few inches in front of my body, unsure what to do.

"Stay there. Now," he walked a slow circle around me, "most attacks happen from the back." With incredible speed, he braced one forearm against my throat and the other around my waist. "What do you do in this situation?"

Beg you to fuck me?

"Um, I dunno." His heart kissed my back in steady, calming beats through the solid wall of his chest. His clean, fresh scent, the heat of his skin, everything *him* made it incredibly difficult to concentrate.

"You have a few options," he rasped into my ear. "I have your shoulders, so your arms can't move much. But your legs are free and much stronger."

"I can't kick you in the balls from here."

"No," he laughed. "But look, you can kick my knee joint. Kick it from the side, the direction it doesn't bend."

I lifted my foot and found the side of his knee with my boot. "Right there?"

"Yeah, good. One good kick there will force me to put all my weight on the other leg." The weight of his chest rested heavier on my back as he raised one foot to demonstrate. "Now what?"

"Now…you're off-balance."

"Exactly. That puts you at an advantage, baby girl." The pride in his words made my skin tingle from head to toe. "Bend your knees, lower your center of gravity, then take a big step forward. Shift all your momentum forward hard, like you're about to take off running."

I did as he instructed, which, to my surprise, sent him flying over me to land on his back on the mats. He shot a stunning grin up at me. "Now slit my throat with your knife."

I brandished the carved hunk of wood and drew a line across his exposed neck.

"Good." He rolled up to sit, eyes sparkling. "So what did you learn from that?"

"That I need to use the differences between our weight and size to my advantage." I panted slightly. It wasn't easy throwing such a tall man over my shoulder.

"Exactly!" He beamed with pride. "That's the main principle I want you to learn. You can get away from any guy who grabs you, as long as you can take away his balance and use gravity to your advantage. Finishing him off," he nodded to my wooden knife, "just ensures he won't come after you a second time." He patted my leg and climbed to his feet. "Let's go again."

We went for several more rounds. Each time he grabbed me in several different ways, and gently guided me through finding his weak points, until I had them memorized. After nearly an hour of touching, grabbing, and mock-fighting, my body was fatigued and sore, while craving him like mad at the same time.

"Come on, last one." Gunner hovered over me as my back pressed into the mat. My legs were around his waist and he held my wrists pinned above my head. His hair hung down, tickling the edges of my face. "How you gonna break my hold, Mari?"

"Gun, I dunno," I panted, rolling my head from side to side. Sweat coated every inch of my body. "I'm completely wiped out."

"Last one, I promise," he repeated. "Remember your legs—"

I raised my head an inch off the mat, the only

distance I needed to press my lips to his. He shut up instantly, returning the kiss with all the warmth and sweetness I had come to know from him. His hands loosened around my wrists and I seized the opportunity to dig my fingers into his beautiful golden locks.

It was the perfect first kiss, a complete do-over from the harrowing moment I was pretending to be his slave. No one was around to threaten or rush us through this, our lives weren't in danger. At least, not right now. That moment would surely come again, but right now it was just me and the man whose smile captured me from the first moment I saw him.

"I don't recommend doing that with an attacker." His lips, swollen from my kiss, curved amusedly as he looked down at me.

"Hm. I'll remember that." Grabbing the edges of his cut, I rested my head back down on the floor and pulled him down closer.

"Baby girl. Mari..." Gunner's moans were soft and breathy as I peppered kisses under his jaw, trailing down his throat.

"Yes?" I nipped his Adam's apple.

He grinned sheepishly. "I was going to wait until I brought you home tonight before doing this."

"Too bad." I pushed his hair aside and sucked at the crook of his neck. "I want you now."

He let out a heavy groan, running his hands down my sides. I felt him, thick and pulsing against my core already.

"Right here? Where it's fucking dirty?"

"You can still clean me off at your place tonight," I reminded him, grazing my teeth along his earlobe.

"You don't have to keep convincing me," he chuckled, slipping a hand under my shirt.

His mouth returned to mine, tongue and lips caressing as he inched my shirt up over my bra. While we parted so I could take it off, his lips fell to my ribs and belly.

"You looked fucking amazing last night with them." His breath was warm on my skin, kisses shooting pleasure to every nook and cranny of my body. "So beautiful and sexy."

"It didn't bother you, seeing that?" This might not have been the best moment to ask, but I had to know.

He paused, lips hovering over my bellybutton as he looked up at me. "It only bothered me that I couldn't touch you." His mouth returned to mine, tongue diving in hungrily. "I couldn't stand it any longer." His words against my lips became a growl, one hand hurriedly undoing his belt buckle and zipper. "I had to make you mine. I couldn't last another fucking minute without calling you *my* girl."

"But sharing me with them?" I wrapped my arms around his neck, lifting my hips so he could pull my jeans and panties away. "You're truly, honestly okay with that? Because I'm theirs just as much as I'm yours. That's not going to go away, Gun."

"I don't fucking care." He wrapped an arm around my back and hauled me up, unhooking my bra swiftly and pulling it off me.

"Gunner? Ohh…"

He laid me back tenderly on the mat, one hand still supporting my back while the other worked some kind of magic spell between my legs. Two long fingers pressed inside me, the other three somehow teasing my clit from all angles outside. His thumb stroked over the top, while his index and pinky pressed on either side of my pussy. Or at least that was my best guess, it felt so fucking good it was disorienting.

"Reaper was right," he rasped, watching my hips buck from his come-hither motion inside me. "We all just want to make you happy. They know how. I'm gonna try my damn hardest to do the same, baby girl."

"You already do," I gasped, the pleasure hitting me hard. "Oh, fuck!" My orgasm crested without warning, seizing up around his hand.

Gunner's skillful fingers stroked me through, riding the wave of my release and then the aftershocks before withdrawing, leaving me empty. He barely had to move into a position for sex, I was already climbing him.

"I won't let you doubt me." He kissed my throat, pulling my hair back gently to expose more of my neck. "I'll never give you a reason to question how I feel again."

"I never did." I pressed my forehead to his, locking my arms around his neck and my legs around his waist. "Gunner, I never doubted how you felt. You've always been there for me. When you pulled away, you thought you were protecting yourself. It's me that should be making promises." I cupped his cheek, my vision swimming with his large blue eyes, and our lips a hair's breadth away from each other.

"I promise I'll make time for you. I'll never intentionally hurt you. I won't ever make you feel like less than them. Whether I had them or not, I still wanted you. I always did. Gunner, please understand that I'm not adding you to a collection. I want you because you're *you*."

"I know, baby girl." He returned my back to the mat with utmost care, shifting his weight between my legs.

"So don't ever doubt *me*." My lips trembled as I spoke. "Because that won't ever change."

"Mari..."

Together we let out a mutual gasp as he slid into me, slick and effortless, like we were made to fit each other.

"I just hope I can be someone who deserves you," he groaned, framing my face with his forearms.

"You're doing a good job so far." My words were breathless, the air chased away every time he entered me.

He laughed, leaning down to steal more of my breath with another kiss. His movement was fluid, graceful. Gunner made love like he swam through water —long muscles stretching, each breath intentional and heavy. I wrapped my arms around his back, sliding my fingers along the tattoo that matched mine.

Mine, all mine.

My hand slid down to his perky ass, feeling the muscles flex there as I pulled him into me deeper. How did I go so long without this, without him? I needed more of him constantly, always.

He slid a hand under my ass as well, angling my hip

in such a way that had my clit buzzing with the impact of his body.

"Gunner, what…yes…" Words weren't making sense. All brain function ceased at the explosive pleasure shooting off where our bodies joined.

My beautiful gunman had to be some kind of magician, moving so hypnotically while his cock hit every nerve ending inside me at just the right tempo, and even the angle he held me maximized my pleasure. How could he be real?

Like the first one, my release came without warning. The crash sent shudders throughout my body, so intense that Gunner had to hold me in place. I was burning up, slick with sweat, and my pulse raced like a rapid drumbeat in my ears. And I could not get enough.

Thankfully, Gunner never stopped. His hand went to my clit this time as he sat up, circling lazily around the center of my pleasure as his hips rolled back and forth.

"Beautiful," he murmured, his eyes dilated and hungry as he watched my breasts bounce.

I grabbed his thighs for leverage, wanting him deeper and harder, more.

"Oh, baby girl," he groaned, zeroing in on my clit. "You're too fucking good…"

His breathing grew ragged, labored over the next few thrusts. The sorcerer of pleasure was finally losing control. He swelled inside me, making me see stars as his thumb strummed its last few magical notes, and we came together in a crash.

GUNNER

"So, how did you get to be so good at that?"

I looked at Mari innocently. "At what?"

"You know what." She kicked me playfully under the table while Horus cooed in amusement from a nearby fence post.

I took a sip of beer to ponder a good way to answer. At the same time I slid an arm around her shoulders, flicking her hair back to admire one of my love bites on her neck.

Mine. All mine.

"I was with someone for a while who taught me a few things."

"I'd say more than a few." Mari sucked at the straw on her margarita. "She gave you the cheat code."

"A satisfactory performance, then?" I smirked at her.

"Highly satisfactory." She leaned against my shoulder. "Ten out of ten, would fuck on the dirty floor of a shooting range again."

We laughed together and I pressed a kiss to her hair. "Happy to be of service."

"Are you happy, Gunner?" She peered up at me. "Really?"

I needed to take my time to answer. Not because I had any doubt, but to really sink into the feeling, like a cool body of water on a scorching day. After we made love at the range, we got back on the bike and headed to this cantina about an hour away. They had a great bar, shaded outdoor seating, and the best taco truck in the Southwest parked outside.

I had a belly full of beer and carne asada. Horus was chilling on a fence post, keeping an eye on us, while Freyja meandered around the patio and made friends with some stray cats. And I had my girl with me. Sure, she'd been on the back of my bike before. We'd had drinks and flirtatious jokes before. But this time, she was really mine.

"I'm happy as fuck," I blurted out like the eloquent bastard that I was. "Everything is fucking perfect right now." I leaned over to steal a sip of her margarita. "Are you?"

"Yeah, I am." She radiated happiness like sunlight, her cheeks still flushed from all the orgasms I gave her.

Not one of her other guys, *me*. She looked every bit as sexy as last night, sandwiched between Jandro and Reaper, but knowing that I alone pleased her today made it a little extra special.

We sat quietly for a while, watching Freyja wrestle with a fluffy grey kitten. Horus made clicks and chirps, as though giving her pointers like some kind of coach.

"How long were you with her?" Mari asked out of the blue.

"With who?"

She tugged on a lock of my hair playfully. "The girl who *taught you a few things.*"

The resurfacing memory brought up an uneasy feeling in my gut. "Jealous?" I chose to deflect, teasing her with a squeeze around her waist.

"Not exactly." She squirmed against my side, the ice in her margarita sloshing. "I mean, I have no room to talk. Just curious, I guess."

"It wasn't really like that, baby girl," I sighed. "She wasn't my girlfriend or anything. We just messed around every so often. We had to sneak around, keep it a secret."

"Why?"

"Well, she was older than me and um," I drained the rest of my beer before finishing my answer. "She was a maid in my parent's house."

Clarity and understanding lit up her hazel eyes. "Oh, I see."

"Yeah." I stared at my empty beer glass, willing it to magically refill. "Long story short, we got caught and my parents sent her away."

"How old were you?"

"Old enough to know exactly what I was getting into," I answered curtly. "She didn't take advantage of me or anything like that. We were just friends for a while before getting physical." I let out another sigh. "Unfortunately for her, I wasn't old enough to think with the right head, and she took the fall for me."

Mari gave my arm a sympathetic squeeze. "Do you know what happened to her?"

"Shipped her off to one of those women's correctional camps, most likely." My tone was laced with bitterness. "Typical move for my folks. Disposing of people who could ruin their image. They didn't even care that she was my friend. I only saw them and her when they hosted parties. They paraded me around like the prodigal son, then forgot about me when the charade was over. So I'd go off to find Beth, and we'd have our own fun. But the son of Hollywood royalty messing around with household staff? Oh no, they couldn't have that."

The whole time I rambled, Mari listened patiently with her head on my shoulder. When I finished, she kissed my cheek and slid her arms around my waist. Even her touch and affection seemed to have healing qualities. It didn't feel great to be dredging up the past, but I did feel lighter. A little less burdened.

"I'm sorry, Gun. Your parents really were assholes." She looked up at me with her chin on my chest.

"That's not even the half of it," I sighed, running my fingers through the ends of her hair.

"Your grandparents, though. They were better, right?"

"Yeah. My grandfather died when I was fifteen, so it was just me and Gram for a while. Grandad's vintage Harley was my first motorcycle. Jandro fixed it up for me."

"Still got it?" Mari smiled at me.

"Yeah, it's in my garage. I take it for short rides

sometimes. It's so old now, and I just don't want to ruin it beyond repair."

She snuggled her head into my chest. "I'd love to see it when we get back."

"Sure thing, baby girl." Another quiet moment passed, the two of us just wrapped up in each other. "My grandparents were married for over fifty years. And even until the end, they couldn't stand to be apart."

"Aw, that's beautiful."

"My granddad said," I swallowed thickly, "that he and Gram were like a pair of scissors. When together, they worked perfectly. Separated, they ceased to work at all."

"Soul mates." Mari pressed a small kiss to my throat.

"I guess."

Mari pulled away to look at me. "What, you don't believe in soul mates?"

"I dunno anymore," I admitted. "I mean, this feels right with you. It would feel right if you had a hundred other guys, as long as you still had time for me—"

"Always," she interrupted with a quick kiss to my mouth.

I smiled lazily at her. "I guess the main reason it took me so long to jump in was because I wanted what my grandparents had. They set up this big expectation that there's one person destined for all of us, and life is all about finding your other scissor blade."

"What we have doesn't make that *not* true," she replied. "Your grandparents had something unique, but so do we. So did you and Beth. Just because you're with me now, it doesn't invalidate your time and memories with her." A wicked smile curved on her lips. "Wherever she is, I hope she's well. And I'm grateful for what she taught you."

"Hm, me too," I chuckled and pressed a kiss to her hair. "Especially if it makes me your favorite."

"Nope, I don't pick favorites." Mari shook her head insistently. "It's impossible to choose."

"That sounds like I have to try a little harder," I grinned, pulling her leg over my lap to straddle me.

"Gunner…" She said the first half of my name with a soft growl, like a warning. The second half left her mouth in a decadent sigh as I kissed her neck, pulling her flush against me.

My lips moved lower, tracing the swells of her breasts as my hands memorized the winding curves from her ass to her waist. She writhed in my lap, rolling her core against my dick that was already hardening for her again. I started to wonder if we could really get away with fucking on the patio of this establishment, when a stray glance over her shoulder alerted me to the three massive bikers approaching our table.

Horus screeched, extending his wings to the sides. Freyja arched her back like a Halloween cat and hissed.

I slid Mari off my lap and warily examined the guys on the other side of our table. "Can I help you, gentlemen?"

The big dude in front lifted his chin at me. He had a shaved head, dark beard coating his lower jaw, sharp amber eyes, and was covered in tattoos. The patch on his cut read *Sgt. At Arms*, essentially the same title I had. His road name read T-Bone. But what caught my attention was the raven perched on his shoulder, its glossy black feathers reflecting the sun like obsidian.

"You Gunner Youngblood?" he asked in a low, gravelly voice.

"Depends who's asking." I reached slowly for the gun in my holster, watching every breath of movement he made.

One of the guys behind him stepped up, a taller, lanky dude built similar to me. His head was shaved too, except for a strip of dark hair along the top of his head tied off in a topknot. He went by Dyno according to his patch, and was his club's Road Captain.

"That's him, T. The Steel Demons arms dealer, couldn't be anyone else."

"I'm flattered y'all can recognize me from afar. That still don't tell me who the fuck you dicks are." My hand wrapped around the pistol's grip, finger hovering over the trigger.

The third guy walked up. He had more than enough hair on his head and in his beard to cover both of his friends. I didn't get a chance to look at his cut before he tossed something onto the table.

It landed with a thump and rolled a few times. I braced my arm in front of Mari, not knowing what to expect. Once it stopped moving, I realized it was a leather, drawstring bag. Parts of it were discolored, like dried blood had soaked through.

"A present for me? Aw shucks, boys, you shouldn't have," I sneered up at them.

T-Bone jerked his chin at me again. "Your uncle. He could've used a hand from his family."

The blood drained from my face, as did all bravado, as I stared at the bag on the table. Slowly I reached over and pulled open the top.

"Oh my God," Mari whispered, covering her mouth.

Uncle Jerry's hand had been crudely sawed off at the wrist. Dried blood coated his fingernails and the gaudy, jeweled rings he wore. It was *his* hand, no mistaking it. The same hand that ruffled my hair as a boy and snuck me hors d'oeuvres in napkins from my parents' parties.

It didn't take much effort to school my features. I felt oddly blank. The biker might as well have dropped a pineapple in front of me. Uncle Jerry was never outwardly horrible to me, but he was every bit as manipulative and self-serving as my father. That said nothing of the atrocities he committed while killing and enslaving his way to ruling the Colorado territory.

When I didn't fit my dad's mold of me well enough, he cast me aside. Uncle Jerry, with no kids of his own, then tried to groom me into his perfect successor.

Both of those fuckers failed.

"Where's the rest of him?" I asked impassively.

"His top half might be somewhere down in Texas by now," T-Bone answered in a bored tone. "Cock and balls fed to the buzzards. Other hand probably up in the Dakotas. Oh yeah." He snapped his fingers as though suddenly remembering. "His head's been spiked through on that god-awful fucking front gate to his mansion."

"And I take it you boys did this?" My gaze moved

over all three of them, taking in and memorizing every detail.

"We did." T-bone rested his hands on his metal belt buckle, some kind of intricate design in silver that looked like a Celtic knot.

No risk, no reward, I thought as I pulled my hand away from my holster, and held it out across the table to shake his.

"You did me, and the world, a favor." The shock in his amber eyes was palpable as he stared at my hand. "Did he scream and beg like a little bitch?"

"Worse than any woman I've heard." T-Bone's lip curled up in a smirk, but he still didn't shake my hand. "No lost love between you two then, huh?"

"He had a chance to prove he'd help out family when called upon, after the Steel Demons saved his ass from his citizens' first uprising." I let my hand drop to the table. "And he sided with our enemy instead."

"Tash." A muscle jumped in T-Bone's jaw when he said the name.

I stayed silent, choosing not to confirm any details of my club's personal business. This guy would have to draw his own conclusions on whether I was a friend or foe.

He relaxed slightly, his men following suit.

"We'll be seeing you, Steel Demon." The raven on his shoulder cawed in agreement.

They turned and walked, allowing me to finally see the club patches on their backs—a raven with its wings spread out and the words, *Sons of Odin MC.*

SIXTEEN

MARIPOSA

Gunner pulled straight into his garage and cut the engine. He lowered his feet to the floor while I remained with my arms locked around his waist.

"Are you gonna tell Reaper about those guys?"

"Yeah, I will." He took his helmet off and shook his hair out. "In the morning."

"You sure?"

"Yes, baby girl." He turned in his seat and gave me an affectionate stroke on my cheek. "They're no threat to us. I'm not worried."

He hopped off the bike and started stripping out of his leathers, but I wasn't convinced.

"Why would they do that to your uncle?"

"Probably because he fucked them over." Gunner hung his helmet on his handlebars, then lifted me off my seat by my waist. "Trust me, my uncle was no peach. If those dudes wanted to jump me, they would have. Running into them could be a good thing, actually." He grabbed the edges of my jacket and pulled me into him with a boyish grin. "Now, can we enjoy the rest of our evening together? *Without* talking about other men?"

"Fine," I sighed in mock disappointment, reaching up on tiptoes to kiss him.

He hesitated at the door leading inside, chewing his lip as he turned to me. "Before we go in, I just want to say, don't get freaked out by the stuff I'm into." He rubbed the back of his neck sheepishly. "I never have women over, so it's a bit of a man-cave. Just, you know, it doesn't define who I am, okay?"

"Gun," I laughed, threading my fingers through his. "I don't know if there's much more about MC life that can shock me."

"I guess we'll see," he muttered, pushing the door open. Horus immediately sailed from his shoulder into the house.

From the outside, his house looked like one of the smaller ones in the compound, but the inside was as open and spacious as a cathedral.

The house only had one story, with high arching ceilings and an open floor plan. It resembled a hunter's cabin, with dark wood accents, exposed beams, and a massive stone fireplace. Horus had perched on a hunk of wood mounted to the wall near the ceiling, which blended in seamlessly with the beams.

Gunner had minimal furniture and the space was spotlessly clean. Skylights and huge windows made it seem even bigger, bringing the dark desert wilderness inside. Once I had a moment to admire the house itself, my eyes fell upon what he must have been warning me about.

The wall surrounding the fireplace was completely covered in a display of weapons. My eyes took in the massive assault rifles first, then moved across to the hunting rifles, then shotguns and revolvers—some of which looked to be antiques. He had a small collection of more modern-looking handguns, then blades of every size, shape, and curvature along the far side.

"You already knew I liked weapons," he said. "I'm kind of a collector, too."

"Gun, these are beautiful." I moved closer to inspect a wicked-looking machete-type of blade with a golden handle. The blade itself was inscribed with some kind of pictographs that looked hundreds of years old. "Where did you find these?"

"Here and there," he shrugged. "That one at a market in Tijuana a couple years back. The guy tried to tell me it was Aztec, which is probably a load of shit. I knew it'd look nice on my wall, though. Got a good deal for it."

I dropped down next to him on his low sectional couch, still taking in the artifacts on his wall. "So why the fascination with weapons?"

He propped his feet up on an ottoman, sinking low into the cushions. "I dunno. They gave me a sense of...*control*, I guess. Which I had so little of growing up. Every decision in my life, from the clothes I wore, to the people I hung out with, was predetermined for me based on my family name. It's kind of morbid, but," he laced his hands behind his head, "it's fascinating to me, how many methods we've invented to fight. To defend ourselves."

"To kill people," I said.

"No, baby girl." He looked at me. "I mean it when I say *defend*. Weapons were invented out of the need to survive, and later, for protection. I've never killed anyone unless out of absolute necessity."

"I get that, love, but," I tried to choose my words carefully, so as to not make this an argument, "you can't deny that weapons have been used to achieve terrible things since the Collapse. It's how your uncle and General Tash rose to power, for instance."

"You're not wrong." Gunner smiled gently, humoring me. "But against them, I'd rather have a weapon than not, wouldn't you? To increase your chances of survival, even a little?"

"Sure, I guess."

"This is why me teaching you this stuff is so important." He slid an arm around me, drawing me in close. "'Cause if some small-dicked fucker tries to touch my girl again, I want to give her the power to make him regret laying eyes on her. If I gotta arm my girl to give her a fighting chance? So fucking be it."

I smiled at the protective growl in his words, remembering the surge of power and fearlessness that came from handling the weapons today. It filled me with a deep appreciation that he didn't want to just protect me from danger, but give me the opportunity to protect myself.

I then traced the 2A patch on his cut, which he had yet to take off. "What does this have to do with it?"

"A well-regulated militia, being necessary to the security of a

free state, the right of the people to keep and bear arms, shall not be infringed," he recited.

"Pretty sure that document got shredded when DC got ransacked," I pointed out.

"Sure, it's not law anymore, but the idea behind it is why we're alive and free to govern ourselves." His lips brushed across my forehead. "And so many others aren't."

I nestled my head under his chin. "Do you think life will ever go back to the way it was before? You know, just…normal?"

"Nah." He wrapped both arms around me. "I don't ever want it to, honestly. The cycle will just start over again, and our great-grandkids will be in this same fucking mess a couple hundred years from now. Besides," he squeezed around me, "I never would've met you in a normal, boring life."

"That's true." I placed a kiss on his throat, shifting across his lap to get more comfortable.

Gunner's Adam's apple bobbed as he swallowed. "Can I tell you something kinda fucked up?"

His pulse began to accelerate as I kissed his neck. "You can tell me anything."

"I'm glad the Collapse happened. Not like I'm happy that people died, lost their homes, and rights and stuff. But I hated my life before. Sneaking off to ride with Reaper and Jandro on weekends was the only freedom I had. After everything went to Hell in a hand-basket, it was like I could suddenly do anything I wanted. No one had control of anything, which meant my family couldn't control *me*." His nose nudged against mine. "What kind of person does that make me, baby girl?"

I curled my legs up, wrapping my arms around his neck. "It doesn't make you anything, Gunner. You're just a person. Your story is unique, but so is everyone's, in a way. If I could go back, I…I don't know if I'd do anything different, to be honest."

"You could've become a doctor." His fingers lightly grazed over my back. "Delivered all the babies you wanted, get paid lots of money, married some rich guy who'd spoil the shit out of you."

"Bo-*ring*," I snorted. "Being a trophy wife is not for me."

"Yeah, you'd rather run around with a bunch of outlaws?" He smiled against my cheek. "Deal with knuckleheads like us, when we just make your life harder?"

"Life is hard, regardless," I sighed into his shoulder. "But I think the worse thing would be feeling alone. Not having a friend, family, or even an animal to care about you. That time between leaving Texas and meeting you was the darkest time of my life."

A shuddering breath escaped me. I'd never told anyone this, not even Reaper. Gunner's palm—running up and down my back in a soothing pattern—gave me courage I didn't know I had, to voice a deep fear I never before had put into words.

"I wanted to lay down in the desert and give up so many times," I whispered. "I'd fall asleep alone and hungry, wishing I wouldn't have to wake up. I had noth-ing. No parents or family left. No friends after East

Texas was annexed and everyone tried to flee. I didn't even have a degree to validate my education."

"I'm so glad you didn't," Gunner murmured against my temple, rocking me gently in his lap. "I'm so glad you're here with us, baby girl."

"The only thing that kept me going," I clutched tightly to his shoulder, "was having patients to care for. Sometimes I'd be the only medic for miles, and I couldn't leave people in pain or with treatable injuries. I had no one to turn to myself, but I was *something* to complete strangers. So I couldn't let myself stop. I couldn't let anyone else feel as low as I was."

"You *matter,* beautiful." Gunner spoke each syllable with heavy weight and intention. "Not just because you're a medic, or that you're gorgeous and smart and care so much. You're even more than the sum of those things. You're *you.*" He squeezed around me tightly, like I would slip away at any moment. "And you're ours. And you're loved. You're never alone, Mari. I promise you."

I touched the tip of my tongue to his ear, my insides fizzing like a bottle of champagne. "Thank you, but you didn't let me finish."

"Oh, sorry." He grinned, planting a kiss on me. "Go ahead."

"I was about to say," I nestled my head into the crook of his shoulder again, "that I'd go through that all again if I knew the outcome would be this."

"*This* being?"

"Loved. Supported. Beyond any measure that I could ask for."

"You deserve it," he told me, blue eyes shining. "Reaper was right, as usual. You deserve more love than a single man can give." He brushed a gentle caress across my cheek. "I just hope mine is good enough for you to hold on to."

"Gunner." I caught his hand, threading my fingers through his. "That's never once entered my mind. If what I give *you* isn't enough, just—"

"Stop right there, baby girl." He held our clasped hands over my mouth. "You're more than enough. You're *everything*."

He leaned us over slowly, until my back pressed into the couch and he hovered above me. His hands supported my head when our lips came together, while my palm kissed the beat of his heart.

Every kiss and touch throughout that night was heavy with the weight and depth of his love.

SEVENTEEN

MARIPOSA

"Did Gunner tell you about the bikers we met?"

I looked at Reaper over my shoulder, watching his eyes narrow in concentration as he gently washed my back with a damp, sudsy cloth.

"He did." Reaper squeezed the water out of the cloth and hung it over the side of the bathtub. "They must be what's left of the torched club we checked out. Must've not been home when the match got lit."

"You think they're on our side?" Freyja kept peeking at us over the edge of the tub with wide, concerned eyes, so I reached up to boop her nose with a soapy finger. She zoomed out of the bathroom and Hades took off after her with a bark.

"Seems that way, although it's still unclear what they actually want." Reaper reached around my waist, pulling me back to lay on his chest. "I think their little hand gesture was to test Gunner's loyalty, to see how he'd act when faced with his uncle's brutal death."

"Especially if he was away from the rest of you

guys," I mused. "Like, in case we had another hidden betrayer. I wonder if they had one of those too."

"It's possible. Tash likes to fuck around with people's loyalty." The bathwater sloshed around our naked bodies as he picked up his whiskey glass from the edge, then held it in front of my face. He laughed at me shaking my head, kissing my hair before he sipped from it. "You didn't develop a taste for it last time?"

"It tastes better on you," I purred, leaning my head back on his shoulder.

"Mm, hang on." He took another sip before pressing his mouth to mine. When my lips parted, expecting his tongue, I got a mouthful of warm, bitter liquid instead.

"Ugh, *Rory!*"

He just laughed and laughed as I coughed and sputtered over the whiskey. The sound of his laughter was deep, throaty music echoing off the bathroom walls as he wiped tears from his eyes.

"Sorry, sugar," he grinned, reaching for me across the bathtub. "That was a lot sexier in my head than real life."

"Hmph," I pouted, but allowed him to pull me back into his arms. "You owe me."

His body went stiff for a moment. I felt his heartbeat accelerate in his chest. "I might have just the thing." He dropped a kiss to my shoulder. "Ready to get out?"

We stood and dried off with fluffy towels. I grinned to myself as I rubbed the towel over my face and hair. Every day that I washed up or got dressed in here, I felt like a princess, not a biker's old lady. Sometimes I still had to pinch myself to realize I wasn't dreaming.

Hades and Freyja watched us from the dog bed in the corner of the bedroom as we made our way out of the bathroom.

"What you lookin' at, perverts?" Reaper muttered to them as he tied the towel around his waist. He seemed nervous, and started rummaging through his dresser drawers in search of something.

"Tessa told me something interesting today." I sat naked on the bed and continued rubbing the towel over my wet hair.

"Yeah?"

"She said this last pregnancy was the most painless out of all of them." I patted the towel over my back where my tattoo had started to itch. "I think it had to do with Freyja being there."

Reaper paused in his rummaging and turned to look at me, brows furrowed. "You think so?"

"I can't remember, but," I rubbed my forehead, "Freyja is a sex and fertility goddess, I think? I read about it so long ago."

"Well, in that case," he grinned wolfishly, "no wonder you can handle all three of us."

"Just barely." I stuck my tongue out at him.

He came over to sit next to me on the bed, holding something just out of view on his opposite side. "I'm glad you and Gun had a good day together, and that he finally got his head out of his ass." He slid a hand around the back of my neck, thumb circling gently. "And when all three of us get up in here? Damn, sugar. You're gonna be wrecked."

"Tell me about it," I groaned, but smiled wickedly

at the thought. Getting lost in the hands, mouths, cocks, and firm bodies of my men sounded like utter heaven.

"But I'm glad it's just me and you tonight." Reaper's hand fell to clasp my fingers on the mattress. His gaze darted away. He was nervous again.

"Me too." I leaned in to plant a peck on his lips. "Is everything okay?"

"Yeah," he laughed sheepishly, meeting my gaze again. "I love you, Mari. So fucking much."

"Oh, Reap." I somehow managed to wrap my arms around his neck, despite melting into a puddle. "I love you, too. So fucking much."

"I can't marry you," he blurted out. "Not legally anyway, but I was hoping…" His words trailed off as he showed me the small, velvet box he'd been hiding.

"Oh my God, Reaper." I slapped a hand to my chest. "Is this…a proposal?"

"If you have to ask that question, I'm doing a bang-up fuckin' job," he muttered. "Look, let me do it this way."

He lowered one knee to the floor, and opened the ring box to show a beautiful stone in a dazzling array of colors. It sat in a simple, silver bezel with a twisted rope design on the band.

"Mari, will you be mine forever?" He swallowed thickly. "And only fuck other guys that I approve of?"

The crude second half of his proposal made me giggle, but the fearsome Steel Demons president looked dead serious, if even afraid.

I held the sides of his face and kissed him deeply.

"I'm yours forever," I repeated back to him. "It's beautiful, but ring or no ring, I will always be yours."

His grin was equal parts joy and relief. "Put it on, then. I want to make sure I guessed your size right."

I extended my left hand, and he slid the artfully crafted band over my ring finger knuckles with little resistance. It fit comfortably, with a noticeable weight to it. Once on my hand, I noticed the R and M stamped into opposite sides of the stone.

"It's beautiful, Reap." I tilted my hand back and forth to admire the color shifting in the light. "Did you get this at the market?"

"I had a metalsmith there put it all together, but I already had the stone and the setting." He swallowed again, staring at the ring on my hand. "They were my mother's. She used to make jewelry."

"Reaper." I fought back tears as I brought my hands to the sides of his neck, beyond touched at the significance of what he just gave me. "Are you sure you want to give me this?"

"Never been more sure of anything in my life." His green eyes lifted to mine, somehow hard and serious, while filled with so much emotion. "It was my mom's dream, for me to give one of her pieces to the woman I'd give my heart to forever." He laughed softly. "I was such a dumbass. I told her I'd never get locked down, never do something as cheesy as that. But fucking look at me now."

"I like you cheesy," I chuckled. "And I love how you love me. I'll never abuse that, Rory. I was always yours first. I'll love you until the end."

For once, he didn't balk at me using his birth name. For once, I wasn't making fun of him. He must have understood I was speaking to the man his mother named and raised, the person he was before becoming Reaper, the Steel Demons president. I loved them both —who he was before and now. They blended into each other to make an incredible, complex person—one capable of loving and caring so deeply, while striking fear in the hearts of all who threatened him.

One did not cancel out the other. And I loved it all.

"Mari," he groaned, hands sliding to my waist as his torso moved between my legs. "In a world that has gone so fucking wrong, you are the one thing that's right."

His kiss was warm, a soothing balm without its usual rough, biting edge. The weight of him leaned me back on the bed, and his hand was quick to support my head on the mattress. A quick shimmy of my thighs around his waist made his towel drop. His naked, freshly bathed skin covered mine with a delicious heat.

When his mouth moved to my neck, I stared at the ring on my hand. It was mesmerizing, shifting greens and pinks as it caught the light. And it looked so perfect and regal on my hand, which now rested on his shoulder.

"I love this stone," I whispered, dancing my fingers on his skin. "What is it?"

"Watermelon tourmaline," he answered, lips between my breasts.

"I'm honestly relieved that you didn't give me a diamond." My hand flattened and sailed down the wide muscles of his back. "Always thought they were kind of boring."

"Huh. Mom said the same thing." His rough, calloused touch swept over my flesh, bringing my nipples to hard, aching peaks. "She liked stones with colors and flaws. Depth. Hidden character, she called it."

"Funny." I sucked in a breath, sensation pulsing through me as his teeth and tongue grazed over my nipples. "I like my men the same way."

His laugh sent ripples of goosebumps along my skin. "That's why you're so perfect for us."

He made it as far down as my navel before I touched his cheek. "Come back up here."

"Not happening, woman. You know my rules." He smiled lazily, dragging his fingers down my belly, teasing toward my entrance.

As tempting as it was to lay back and let him work his magical tongue and fingers, tonight my body called for something different.

"Would you believe me if I said I didn't feel like coming half a dozen times before you get inside me?"

"Hmm." He pretended to think. "No."

"Reaper," I sighed. "Will you please come up here?"

He slid up my body with a frown, green eyes hovering above me while his cock rested on my hip. "Something wrong, sugar?"

"No, my love. Not at all." I wrapped my arms around his neck to pull him down. "Kiss me."

His arms slid around my back, the heat and weight of his whole body lowering gently as his mouth pressed to mine. Our lips moved against each other, tongues caressing and penetrating, a perfect prelude for what we were about to do. I shifted my hips underneath him, nudging my thighs up so his silky head kissed my entrance.

"I can't fuck you before you're warmed up," he groaned, forehead heavy on mine.

"Reaper, I'm warmed up every time I look at you."

He kissed the bridge of my nose with an amused huff. "On top of everything else, you're good for my ego, too."

"I just want to feel you inside me," the confession came out with a light whimper. "I want to come wrapped around you. I want to look at you and feel you on top of me."

He paused, looking at me with curiosity. Then a corner of his mouth quirked up as he dragged one finger down the length of my body.

"My dirty girl wants to make love to me, is that it?"

"I know. Kinky, isn't it?"

His finger found my core, nudging his cock out of the way so he could touch me. He dipped inside, releasing a groan at the discovery of how wet I already was. The pad of his thumb circled lazily around my clit as he pressed another finger into me, stroking my pussy in a way that brought my hips lifting off the bed.

"Reaper," I whined.

"I know, babe. Just checking you." His grin was wolfish as he withdrew his hand, aligning his hips with mine again. "I don't think I've done this before."

"Huh?" I stared at him.

A deep kiss pressed me down into the mattress. A

full-body shiver wracked me as his cock slid across the aching wetness between my legs.

"You're a lot of firsts for me," he admitted, settling over my body. "The first woman I really loved. I loved your mind first, I think. Then this smart little mouth." He traced my lips with his thumb before skimming down my chest. "Then your heart."

"Not my body?" I gasped jokingly.

"Of course I love your body." His hands ran down my sides as he stared at me reverently. "But have I really loved you with *my* body before now?"

He slid into me in one fluid stroke, clutching my hair in his fist to keep our gazes locked. All the air felt shoved out of my lungs as my head leaned back, my hips raised up for more.

"You know why I love making you come so much?" Reaper locked both hands in my hair, his body rolling over me with the slow, intentional penetration I'd been craving.

"Because…you love me?" I was half joking, half unable to form a coherent string of words.

He was right. I never felt him like this before either —stretching and filling me with such relentless care.

"Because I'm selfish." His forehead lowered to mine, lips hovering a hair's breadth away from a kiss. "I want to please you so fucking good, you'll never have a reason to leave me."

Noelle's premonition crackled through my head like lightning, just as his mouth fell to mine, and his cock hit new depths within me. Reaper's lips dragged to my neck with a groan, his shoulders flexing with restraint. He wanted to unleash that dominance, that strength and power he usually fucked me with. But he kept his thrusts slow, pressing all the way into me before slowly withdrawing.

He can't be, I thought, a cry on my lips as he filled me up again, lingering there before pulling his hips back. He couldn't be the one to break my heart. Everything he did was for me—my happiness, my safety. But if not him, then that meant…

I pushed the thought away, turning my hand so his mother's stone in my ring caressed his cheek.

"I'll never leave you," I panted in his ear. "Even if you don't give me ten orgasms a day, this ring is never coming off."

"Mmm." His mouth found mine for another kiss. "What's a good number then? Eight? Nine? How much slack are you willing to give me?" His serious face morphed into a devilish smile as he cupped one side of my ass, angling my hip higher.

"I mean… fuck!" He kept up the deep, slow tempo, but my clit was buzzing from the new friction. "Don't make me think of numbers right now."

"What would you rather think about while I'm so deep inside you?" he grunted out. "Christ, you feel so good. I need to love you like this more often."

My reply was a mix of wordless moans, gasps, and whimpers as the pleasure built, coiling like a spring where our bodies conjoined. Fingers dug into hard muscle. Flesh and heat collided and broke apart, again and again.

"What was that?" Reaper chuckled into my ear, his

voice raspy and ragged. "Do you want more of this from me, sugar?"

He swelled inside me, pulling a scream from my throat.

"Worshipping you," he groaned, his control unraveling with every breath. "Revering you. Loving you. With every inch of me."

My climax crashed over me, sending ripples of shivers from my head to my toes. Reaper did the opposite, his body stiff as he held me twitching in his arms, until his release spilled with a heavy groan. He melted over me, a heavy blanket of heat with a rapid pulse that matched mine.

I licked a bead of sweat from his neck. "That," I panted, "is definitely worth repeating."

EIGHTEEN

SHADOW

Why do you do this to yourself, my son?

"…what…?" I rolled over in bed, not ready to wake up. Sleep had become so pleasant now, and I wanted to stay there for a little bit longer.

I showed you the sky. I gave you my sight. Why do you continue to shroud yourself in darkness?

I cracked an eyelid open, squinting against the tiny strip of sunlight peeking through my blackout curtains. It was so reminiscent of my only view of the outside world from my tiny dungeon years ago.

No, the light wasn't coming from that. Someone was in my room. A tall figure, with wings spreading out to either side of him. The light was a glare reflecting off of something gold he wore, some kind of collar or chest plate.

I couldn't make out details, like his face or clothing. Sleep still held me in a warm embrace, my vision murky through slitted eyelids.

"Who's there?"

Hades will not take you prematurely, so there's no need to lock yourself in a dark coffin every night. The figure sounded like he was sneering. *You have as much right to the sky and sunlight as anyone else. You didn't know when I gave you my gift, but you must know it now.*

"Who the fuck are you?" I growled through gritted teeth.

You know who I am. I'm Horus.

The tether of sleep snapped and I jolted upright, wide awake. My room was empty. Somehow I knew it would be. He never spoke to me when I was fully lucid. And he had never explicitly told me his name before.

Horus, like Gunner's falcon. Was that why his bird came so close to me that time on the roof? I couldn't understand it, so I didn't bother to try.

Pushing the sheet back, I got out of bed and crossed the room to my window in two long strides. I snapped open the blackout curtains, the sunlight flooding my room making me squint a little.

The sun was already high and people were going about their days. Since taking the sleep medication, I'd been sleeping in later and later. I never knew that sleep could feel good. I'd begun to crave it after a long day, instead of drinking myself into a stupor to avoid it.

I showered and dressed quickly, hoping Jandro left coffee in the kitchen. He was always an early riser, and was likely at the shop already.

"Meow!"

I paused in drying my hair with a towel, cocking my head. Either that was something in the house squeaking or—

"Meow!" This time the sound was followed by scratching at my bedroom door.

It only took me cracking my door open for Freyja to squeeze through the gap and begin climbing up my pant leg.

"Good morning, funny kitten."

To my surprise, the greeting tumbled out of me without me having to think about it. With no other people around, I didn't have to worry about being socially inept.

I plucked the cat off of my jeans when she reached my thigh, carefully dislodging her tiny, needle-like claws. "Your human must be near," I added, more to myself than the animal.

Carrying the kitten in my palm, I left my room and started toward the stairs. Mariposa was already halfway up and shot me an apologetic look.

"Damn it! I'm sorry, Shadow. I'm going to have to put a harness on her or something."

"It's all right." I met her on the stairs and held the kitten out to her.

"She's really taken a liking to you." Mariposa picked up the cat with both hands, her thumbs sweeping over my palm. "The moment I walked in, she zoomed right up to your room."

I didn't know how to respond to that. Freyja's green eyes were glued to me, even as Mariposa scratched her head.

"She's a funny little animal. I really don't mind," was all I could think to say.

Mariposa smiled at me, turned to walk back down the stairs, and paused. "So how are you this morning?"

I realized she wanted to walk down alongside me, so I sucked in a breath and followed her steps. "Uh, I'm good. Quite good. And you?"

"Same. You're still sleeping well?"

"Yes, thank you." I debated telling her about the lucid dream right before waking up, but decided against it. I knew it wasn't from the sleep medication, but wasn't sure how else to explain it. "Are you looking for Jandro?" Something squeezed inside my chest as I asked, like I was secretly hoping for a certain answer.

"No, I know he's at the shop." She turned to me, setting Freyja on the floor when we reached the bottom of the stairs. "Today's my second tattoo session, right?"

"Oh! Right, yes." I hadn't forgotten, not at all. In fact, I'd been counting down the days until it was time to tattoo her again. I just never expected her to be the one to bring it up. I figured her men would have to cajole her into sitting down with me to finish it. But here she was, first thing in the morning, looking bright-eyed and excited.

And pretty. So fucking pretty.

"If you're busy today, I can come back later."

"No, no. Today is fine," I assured her. "I'll just get some coffee, clean and set up, then we can get started."

"Want me to clean while you start the coffee? Jandro took the whole pot."

"Of course he did," I muttered. "But no, you don't have to clean for me."

"I'm just excited to get started," she laughed lightly.

"I'll do it right, I promise. I know a thing or two about sanitizing."

I stood frozen, unsure how to feel about her cleaning my tattoo area. Mostly, I was floored at the fact that she was offering to help.

"Um, if you really want to—"

"I'm on it."

She went straight to my desk and pulled the spray bottle of bleach solution out from a drawer. With a few quick sprays onto a paper towel, she proceeded to wipe down the chair she would be sitting in. Before she had a chance to catch me staring, I abruptly turned and headed into the kitchen to start the coffee.

On my way back, I made sure to grab a clean towel from the guest bathroom for her armrest.

"What do you think?" She stepped back, and held her hand out to my spotless tattooing station.

"Looks great. Thank you."

As we sat down and I began prepping my tattoo gun and ink, I realized with the exception of Freyja, we were truly alone. While in her medic's office, I was forced to think of her in a professional capacity. But now it was just the two of us in my house, and I would have to touch her.

We hadn't been truly alone like this since *that* day.

"Where's Gunner today?" I hoped my tone was casual.

"Off on a supply run." I tried not to watch as she piled her hair into a topknot to keep it out of the way. "Is that okay?"

The question caught me off-guard. Her expression was concerned when I glanced up at her.

"That he's off getting supplies? Um, yes. I'm not sure I follow."

She smiled a bit sheepishly, lowering her gaze to her lap. "I just don't want to make you uncomfortable by coming here alone."

"You don't," I blurted out before I could think.

Her eyes lifted back to me, lit up with surprise. "Really?"

I nodded, heat filling my face before I turned back to my tattooing supplies. "You never have, to be honest."

"So we're okay, then?" she asked hesitantly. "To be unchaperoned, I guess," she added with a nervous laugh.

Her question bewildered me. No one had ever been so concerned with *my* comfort before. What was this feeling? She had a way of bringing up all kinds of sensations I never felt in my body before. I couldn't name what was swirling in my chest right then, but I found myself trying to hide a smile.

"I'm fine with it, as long as you are."

"Good," she beamed, looking genuinely happy. I couldn't completely understand why, but I liked seeing her happy, regardless.

I took a minute to adjust the voltage through my power supply, averting my eyes when she removed her top layer shirt to give me access to her back.

"How does it look?" She spun around in the chair to face away, wearing the open back top she had on last time. "It itched like hell, but I tried my best not to scratch it."

I glanced up. "Looks good." I swallowed, clenching my fist on my thigh. "Really good, actually. You took good care of it while it healed."

"Thanks." She tossed me a smile over her shoulder. "I think having a good artist helped."

Mariposa's back was smaller and leaner than most clients I'd worked on before, and I had to adjust the design as such. The Demon flowed surprisingly well over the contours of her body, accentuating her feminine curves, while also sending a clear sign to outsiders who she belonged to.

Fuck, I was staring again.

"Ready?" I asked when there was nothing left to stall me.

"Whenever you are."

I took a deep breath and laid my gloved palm flat on her skin, much like she did to me *that* night, and began to work.

Several minutes passed with the buzzing of my machine as the only sound. Mariposa sat like a rock, even when I added shading directly over her spine. She really was an easier client than most men I worked on.

"Can I ask a question?" She glanced back at me, her head resting on her arms.

I lifted my foot from the pedal, making the buzzing stop. A sharp claw of anxiety gripped my chest. "Um, sure."

"For a tattoo artist, you don't have many tattoos. Any reason for that?"

I released the breath in my chest and put my foot back

on the pedal. An innocuous enough question, but one I'd still have to answer carefully. "My skin doesn't hold ink well because of all the scar tissue. Lines get blurry faster, and it just doesn't look good. Otherwise, I'd probably be covered."

"The Demon you have doesn't look blurry. Did you do it yourself?"

I paused, lifting my foot again. She only saw my chest tattoo because of what we did. Or rather, what *I* did to *her*. I didn't even know anymore if it was a mutual act or not. All I knew was that it couldn't be repeated. Talking about it seemed to be off the table too, so why go there?

She's just making conversation about tattoos. Don't be a dumb fuck.

"I did, using a mirror and drawing it backwards. I don't have a lot of scars in that spot, so it turned out okay."

She didn't need to know my lack of scars there was because of the proximity to my heart. A blood sacrifice wasn't any good if it stopped spilling blood. They didn't cut me on the neck for the same reason.

Another few minutes of silence passed between us. As I worked, I felt the tension settling into her body, the subtle shifts and the urge to fidget.

"Do you want to take a break?" I asked her.

"I'm okay." She watched me again over her shoulder as I reached to dip more ink, her eyes following the length of my arm.

"You want to ask me about them, don't you?" Again, the words came out of me without thought. That seemed to be happening a lot today. Usually, I struggled to get words out.

"Do *you* want to talk about them?"

I looked at the crude handiwork decorating my forearm. Years upon years of scars weaved a pattern of distorted flesh. I wavered between disgruntled acceptance of my scars, and seething disgust. It wasn't really about my appearance, though. Most people had some amount of scars. What I hated the most was never getting the chance to be normal. The scars were a constant reminder of how I was shaped and molded into the socially-stunted freak I was now. I didn't know how to be anything else. I never got the opportunity.

"No, not particularly." I resumed shading Mariposa's tattoo, trying to filter out everything else but the artwork.

"Then I won't ask."

That too, made me pause. I could tell she was curious, and appreciated that she didn't push. The only conflicts I ever had with newer club members were with those who got too fucking nosy about me. I knocked Big G on his ass once years ago, after multiple warnings to stop getting in my face. No one asked nosy questions about my past or my scars again after that.

We continued on with little words between us, mainly me checking in on her pain level and her assuring me she was fine.

"How did you get into tattooing?" she asked at one point.

I took an extended pause to refill ink. The questions she asked were so simple, so entry-level to normal people. But I felt the need to answer in a particular way in order to keep...whatever this was between us. Talking to her gave me a sense of ease and comfort that I didn't want to end. Socializing was not my strong suit, but even I knew certain subjects were off-limits for casual conversation.

"I was, um, not formally educated," I began, returning my hands to her back. "I didn't learn how to read and write until a later age than most. So drawing pictures was how I expressed myself, how I communicated."

"That's really cool, actually."

A small surge of pride welled up in me, before quickly deflating. Of course she would think that. She didn't know any better.

"I started drawing with a stick in the dirt," I went on. "When I had access to pen and paper, I used that. I learned about tattooing in prison from another inmate. He showed me the stick-and-poke method, which was all we had. After Jandro and I left, he rigged up my first machine for me."

My voice sounded strange coming out of my own head. When was the last time I talked so fucking much? Probably never. But the words poured out of my mouth like a waterfall, and the smile over her shoulder grew wider as she listened. I started to feel like I'd tell her whatever she wanted to keep that smile going. Even the sordid details of my past I never told anyone before, if she wanted to know that.

"That's really amazing, Shadow. Did you design the Steel Demon logo too?"

"Yes, I did." I tried to keep my eyes focused on her skin, but couldn't resist meeting her gaze again just to see if that smile remained. "Reaper told me what he wanted, and I gave him a few rough sketches based on that. He picked the best one, in my opinion."

"Your *expert* opinion," Mariposa corrected me with a soft laugh.

"Hmm, maybe. I don't know."

"I do know. You're great at what you do, Shadow. Not just with the artwork itself, but you have a good bedside manner."

I pulled away to stretch my hunched-over position, mulling over her words. "I'm not sure what that means," I admitted.

"It's a medic term," she explained. "A medic's visit, or a tattoo, can be an uncomfortable experience. But if we can make the client feel at ease, less worried or uncomfortable, we can transform the experience into something good." Again came that smile over her shoulder. "That's what I mean by bedside manner. You've made my first tattoo a painless, fun experience, Shadow."

"I...I'm glad." My throat worked uselessly, my pulse going crazy as I processed what she was telling me.

She was...enjoying this? Not in spite of me, but *because* of me?

"Are you okay?" Her brows furrowed slightly.

"Yes! Yes, sorry. I—" I shook my head, nearly running a hand back through my hair, before I remembered and stopped myself. "It's just no one's ever told me that before."

"Someone just did," she smiled.

We continued on, Mariposa insisting she was good every time I checked in. Finally, I lifted my foot from the pedal and set my machine down. With a clean cloth, I wiped all the remaining excess ink from her back.

"I think we're done." A tinge of longing crept from my chest into my throat. "Go ahead and take a look."

Mariposa stood and stretched with a soft groan. I jerked my gaze away, the combination of that sound and the fluid movement of her body sending heat straight to my dick.

"Shadow, I love it!" She looked over her shoulder in the mirror, swaying her hips and shoulders to look at the tattoo from different angles. "Seriously, it's so badass!" She twirled until she faced me, her smile bigger than ever. "I'll have to come back to you for more."

"I'm glad you like it." I peeled my gloves off, sounding nonchalant, but the inside of my body sparked and buzzed like fireworks in a beehive. "And you know where to find me if you'd like more."

She took one step toward me, opened her mouth to speak, and promptly crumpled to the floor.

"Mari!"

I rushed over, not even realizing I'd used the shortened version of her name, and knelt at her side. "What's wrong?"

"Well, that's embarrassing." She let out a sheepish laugh and leaned to one side, bracing a hand on my arm.

"Are you hurt? Should I get Jandro?" Panic tightened around my heart like a vice. Jandro would be the best person to help. Gunner was gone, and Reaper would definitely kill me.

"No, no. I'm fine." She laughed again, this time nearly leaning her head on my shoulder. "I think I just stood up too fast after sitting for so long. I felt my leg going to sleep, but didn't think it would give out on me."

"So...you're not injured?"

"Just a bruised ego," she snickered. "As a medic, I should know better." She tilted her head, and this time it did touch my shoulder. "Sorry to worry you."

"I'm just glad I didn't—I mean, glad you're okay."

She let out a huff of breath, still laughing at herself. "You're sweet, Shadow."

More feelings erupted in my chest, foreign sensations I didn't have words for. Needless to say, no one had ever called me sweet before, either.

A slight turn of my head would bring my cheek in contact with her forehead that was still resting on my shoulder. Even such a small movement felt too close, too intimate. I'd seen her men touch her in such a way, which meant it was wrong for me to do.

But I never saw her put her head on anyone but her mens' shoulders before either.

"Can you stand?" I asked.

The confusion and anxiety about this close contact made my chest ache, even though I liked feeling the weight of her head on me. I liked the delicate scent of her hair and seeing her smile up close.

"Yeah, I think I'm good."

She lifted her head, but kept her hand on my arm. I closed my hand around her elbow to steady her as we rose from the floor together. And then, all contact was gone. The few feet of distance between us felt like a barrier that I dared not penetrate.

"I'd really appreciate you not telling anyone about my little spill." Her face flushed red, the embarrassed smile lingering.

"What little spill?"

The joke worked and she laughed, the pretty sound filling up the empty space in the house. I felt it almost like fingertips over my skin. I didn't say it out loud, but I'd also never breathe word of her head on my shoulder, her hand bracing against my bicep. Maybe it was wrong, but I wanted to keep those small moments of touch to myself. Just like how I selfishly recalled the feelings of her hands on my chest, her knee on my fingertips, and the silky warmth of her pussy wrapped around me. I lingered in that forbidden memory more than I would ever admit.

"Shadow, I'd like to tell you something." Mariposa clasped her hands nervously in front of herself, chewing on her lower lip.

Her nervousness made my anxiety dial up to an eleven. Could she tell what I'd been thinking about just from looking at me?

"Yes?"

"I just want to say," she took in a deep breath, "that I'm proud of you."

"Proud of me?" I blinked. "For what?"

"For everything," she breathed. "You taking steps to treat your sleep issues, and trusting *me*, a woman, to provide the medication. For cutting back on the destructive drinking, which is going to do wonders for your health. For talking to me, tattooing me, everything! I know it hasn't been easy for you, but you're taking all these new experiences in stride." She glanced down at the floor before looking back up at me. "I figured you don't have many people saying this to you, so I just wanted you to hear it from me. You're doing great, and yeah, I'm proud of you, Shadow."

I was stunned, rendered completely unable to do anything but stare at her. *She* said all of that to me? This woman, with her shifting brown-green eyes, the smile I couldn't get enough of, and the strands of dark hair falling out of her bun to caress her graceful neck?

This woman—so warm, captivating, and beautiful that three Steel Demons fell hopelessly in love with her, said she was proud of *me?*

The softest breath of air from her lips could have knocked me to the ground.

"Please say something," she laughed nervously.

"I don't—I just—" I stammered uselessly, the words out of my grasp. I forced a swallow and a deep breath. "Thank you. I don't know what else to say. It...It means a lot to hear you say that."

Her smile returned, and my heart truly stopped when she took a few steps toward me, shattering the barrier between us like it was nothing.

"Is it okay if I give you a hug?"

No amount of deep breaths and mental preparation could bring words to my mouth in that moment. I wasn't supposed to touch her at all, but that got blown out of the water because of her fall, never mind her tattoo. A hug was a completely foreign gesture to me, but that meant nothing in the grand scheme of things. Men hugged each other. Adults hugged children. It wasn't harmful. Not sexual. I understood logically that it was a platonic thing, but I never in my life had that much of my body touch another person.

But I wanted to.

Only with her.

My mind screamed *yes*, but my throat and tongue froze up. So I jerked my chin down in a sharp nod.

She came to me slowly, small hands skimming across my ribs to land gently on my back. Her head turned to rest one cheek in the center of my chest. Then, with a light squeeze of her arms, pulled her body flush against mine.

My hands stayed low at my sides as I just stood there, soaking up the most physical contact I ever had with a woman, or anyone.

The front of her body felt soft pressing into me, her cheek bringing a soothing warmth near my heart. Her hands moved with gentle pressure on my back, pulling forth a sensation that was so good, so intense, I wanted to release it with a moan.

"You can hug me back if you want to," she said in a small voice.

My attention returned to my arms at my sides. I knew hugs usually meant both people wrapped arms around each other, but what if I did it wrong? Plus, I had to be careful with her fresh tattoo.

Tentatively, I brought one arm around the back of her shoulders, just above the tattoo. She didn't seem at all fazed by my scars touching her, even tightening her arms around me when I used the weight of that arm to press her gently into my chest.

Mindful of her fresh ink, I kept my other arm lower, ultimately deciding to wrap it around her waist. With both arms, I returned the light squeezing that she initiated.

So this was my first hug.

I closed my eyes and willed my body not to shake from everything running through me.

NINETEEN

REAPER

I rapped my knuckles on Jandro's door while Hades sat like a good pup at my side. It was hard to look at him lately and remember that he wasn't just my dog, my most loyal companion and friend. There was some higher power at work here, using me for some divine purpose. Was that toothy smile mocking me or was this being in a dog's body truly happy to follow me around and guard my loved ones?

I questioned everything now. How he seemed to understand everything I said. The way he guarded Mari so fiercely, and even the circumstances of how I found him. After Mari told me what happened as Tessa was in labor, I couldn't bury my head in the sand any longer. I needed answers now.

"Shadow," I greeted the large man who pulled the door open. "Just the person I wanted to see."

His dark eye, uncovered by his hair, blinked at me in confusion. "Me, president? I...wasn't expecting you. Did I forget about something?"

"No. I apologize for dropping by unannounced, but I would like your help with something. May I come in?"

He pulled the rest of the door open and stood aside for Hades and me. The dog wandered in first, giving Shadow a cursory sniff and huff of approval before moving on.

The first thing I noticed upon walking inside, aside from all of Jandro's mechanic shit, was Shadow's desk with a sketchbook and his disassembled tattoo machine.

"Oh, hey, thanks for doing such a badass tattoo on Mari. It looks fucking great on her and she's already talking about wanting more."

Shadow cleared his throat and, unless my eyes were tricking me, even seemed to blush. My old lady had that effect on people, so it didn't concern me. If anything, I was pleasantly surprised she was able to have a positive effect on him at all.

"Of course," he muttered, closing the door behind us. "She's a good client. I'm glad you're pleased with it too. So what can I help you with?"

"You still have all those old books?" I asked. "There's some...ancient knowledge I want to look into."

That piqued his curiosity. "How ancient do you mean?"

"I'm not sure," I admitted. "Possibly thousands of years. I want to know about gods. Pre-Christian, all that pagan shit."

Shadow nodded and led me through his side of the house. "I may have some old books that used to teach about this kind of subject matter. Any particular pantheon?"

"Pardon?"

"Pantheon," he repeated. "Different cultures used to worship multiple gods. A grouping of gods worshipped by a single society is called a pantheon."

I stared at him as we walked into a small room lined with bookshelves. Each shelf was near-bursting full of books.

"How do you know all this shit?" I asked him.

Shadow scanned the titles on the shelves. "After we settled here, I asked Gunner to find me books on every subject that used to be taught in schools." He glanced at me over his shoulder. "I was never truly educated, as you know. I figured this way, I could learn some of the things I missed."

"It's an impressive collection," I mused, eying one shelf that was all about US military history. "Maybe we can use these to educate the kids when they're old enough."

Shadow coughed with surprise. "If you think they'll be useful, I'll be happy to loan them out. I have multiple copies of a few things."

"I'll talk to Andrea. She homeschools their little ones now. I bet she can make a curriculum for when they're older, too." I scratched my jaw. "But to answer your original question, no. I don't know what pantheon I'm looking for."

"What about names of gods? Any in particular?" Shadow began pulling books from shelves and setting them on a side table.

I swallowed, meeting the bright eyes of my dog. "Hades, Horus, and Freyja."

Shadow looked at me again with surprise. "You all named your animals after gods without knowing their origins?"

"We didn't name them. They told us their names."

This wasn't information I planned to spread to the whole club, but I trusted Shadow. Maybe he didn't have an animal bond, but with his inhuman strength and uncanny ability to see in the dark, I'd place all bets on him being something not-quite human as well.

Just as I thought, he seemed surprised, but not more than that. After a bit more shelf-scanning, he placed an impressive stack of books onto a side table. "These are all the books I have on ancient mythologies. You can look for the names of gods in the index in the back."

I grabbed the first book off the top of the stack, which was on the Aztec religion. One flip through the index told me I wouldn't find anything useful in there. The names of the Aztec gods were no less than twenty letters long and used too many Xs and Zs.

"They're not in this one." I set the book aside and moved onto the next one—Greek mythology.

Something about it rang a bell. Was it Mari that asked me if I took Hades' name from a Greek myth?

My pulse shot up as I scanned down the list of names in the index.

"There it is!" I declared, before running my finger across to find the page number.

"All of them?" Shadow asked me.

"No." My hands were damn near trembling as I flipped to the section in the book. "Just Hades."

And of fucking course. Hades was the god of death and ruler of the underworld.

"The gates of the underworld were guarded by his three-headed dog, Cerberus," I read aloud, before sliding my gaze over to *my* Hades. The damn mutt was goofing off, rolling around on his back on the floor.

"I found Horus," Shadow announced, showing me another book. "The falcon-headed god of the sky."

"For the Greeks too?"

"No," Shadow shook his head. "The ancient Egyptians." He sucked in a hard breath and nearly dropped the book he was holding.

"What's gotten into you?" I asked.

"There's...a story here." He shoved his hair back, odd-colored eyes moving rapidly over the page. "Horus battled with another god, Set, and lost his eye in the process." A hand floated up to the scarred side of his face. "I didn't lose my eye, but was blinded before being able to see with it again."

I looked back down at my book, reading more thoroughly on Hades rather than skimming like I just did. What I read legitimately made me drop the book. "Fuck me, this shit is freaky."

"What?" Shadow stared at me.

I looked back at my dog, still acting like a fool on the ground, twisting on his back with his tongue lolling out.

"Hades kidnapped his wife, Persephone."

The dog finally rolled over to his belly, barked once, then grinned at us.

"She was his prisoner at first but," I shook my head in utter bewilderment, "they eventually fell in love."

"Like you and Mariposa," Shadow breathed, voicing the connection I didn't dare say myself.

"What the fuck is happening here?" I raked my fingers over my scalp.

"Freyja." Shadow picked up another book and frantically flipped through it. "What can we find out about her?"

I went over to Hades and kneeled down to his level. "Anything you want to say about this?"

No response, but a big doggy smile, naturally. Still looking through the book, Shadow let out an amused huff.

"What'd you find?" I asked.

"Freyja drove a chariot pulled by two cats," he reported. "And she slept with four dwarves for some rare necklace."

My stomach turned in on itself. Clearly, Mari having a cat companion was no coincidence.

I recalled Noelle telling me her dream, supposedly from Daren, that Mari would love four men. So aside from me, Jandro, and Gunner, she would bring in one more. I couldn't even speculate as to who that was—there were no other men I trusted enough to be with her. It wasn't even the mysterious fourth person I was concerned about—but the other part Noelle told me.

That if I killed one of Mari's lovers, she'd never forgive me. So typical of Daren's uncanny ability, to give me a warning with no context whatsoever. Not that I believed my dead little brother was actually communicating with Noelle. Hades' amused smile and head tilt seemed to disagree with me, though. Like this vessel of an ancient god, or whatever the fuck, could actually hear what I was thinking.

"Anything else?" I rose from the floor, turning my back to the dog as I meandered back to the stack of books.

"She's the goddess of erm, love, lust, beauty, sex, and fertility." Shadow appeared deeply uncomfortable with all of those words. "She takes half of those slain in battle to her heavenly field."

"What happens to the other half?"

"They go to Valhalla, Odin's hall."

"And what pantheon is this?"

"Norse mythology."

"Gods from three different pantheons, all right here," I muttered under my breath. "How the fuck does that make any sense?"

"I'm not sure." Shadow held his chin, eyes darting over the open books spread out in front of us. "I wonder if it even matters."

My eyes narrowed at him. "What do you mean?"

"Death, the underworld," his finger tapped down on the section about Hades, "The sky and sun above," the finger moved to Horus's book, "and between the two, life and love." His fingertip made a small caress over Freyja's depiction. "What do they all have in common?"

"I don't fuckin' know," I groaned, rubbing my forehead.

"All these…human experiences were personified by ancient cultures. Deified, you could say. They were given a name, an image, and were worshipped."

"So?"

"Every ancient culture had a deity associated with death, the sky, and with fertility and beauty. Their names are different and they may be depicted slightly differently, but they're all the same ideas." Shadow approached another bookshelf, scanning the titles before pulling out one particularly ancient-looking volume. "I read about something called a collective unconscious by this psychologist in the early nineteen-hundreds."

"Give me the watered down version, if you will." My head was already spinning.

"Okay, so," Shadow paused in his rapid page-flipping. "The collective unconscious is this *something* that connects all humans. It's what unites us, in a sense. We're fascinated with death, we get, er, anxious about being accepted, we seek out, uh, love and partners—all of that is part of the human experience. The theory is that it's the collective unconscious that drives those desires."

"Okay," I sighed, rubbing my temples. "What does that have to do with gods?"

Shadow closed the book and put it back on the shelf. "Well, one theory is the collective unconscious is the divine part of humanity."

"I'm not following," I admitted.

He cocked his head toward the table where the open mythology books laid. "Did those ancient cultures create their gods, or were the gods inside them all along?"

"Fuck me. You really expect me to answer that?"

"It's just something to ponder. We can't prove whether the collective unconscious is real or not. But if they just made gods up, they would be more unique to that culture. We wouldn't have divine beings associated with love, death, and whatever else across *all* cultures."

"So say, the god of death," I turned toward my dog, who cocked his head at me, "he exists across all of humanity, all cultures. He's just given different names."

"That is the basic theory, yes."

Glancing back at Shadow, I tossed him a smirk. "You're a lot smarter than you put off, dude. I had no idea you knew half of this history-psychology shit."

"Ah—um, thank you, President."

"It's Reaper," I reminded him. "You earned the respect of calling me by name a long time ago." Crossing my arms, I turned in a slow circle to take in his library again. "Mari would get a kick out of this, I bet. She likes research, pursuing knowledge and all that."

"She's welcome here anytime," Shadow said, his dark eye brightening.

"Really?" I didn't hide my surprise. "Her presence doesn't bother you like other women, huh?"

"No, I uh…" A deeper shade of red crept up his face as he stammered. "I'm comfortable around her. It felt strange at first, but I think she's helping me get better at this in general." He gestured a hand between us. "You know, talking. Socializing."

"You have been more talkative lately," I observed. "Not a Chatty Cathy by any means, but I've noticed the change, Shadow. Your whole demeanor is more confident around people now."

"Thank you, Pres—ah, Reaper."

A sudden growl from Hades startled us both.

The dog lunged for the window, hackles raised and

teeth bared. A deep coldness settled over me. I hadn't seen him act like that since Mari was kidnapped at the market.

"What is it?" I followed him to the window to look, but saw nothing amiss.

Hades barked menacingly, then abruptly whined, rubbing a paw over his snout.

"Do you smell that?" Shadow cracked the window open.

I felt it in my throat first, like someone shoved sandpaper down my gullet, then saw it outside.

"Shut all the windows!" I rasped before a dry cough overtook me, my lungs already heaving for fresh air. "Do you have gas masks?" My eyes started to water, like someone rubbed peppers into them.

"I'll get them." Shadow coughed into his arm before running out of the room.

Outside, I watched the small canisters rolling over the street, releasing dense, fluffy smoke that burned the inside of my lungs and made my eyes water. Tear gas. Someone was attacking us *again*.

And then an explosion knocked me off of my feet.

TWENTY

JANDRO

I pulled the garage door down with a heavy clank of metal on concrete. Wiping my brow, I locked it securely before heading down the driveway.

Mari would be at Tessa's house until later, checking on her and the baby, while helping around the house, so I meandered to the front gate where I knew Gunner would be posted.

He and I were always cool, though not especially close. We disagreed more often than not, but respected each other enough to not start shit. Because of our differing opinions, Reaper often listened to us in equal measure. He balanced both of our viewpoints before coming to his own conclusion.

Reaper had always been my brother. I knew him almost as well as myself. In contrast, my friendship with Shadow grew out of him having no one else to help him lead a somewhat-normal life. So even though I knew the big guy for the shortest amount of time, I felt closer to him than Gunner.

Now that Gunner was part of our little love-rectangle, I felt an inkling to spend more time with him. Just to kick back as a couple of dudes who loved the same woman.

A screech and the feathered bullet flying over my head alerted Gunner to my approach. Or more likely, he saw me coming from down the street as soon as I closed the garage.

"Vice president," the posted guards mumbled in greeting as I approached the front gate.

"Just come to bullshit with your boss," I announced, shielding my eyes to look up at Gunner, sitting on the edge of the brick wall surrounding our compound.

The blonde Demon jerked his head at me in invitation to join him, a black cigarette between his lips. "Come on up, VP."

I grabbed the wrought-iron bars of the gate, hauling myself up and scooting onto the pale, sandstone bricks next to him.

"Smoke?" Gunner held his soft pack out to me.

"Sure. Thanks, bro."

He lit us both, then leaned back to address his posted guard. "Y'all nosy fucks can keep an eye on shit over there." He pointed at unguarded areas of the perimeter to the guys who'd been coming in closer to smoke, chat, bullshit.

They returned to their posts and Gunner exhaled a white cloud of smoke. "They're bored," he sighed. "Nothing's come near us for weeks. They're getting lazy, but I can only bark so much if I don't know what we're guarding against."

"You been rotating shifts?" I blew smoke out through my nose.

"Yeah, as much as I can. Problem is, we just don't have enough people for a compound this big. I can't exactly have guards twenty-four seven, then give 'em a week off for R&R."

"Reaper being extremely selective about who joins has only been good for the club," I reminded him.

"Yeah, I get it. This place is just kinda big for our britches, don'tcha think? We've got like what, ten empty houses? Mari's office was just a storage closet before Reaper made it a mission to get a medic."

"It's what we got. We'd be fools to give this place up." I took another drag. "Me and Shadow don't run into each other at home if we don't have to. I even got room for my chickens."

Gunner huffed out a dry laugh, exhaling smoke. "You and those damn chickens."

"They're great, dude. Low-maintenance care, free eggs. They walk around like funky little dinosaurs. Chela even jumped into my lap the other day."

"They make a great snack for falcons," he grinned.

"You keep that damn bird away from my girls. Plenty of ground squirrels and shit for Horus to eat."

"Yeah, yeah."

I flicked ash off the end of my cig. "So how are things?"

He lifted an eyebrow. "What *things* are you referring to?"

"You know, things in general." I blew out more smoke. "With the new woman in your life, for instance."

"She hasn't told you everything?" His voice revealed some surprise.

"Nah. Mari tends to keep the one-on-one stuff private. Not *everything* has to be shared, you know."

Gunner turned a thoughtful gaze to the horizon. "I guess I didn't really think about that part."

"I didn't either, 'til just now, really. Lots of things to learn and discover about sharing a woman." Now finished with my smoke, I stubbed it out on the rock wall. "So how *are* you handling it?"

He didn't answer for a time, just smoked pensively while watching the horizon like some damn romantic cowboy. "Good," he answered finally. "Like, I'm kind of amazed at just how good and easy it is to be with her."

"See?" I nudged his arm. "I told you, dude. It's not always easy, of course. Especially now that she has three of us to consider. But she's got a way of making you feel like the only man in her life, right?"

"Yeah," he admitted. "That whole day we spent together, I kept feeling like I had to hold onto it. To savor being alone with her because it would come about so rarely."

"Nah. Even when we're all together, her connection with each of us is pretty special. It takes getting used to, but it's worth it."

"I'm starting to see that." He barked out a laugh as he tossed his cigarette butt. "Listen to us fucking saps. I'm glad I told my guys to go away."

I looked over both shoulders to make sure no one was in earshot, but still lowered my voice. "Now, be honest. What did you think of the whole group bedroom scenario?"

"Huh, I forgot you were in the shower so you missed the ending." He rubbed a hand down his face to hide his smirk. "Honestly, it was fucking hot, man. She wanted to watch me finish myself off, so I got closer to her. Reaper was pounding her and, well…I made a fucking mess of myself."

"Atta boy." I slapped his back. "Other dicks in the bedroom don't have to be weird, if you don't let them."

"Guess not," he chuckled before a stern mask took over his face. "Be right back," he muttered, then his eyes rolled back until only the whites were visible.

"Aw, fuck," I grumbled, grabbing his arm to prevent him from tumbling over the wall. "This can't be good." I looked up in search of Horus, knowing Gunner was looking through the falcon at that very moment.

His blue irises rolled back into view less than a minute later, as did the control of his body. "We need guns and gas masks," he hissed, climbing down the wall. "We're about to be attacked."

In disbelief, I looked out at the empty, silent desert beyond our walls. "Gunner, what the fuck?"

But he was already running along the perimeter, whistling loudly and yelling to the guards, "Rifles up, fuckers! Goggle and mask up! This is not a drill! Our enemy is airborne!"

They sprung into action, following their captain's orders, but looked just as confused as me.

"Gunner, where—"

Something small and metallic whizzed by my head.

Another hit me square in the back and clattered down the wall to the ground. A dense, white smoke began pouring out of the canister. By the time I felt the stinging in my eyes and throat, it was too late.

Hundreds more of the tear gas canisters sailed over the walls, seemingly out of nowhere. Coughs and cries of confusion filled the air. Even without the burning in my lungs and eyes, visibility was reduced to nearly nothing as smoke filled the air.

I scrambled off the wall, covering my nose and mouth with my shirt as I headed for the clubhouse. We needed guns. We weren't getting choked and blinded for no fucking reason. I had to reach the armory.

Half-blinded by tears and stinging pain in my eyes, I spotted my woman running to rush out of the clubhouse while I, and a dozen others, crowded the doorway to rush in.

"Jandro, what's happening?" Mari moved away from the door, flattening herself against the wall to let the stampede of people through.

"Attack," I rasped through my body-wracking coughs. "Smoke and tear gas. Keep everyone insi—"

A deafening *BOOM* rocked the building, knocking me off my feet and directly into her. Hysterical screams from outside made my blood run cold.

"You okay?" I turned my head to cough into my arm, which I braced against the wall to not crush her.

"Yes, but we need to help those still outside!"

"Follow me," I coughed. "Armory."

I grabbed her hand and pulled her down the hallway, my sight and breathing only marginally better away from the smoke. Two more blasts went off, rattling the windowpanes and creating even more chaos outside. I could only hope Gunner and his guys were handling it out there.

Our armory was once the cash vault of this ritzy, gated community. Nothing was left in it when we took over the place, but the impenetrable steel and concrete walls made it a great place to store guns.

"You know how to shoot now, right?" I held a rifle out to Mari.

"Um, kind of."

"Good enough. We need you." I showed her how to load the Mini-14, then shoved it into her hands, along with a spare box of ammo.

Next, I pulled out the box of gas masks and dug until I found one of the smaller sizes for her. "Put that on and adjust it as needed. The bottom part needs to seal to your skin."

I found one for me and put it on, grateful that I shaved that morning, as the mask created a seal. At that point, more of the guys started coming into the armory and taking their own guns and masks, their eyes red and noses runny from the gas.

"Make sure the women and kids are safe," I instructed, my voice muffled by the mask. "Have them hide under tables, beds, in closets, maybe. We don't know if they're bombing houses or what."

"It looks like grenades, VP," Slick reported. "Being dropped off by drones."

"Son of a bitch," I cursed. "Then we need to shoot down some motherfucking drones, don't we?"

A chorus of bloodthirsty cheers answered me, their guns raised in the air and red eyes narrowed with vengeance behind their masks. These were the Steel Demons I knew. This attack would not maim us.

I turned to Mari. "Stay by the building to help people find their way in. If you see something flying, shoot it. If you see anyone without a Demons patch, shoot them."

She nodded, but before I could leave, reached out and clutched the front of my shirt in her small fist. "I love you. Be careful."

I wrapped a hand around the back of her head, touching our foreheads together as best I could without my mask knocking into hers. "Can't kiss you now, but I will later, *Mariposita. Te amo.*"

"You better." She stepped back, brandished her rifle in front of her, and cocked it. "Now go."

Damn if I didn't get just a little bit turned on, seeing my woman dressed up like a post-apocalyptic vigilante. I had to give it to her good, after we were done with all this shit.

Leading my guys, I jogged out of the building into the war zone outside. You'd think there was a forest fire nearby, the smoke hung thicker than coastal fog. The air through my respirator was now just mildly irritating, rather than choking.

"Spread out," I commanded. "Stick to walls and what you can see. Don't run out into the smoke unless you see someone who needs help. If you do, send them back to Mariposa."

"Drone! Three o'clock!" Slick raised his rifle in the

air and fired off a shot. A choking, sputtering sound like a dying engine roared above us until a white object crashed into the street ahead of us.

"Wait, wait, wait!" I screamed at my guys who started running toward it.

My instincts were right. The crashed aircraft exploded, sending burned metal and melted plastic flying in all directions.

"Nice shot, bro." I clapped Slick's shoulder. "Be careful where you're shooting, though. Make sure no one's close by or under. That goes for all of you."

They gave me an affirmative and we kept moving. My eyes strained through the smoke that never seemed to clear up. White drones camouflaged well against this bullshit. Fucking Tash thought of everything.

I saw no signs of Gunner, so he and his guys still had to be at the front lines. My stomach clamped with worry, but I couldn't get to him just yet. I had to make sure no one in the residential areas was still out, possibly hurt and unable to move.

Keeping my head ducked low, I crept along the sidewalk toward my own house. Another blast sent my ears ringing, and I covered my head and face against a shower of dirt and rocks. The grenade had gone off in the small hill beyond the retaining wall next to me.

I scanned the smoke-filled sky, listening for the tell-tale buzzing of the drone through my ringing ears. Only by chance, I saw it as it swerved to head in another direction, and took it down with two shots. The white aircraft didn't explode on impact, which told me these things were only carrying one grenade at a time.

"Jandro!"

Two dark figures ran toward me, their features so obscured by the smoke that I didn't recognize them until they were right next to me.

"What the ever-loving fuck is going on?" Reaper roared behind his mask.

Hades hunkered down close to his side, an extension of his human master. Shadow loomed over all of us, his hair pulled back so the mask could seal to his face. The big guy's odd-colored eyes focused skyward.

Another blast went off and the three of us crouched low on the other side of the retaining wall. Shadow raised his rifle and fired off one shot, picking off the drone I had no idea was there.

"You can see through this shit?" I asked him.

"Not well," he admitted. "I can make out rough shapes in the smoke, though."

"I want his fucking head." Reaper was practically frothing at the mouth, rage in his eyes like I'd never seen before. "Tash is right outside our walls, I just fucking know it. He's sitting back and smiling. I want to hear him scream."

"Bro, take a breath." I clapped hard on Reaper's shoulder to get his attention. "We're blind right now. We've got to stay calm and get our people out of the way of these blasts. Then we can go after him."

Hades barked suddenly and took off running, his black fur becoming little more than a shadow in the smoke.

"Someone's in trouble. Mari!" Reaper bellowed.

"Stay back." I shoved a hand against his chest. "I

just came from there. I'll get her. You two keep picking off these drones, and sweep the residential areas."

I took off after Hades before he could argue. Reaper wasn't in a good state of mind right then. His obsession with bringing Tash down got in the way of his rational thinking. If he saw Mari in trouble, he'd positively lose it.

A blast knocked me to my knees. Hard asphalt bit into my palms, but the harrowing scream up ahead made the sting feel like nothing.

"Mari!"

I hurried to get my feet underneath me, but felt like I was moving through sludge, no matter what.

Dark shapes lay motionless on the ground up ahead and I still couldn't move fast enough. *Not her,* I begged whatever powers were listening. *Please not her.*

"Jandro, help!"

Her voice. Raspy and full of terror, but it was hers.

I dropped to the ground, only seeing her. "Why aren't you at the clubhouse? I told you to stay there!"

"It's Dallas!" Mari sobbed. "He blocked the blast from hitting them. Help me, I can't move him."

Only then did my gaze drop to the motionless figure on the ground. The cries underneath the limp body were barely discernible through the ringing in my ears. Together, Mari and I turned him over, rolling Dallas off of his two hysterically sobbing children underneath.

"Hey, guys." I tried to keep my voice calm as I moved between the kids and their father's body. "I need to get you inside, okay?"

"Dad!" Avery, his daughter, shrieked. "Why's Dad not moving?! I want my dad!"

Blocking their view with my arms, I looked at Mari over my shoulder. Leaning over Dallas, her hands were slick with blood as she searched for a pulse. When she caught my gaze, she gave a tiny shake of her head, her eyes glittering with tears.

Fuck.

Fuck everything about this.

"Daaaad!" the kids wailed, pushing on my arms as they tried to get around me.

"We need to get you guys inside," I repeated, numbness taking over me.

Dallas was dead.

No fucking way, how could we lose *him?*

Hades' growl pulled me back to the present. He grabbed Dallas's son by his shirt and started yanking him back toward the clubhouse.

"Mari, get them inside."

"We can't just leave him out here—"

"We can't leave *them* unprotected either. Go!" An increasingly loud buzz alerted me to another approaching drone. I jumped to my feet to make a shield over them, scanning the sky with my rifle ready. "Get them out of here! Get somewhere safe!"

"Jandro, look out!"

I didn't feel the blast. First I was on my feet, looking for the drone through the smoke. Then I was either falling or flying, maybe both. And then nothing.

———

BLACKNESS SURROUNDED ME, like I was floating in a pool of ink. I felt weightless, even bodiless. I tried to move my fingers and toes, but couldn't feel them in this space.

"Fuck no. Am I dead?"

Was I actually speaking, or just thinking? I couldn't tell.

If this was death, how fucking boring.

I just hoped Mari and the kids were okay. The guys would take care of her. Poor Dallas. Would I see him here? It didn't seem like anyone else was here but me.

Something appeared to shift and materialize in the blackness. I couldn't see clearly, but I could make out the rough shape of a man in front of me. He had no discernible features, but the solidness of his presence was a small comfort in this weird, floating blackness.

"You shouldn't be here," the figure said in a deep masculine voice, almost with an air of snobbery.

"Well, excuse me," I huffed. "I didn't exactly intend to stumble in here, wherever the fuck this is. Death? Hell? Some signage would be helpful, you know."

"Neither. You're close, though." The figure seemed to cock its head to the side, like a dog. "But it's not your time, Jandro."

"Sweet. Send me on back then." I tried to ignore how unsettling it was that this figure knew my name.

"I can't *send* you anywhere. You have a choice to make—fight and live, or give up and pass on. Mariposa is doing everything in her power to save you right now. The least you can do is fight for your own life."

How the fuck was I supposed to respond to that? I

was hanging by a thread, and my girl was probably scared shitless.

"Who are you?"

Not that I could see anything, but I *felt* like the figure smiled.

"I'm Hades."

"Hades?" I repeated. "Hades, the dog?"

"Part-time dog. Full-time lord of the underworld."

"…What…the…"

"I suggest you make your decision soon, Jandro. I would hate to open my gates to you prematurely. Unless," he paused, his tone changing as if talking to someone else, "you'd be interested in taking him, dear? He did fall in battle, after all."

A second figure materialized, this one definitely feminine. Like the masculine one, I only saw the rough outline of a waist and hips to die for. She may have had long hair, I couldn't tell. If the weight of their presences didn't feel so heavy and real, I would've been convinced I was hallucinating.

Fuck, for all I knew I *was* hallucinating. Didn't mean it wasn't real on some level.

"No, darling, I can't take him," the feminine figure protested. "It's far too soon. He's too young and handsome."

"Precisely what I was saying," Hades muttered.

"And who are you, the tooth fairy?" I asked. "An angel?"

The feminine figure chuckled, and I swore soft fingertips caressed my cheek. "Perhaps you'll recognize me with this sound?"

A rumbling purr filled the air, the fingers on my cheek now digging in like tiny claws.

"Freyja?" I whispered, dumbfounded.

"Oh, *Alejandro,*" she murmured, with a perfect Spanish accent. "You have so much love to give, beautiful children to make. You're a fighter, handsome. Fight for what matters. Don't let go yet. We'll be here when you're ready."

"Wait," I protested as both of their presences started lifting away, like anchors being pulled up. "I can't feel shit! How am I supposed to fight?"

But no answer came. Both of them were already gone.

TWENTY-ONE

SHADOW

"Like hell I'm going wait and see if my wife is fucking dead!"

Reaper was like a rabid dog, face twisted behind his mask with a murderous expression. I always knew he had a temper. Anyone could see the rage he carried just below the surface. In situations like these, he always unleashed it on his enemies. It was one of the reasons our club had a reputation for such violence and ruthlessness.

But today our enemy was invisible, and his rage was aimed at whoever stood between him and his woman.

"Shadow, if you don't let me go, I fucking swear I'll shoot you. She needs me!"

"Jandro has her," I reminded him, tightening my grip on his cut. "President, we need to spread out. Once everyone's contained, we need to get on the rooftops. Get above the smoke so we can—"

A nearby blast sent us crouching to the ground as pebbles and debris showered down on us.

"Fuck, I think that was my house." Reaper waved his hand in front of his face, trying to clear the smoke, to no avail. "Noelle might be inside."

"Go." I slapped his shoulder. "Check on her. I'll swing around to the front of the compound."

"Find Mari. Please," he begged. "I need to know she's okay."

"I will, president." Truth be told, I too found myself concerned about the pretty medic.

It shocked me, this burning need to see for myself that she was unharmed. I never worried about Jandro, he could take care of himself, but he was the only other person I cared about to an extent such as this. A woman I barely knew now occupied more of my headspace than my best friend of several years. This worry was unsettling.

I took off in the opposite direction as Reaper, with only the few feet of road ahead of me as my guide. The rough shapes of roofs and streetlights all looked the same in the dense fog. And with the sun blocked out, it was impossible to tell which direction I was going.

I jogged blindly down the street, trying to listen for the drone propellers, but these aircraft were nearly silent. They had to come into my line of sight before I shot them. I took down three as I ran, all with their grenades already released. Fuck, this was bad.

How long had Tash been planning this attack? Since I shot down that first drone weeks ago? Earlier?

A loud blast stopped me in my tracks. I crouched low, covering my head, my ears ringing. That one was close, probably no more than fifty feet away. The harrowing scream that followed it pushed me to my feet.

"Jandro!" a woman's voice wailed. Mariposa's voice.

I pumped my arms and legs hard, sprinting toward her voice at top speed. My heart felt like it was going to burst from my chest, and it had nothing to do with how hard I was running.

Dark shapes on the ground slowly became clearer as I got closer. Some shapes were frantically moving, others lay eerily still. "Who's there?" Mariposa waved her hand in front of her face as Reaper had, her hair wild and tangled.

"It's me, Shadow." I reached out and touched her shoulder, not realizing it until I felt her arm trembling under my hand. "Are you hurt?"

"No, but—"

Ear-splitting cries cut her off, coming from the ground near my feet. I took my hand from her shoulder and looked down. Two children huddled together, screaming, next to two motionless bodies.

"Jandro!" I lowered down, laying my rifle next to my barely recognizable friend. An overwhelming burning smell nearly gagged me through my mask.

"He's got a pulse, but it's faint." Mariposa yanked the children close to her, picking up the girl first, then holding tightly to the boy's hand. "We can't waste any time! Can you carry him to my office?"

I grabbed Jandro's limp arms and threw them over my shoulder, letting his torso slide down my back until I could hold him around his waist and legs.

"Who's the other one?" I asked Mariposa, rising to my feet.

"Dallas." She led the way back toward the club-house, fighting against the children who were trying to run back out to the street.

"Is he...?"

She gave me a single look that told me all I needed to know.

"I'll go back for him," I told her, shifting Jandro higher on my shoulder.

"Thank you, Shadow. Fuck, I'm really glad you showed up."

"Me too. What happened?"

"Give me a second," she huffed, pulling open the clubhouse door and yanking the kids inside.

I held the door open with my free hand, blocking the entrance with my body as Dallas's children fought, kicked, bit, and screamed at Mariposa.

"Can you take them, please?" she nearly tossed the girl in her arms to a small group of women huddled inside. "Wait until the Demons say it's safe before you take them to their mother."

Finally free of them, she ran back to me, leading me down the hall to her office.

"Dallas shielded the kids from getting hit with a blast. Then Jandro came to help, and he shielded us from another one."

"Will he survive?"

Fear was the feeling I was most familiar with. I feared pain, confined spaces, and the flashbacks that assaulted me without warning. I recognized fear in the faces of most people who looked at me. But never before had I feared losing someone I cared about.

"He will." Mariposa wasn't afraid. She was tight-lipped, determined. Maybe even angry. She reminded me of Reaper in that moment, holding back a storm with sheer will. "I'll drag him back to life, even if I have to go all Dr. Frankenstein on him."

"I like that book," I muttered, ducking in the doorway to her office to not further injure Jandro.

"Yeah? You like to read? Lay him down on his stomach for me, please."

I lowered myself to the level of her table, while she slid him carefully off of my shoulder. "Yeah, try to read anything I come across, really."

"Jesus Christ." Mariposa's attention was back on the man she loved, lying face down on her table. "Why'd you have to do that, *guapito*? I love you, but you're such a dumbass."

"Do you, um…" I watched as she cut away what little remained of his clothes, exposing the charred, raw flesh of his back. "Do you need me to do anything?"

Her eyes lifted to mine. Maybe it was the shock of everything going on, but I no longer felt uncomfortable with her looking at me.

"Can you get Dallas, please? Wrap him in a sheet and put him somewhere until, you know, until we can…"

"Yes, of course."

"Be safe out there, Shadow."

"I will, Mariposa."

———

I'D MOVED BODIES BEFORE, but never one of my own brothers.

Dallas and I weren't close, but he was a good man, and a good Demon. I didn't know if there was any social etiquette to treat dead comrades a certain way, but it felt wrong to just drag him along the ground.

I found several dark sheets and wrapped him up tightly in the street. All the while I watched for more drones, and shot a few more down that came close. Most of our people seemed to be safely inside, but the drones kept coming. The teargas seemed to be dissipating now. I could see clearer, but the chemicals still itched the hell out of my eyes and sinuses.

When I finished wrapping Dallas's body, I slung him over my shoulder like I did Jandro. I placed the body in one of the empty rooms in the clubhouse and locked the door. Mourning him would have to wait.

Once he was secure, I went back down the main hall to check on Mariposa and Jandro.

"How is he?" I asked from the doorway.

She looked up from examining his back with a grim expression. "Not good. I've got fresh blood going into him, but his pulse is still weak. I can barely detect a breath. And that's got nothing to do with his burns—"

Her voice cracked and she quickly wiped her eyes with her sleeve. My chest ached at seeing her emotion. I wasn't the only one who cared about him. She loved him, and carried the burden of trying to save his life.

"He'll pull through." I walked in to stand next to

her. "He's stubborn as hell, he won't let this stop him. And you're a talented medic. He's lucky to be in your hands."

She gave a weak smile. "Thanks, Shadow."

I thought of the hug she gave me. Would it be appropriate to hug her now? People hugged to comfort each other, didn't they? My fingers itched to reach out to her, to ease the worry on her face.

"Where are the others?" Mariposa asked, turning back to Jandro. "Have you seen Reaper and Gunner?"

I closed my fingers at my sides. "Reaper was checking on his sister at home when I found you. I haven't seen Gunner, but I assume he's with his guards at the front gate."

"Can you check on them for me? I should get multiple stations set up in case there are more injuries." She looked worriedly around her small office. "God, I wish I had clones of myself."

"I'll head to the front gate now." I retrieved my rifle from my holster, checking it for ammo. "I'll let your men know you're safe."

"Thank you, Shadow." Relief softened her features slightly, which eased the ache in my chest.

I looked down at Freyja, who was nuzzling Jandro's hand that hung down from the table. "Watch over your human, little one."

I had barely turned to leave when crashing sounds came from outside. Mariposa and I braced ourselves, but it didn't sound like grenade blasts.

"Stay here. Lock the door," I instructed, cocking my rifle.

Silently, I moved out into the hall with my weapon raised. Keeping it against my shoulder, I pushed the clubhouse door open and surveyed the outside. Visibility was much clearer now, I could see all the way down the street.

And three drones hovering in the air.

I took aim, curling my index finger around the trigger, when the one I set my sights on suddenly jerked to one side and dropped sharply in altitude.

"The fuck?"

Out of nowhere, it simply dropped out of the sky and crashed to earth. The two others did the same, one after another.

"Yo, you seeing this?" someone yelled.

I looked to the left to see Reaper running up the street toward me.

"She's fine," I told him before he could ask. "But Jandro's badly hurt. She's in her office with him."

He nodded, the relief palpable on his face. "What do you make of this?" He gestured toward the sky.

"That they're crash-landing all of a sudden? I have no idea."

The president clapped my shoulder. "I think the worst of it is over. Gunner's on his way in. Cover him at the gate, will you? We'll be with Mari."

"Yes, president."

Gunner ran past me, not a minute later, on my way to the gate. "Thanks, Shadow. A lot of the same shit, just dropping out of the sky for no reason. Keep your eyes peeled, though."

I climbed the metal rungs embedded in our

perimeter wall and squinted at the landscape beyond our once-safe home. Broken drones and their parts lay strewn across the desert like some kind of robot cemetery, but nothing else seemed amiss.

"See anyone out there?" I asked Benji.

"Not a damn soul," he spat. "Some of the tear gas didn't make it over the wall, so we got faces full of it. Then, still nothing once it cleared. It was like some damn robot uprising. 'Til their batteries went out."

"That's impossible," I muttered.

The tear gas cleared up hours later, with no drones coming back to life. Near dusk, I took my mask off and filled my lungs with sweet, fresh air. In the last sliver of sunlight, I spotted movement that made me look closer.

Three figures approaching on motorcycles, with a black bird flying above them.

TWENTY-TWO

MARIPOSA

"God fucking damn it, Jandro."

I wiped my face with my arm, tears and snot making a mess on my sleeve. But I couldn't stop. I wouldn't stop until I saw a fucking heartbeat on that monitor.

"Clear!" I yelled before pressing the defibrillator paddles on his chest again.

His body jumped with the jolt of electricity. But the monitors still displayed a flat line. His kissable, pillowy lips were turning blue.

"Fine, Jandro." I set the paddles aside and ripped off my gloves. "You want to play that way? You're just going to make me even more pissed off for when you wake up."

I went to my cabinet and pulled out the small glass jar of adrenaline. Ripping open a fresh needle and syringe, I stuck the lid and withdrew the highest safe amount to give a human without throwing them into cardiac arrest.

Safe was an iffy word when it came to shooting pure adrenaline, but I was desperate. We already lost Dallas. I wasn't about to lose one of my men.

"I love you," I told Jandro's lifeless body stretched out on my exam table. "But I fucking hate you right now." With that, I stuck the syringe directly into his elbow and shoved the plunger down.

Nothing happened right away, so I started up CPR on him again.

"Mari," someone said from the corner of the room. Probably Gunner, I didn't know. I had to fucking focus.

"Shut up," I responded, counting through my chest compressions before breathing into Jandro's mouth again. The butterfly necklace he gave me hung down from my throat, brushing against his chin.

Not a single cell in my body was ready to give up. I would not lose him. I'd break every single rib giving him CPR, before I let him go. But as I kept pressing down, kept giving him my air and trying to jumpstart his heart, the cold grip of fear started to creep in.

Just as I started feeling lightheaded and completely out of breath, the man on the table pulled in a ragged, desperate gasp of air.

The heart monitor beeped to life, almost too fast as Jandro choked and coughed, his body bringing in much-needed oxygen. I slid to the floor, completely drained of energy and also limp with relief. Someone pulled me back up, a solid chest and strong arms wrapping me in a hug. Leather and cloves filled my nostrils as kisses swept across my face.

"You did it, sugar." Reaper's voice was choked with emotion. "You're a fucking lifesaver."

Someone else had pulled the oxygen mask over Jandro's face, his breaths still deep and pained, but steadier as he regained consciousness. His pulse slowed gradually as blood returned the color to his face.

He pulled the oxygen mask from his mouth and looked at me.

"How long have I been out?" he rasped, barely over a whisper.

"You weren't breathing, and had no pulse, for nearly two minutes," I replied flatly. "You've sustained third degree burns on your back from the grenade. You've lost a lot of blood, required a transfusion, and might have brain damage from your lack of oxygen."

Jandro's eyebrows lifted. Most of his body was numbed from anesthesia, but he still had strength to move his head.

"You don't look too happy to see me, *bonita*."

I snapped.

Pulling myself out of Reaper's embrace, I took one long step to the VP's side, and slapped him hard across the face.

To say he was stunned would be an understatement. His jaw dropped as he clumsily raised a partially-numb hand to his cheek.

"Hey, hey." A hand squeezed my shoulder, and Gunner's soothing voice brushed across my temple. "Take it easy, baby girl."

He brought my temper down a couple notches, but I

was still focused on Jandro, seeing him through red-tinted vision.

"It stops with this, Jandro." I willed my voice not to shake. "You're not taking bullets for me anymore. You're not blocking grenades with your body anymore. I need you *alive*, you fucking idiot, don't you understand?"

No fucking way in hell would he break my heart by dying on me. I wouldn't allow it. Fuck Daren's prophecy. I didn't even notice the tears spilling down my cheeks until Reaper wiped them away with a rough thumb pad.

Jandro just shook his head at my demands. "Not happening, beautiful. It was either me, or you and the kids. I wasn't about to let you or them take any force of the blast." He shifted, trying to get comfortable in the makeshift hospital bed. "Why the fuck are all of you in here anyway?" He scanned the room, seemingly noticing Reaper and Gunner at the same time. "What happened? Is it over?"

"Yeah." Reaper scrubbed a hand down his face with a sigh. "It went on for a while after Mari got you in here and tried to stabilize you. We kept picking off drones, and they just kept coming. That was, until..." He looked to Gunner, like he couldn't believe the next part of the story himself.

"Until they all just started dropping out of the sky." Gunner crossed his arms, looking just as puzzled as Reaper. "Like their controllers got switched off, or ran out of batteries or something."

Jandro stared at him, wide-eyed. "All at the same time?"

"No, but one after another pretty quickly. It was

freaking weird. My guys are out combing the surrounding area right now. They couldn't have been controlled from far away."

"Did we lose anyone else besides…"

A dark, somberness fell over the room. I couldn't bear to say Dallas's name either, to refer to him in the past tense. Out of all the Steel Demons men, he was probably the most innocent and least-deserving to be killed in such a way.

"No." Reaper's face was grim, and he couldn't bring himself to make eye contact with anyone. My heart ached for him. I knew, as president, he took Dallas's death as his personal responsibility.

"A few minor injuries, but that's all." I picked up speaking, where Reaper clearly couldn't. "The effects of the tear gas have started to wear off. It was standard law enforcement stuff. Nothing causing permanent damage, thankfully."

"Do you know how Dallas…what the cause was?"

I let out a sigh, exhaustion hanging over me like a massive load on my shoulders. "His spinal cord was severed in multiple places, which was the most likely cause. He also had massive internal bleeding, which would have killed him if the spinal damage hadn't." My gaze dropped to the floor, my head feeling incredibly heavy. "There was nothing I could do."

"Did he go…painlessly?" Gunner and Reaper both looked up at Jandro's question, as if they needed to know this too.

I nodded, trying to turn my exhausted mind away from the image that would haunt me forever. Dallas running out to shield his kids. The blast knocking me off my feet. And he, in its direct path, falling limply on top of his children. He was dead before he hit the ground.

"It was over fast," I assured my men. "He didn't suffer."

They all nodded, that morsel of information a small comfort to them.

"We need to hold a memorial for him," Reaper muttered. "A big one, with the highest honors of our club. One on par with Daren's." He scoffed dryly. "Both of the Steel Demons who've died, did so protecting others. Funny how shit works out like that." He turned to look at Hades, who'd been sitting quietly in the back of the room, as if the dog would offer an explanation. But none came.

A heavy knock pounded at my office door, rattling all of us. Reaper and I exchanged a glance.

"This is your domain, sugar. You decide if you want people in here or not."

"President." I recognized Shadow's rough, but oddly soothing voice from the other side. "I'm bringing news that we've detained three men found outside the walls."

"Come in, Shadow," I called.

The door opened, and the large man quickly filled the remaining space in the small room. Freyja, who'd been curled up asleep on my stool, woke up at the sound of his knocking, and after a quick stretch, trotted over to her favorite human. Shadow picked her up without hesitating, tucking her against his chest with his forearm as he scratched her head with his other hand.

"Hey man," Jandro greeted tiredly. "Do you have

General Tash waiting for us with a bow tied around his head?"

"No. I don't know how to tie a bow." Shadow actually had to raise his voice to speak over Freyja's loud purr. "And it's not the general, regardless. It's three men from another MC."

"Great," Reaper growled. "More of the general's puppets. I hope you broke a few of their fingers? Got them started on at least thinking about talking. How many do you estimate were out there in total?"

"That's the thing," Shadow answered hesitantly. "They said they're alone, that they weren't part of the attack. They came to the front gate and allowed themselves to be detained willingly."

Everyone in the room stared at him. Except for Freyja, that is. Her eyes closed softly with blissed out relaxation in Shadow's arms. There was no place she'd rather be.

"Did they have patches?" Gunner's question cut through the silence. "What's their club name?"

"Yes. They call themselves the Sons of Odin."

Gunner and I looked at each other, clearly recalling the same three men who approached us at the cantina with his uncle's severed hand in a bag. Reaper also rocked back on his heels with surprise.

"Did one of them have a raven?" Gunner asked.

Shadow cocked his head, still scratching Freyja idly. "I spotted a black bird flying over them as they approached, yes."

"All of you, out." I made a shooing motion toward the door. "Question them. Find out what you need. I have to keep tending to this one." I jerked my head at Jandro.

Reaper chuckled, while Gunner beamed at me with a radiant smile. They each kissed me, while Shadow reluctantly slid a very sad-looking Freyja out of his arms. Once they were gone, I put on a pair of fresh gloves and slid a hand behind Jandro's shoulder.

"You should be good and numb back here now, so let me check out this burn."

"Yes, ma'am," he groaned, using his little remaining strength to lean forward.

I pulled away the gauze I'd drenched in antibiotic ointment and did a closer inspection of his back.

"How bad is it?"

"Pretty bad," I admitted. "You're going to have extensive scarring. You might need skin grafts. I'm going to need to keep you on IV antibiotics for at least a week. I already gave you a tetanus shot while you were out, but the risk of infection is still high. You'll need to let me know if you get a high fever."

He looked at me over his shoulder. "You really mad at me, *Mariposita*?"

"Pissed," I snapped. "The last thing I need is any one of you dying on me."

He scratched his head. "I was really only gone for a couple minutes, huh?"

"Yeah. I wasn't about to quit, but I started getting scared that you might…"

"Not come back?"

"Yeah," I sniffed, picking hunks of dead tissue and debris out of his back. "And that would've sucked even worse, 'cause I'd never get a chance to let you know how pissed I was."

Jandro laughed softly. "I'm sorry to piss you off, babe. But I'm not going to stop protecting you. I don't care if I come out on death's doorstep, or end up looking like Shadow—"

"Okay first of all, that's rude," I growled. "He's your friend. He carried your ass in here while I wrangled Dallas's kids. Second of all, there's nothing wrong with how he looks."

"I didn't mean—"

He flinched with a hiss, then stilled. I had most likely probed closed to a nerve with my tweezers. It was impossible for the local anesthesia to reach absolutely everywhere. His back was such a mess regardless, I no longer could tell where I had numbed him or not.

"You're right," he finally voiced softly. "That was messed up of me to say. Sorry, babe. My head's all messed up." He leaned forward, placing his head in his hands. "I keep thinking I saw, or rather *heard*, Hades."

"He was barking his head off for a while," I mumbled absently, steadfast on my task. The stainless steel pan nearby was quickly filling up with dead chunks of Jandro.

"No, I mean like, *speaking* to me. As a person."

I froze, my tweezers hovering in midair. The memory of a man-shaped apparition sitting at the end of the bed came to the forefront of my mind.

"What did he say?"

"That it wasn't my time yet." Jandro raised his head, resting his chin on his hands. "He told me I had a choice

—let go or fight. He would open the gates for me if I let go, but it would be too early." My highly-medicated lover turned to look at me over his shoulder, pupils wide. "Then Freyja shows up and agrees with him. How much oxygen did I have to lose to see that shit?"

"Freyja?" I squeaked. "*My* Freyja talked to you?"

"Well, not your cat. It was some lady. But all I could see was a rough outline, like through fog."

"What did she say?" I demanded, moving in front of him. "What *exactly* did she say, Jandro?"

"Um," he scratched his head. "I had a lot of love to give and beautiful kids to make, so I couldn't die yet. Something along those lines."

"Love and fertility," I realized, muttering the words under my breath.

Reaper had to know about this. I knew he went to see if Shadow had any books on the gods who seemed to present themselves to us. It was right before the attack and I didn't have the chance to ask if he found out anything. Even without knowing, I had no doubt that Jandro really did communicate with Hades and Freyja on the brink of death. I suspected it for weeks, and this confirmed it.

Gods were talking to us. And protecting us.

"Mariposita," Jandro cooed, reaching for my hands. "What's wrong? You look like you've seen a ghost."

I let out a sheepish laugh, closing my fingers around his. "I don't even know how to begin to explain this to you—"

"Something's watching out for us, huh?" he whispered. "Something bigger than us. And they came to us through those animals following you all around."

I blinked at him. "How did you—"

"Reaper doesn't keep anything from me. I've noticed the strange things here and there. Plus," he smirked, "I talked to the source myself. How many guys can say that?"

"Reaper and I have heard Hades," I admitted. "I've heard Freyja only once. Guess I'm just waiting for Horus to say hello now."

"Yeah, he was strangely absent from the conversation," Jandro mused. "But yeah, don't ask *how* I know, but they were real, Mari. I joke about losing oxygen, but they were as real as you or me."

"And if it weren't for them," I leaned in close, "you might not be here now to hear how pissed off I am."

"Still, huh?" he chuckled. "I take it you don't want to practice making some beautiful kids right now?"

"No." I moved to his back and picked up my tweezers, resuming my cleaning of his burn.

"No? Your goddess said we should!"

"Don't care. Still mad."

"That's alright, babe." He turned, aiming a kiss at me. "You can hate-fuck me later."

TWENTY-THREE

GUNNER

I twirled my favorite hunting knife in my fingers as Shadow led us down the hall. Horus clicked his beak, talons squeezing into my shoulder. I swore I could feel his frustration, or maybe I was just projecting my own.

He barely flew during the attack—the tear gas was too thick even for his vision. He was able to get above the smoke clouds, but still couldn't chase the drones that were in the thick of it. My fly boy was almost as blind as we were, and I knew that pissed him off.

Those drones had to have infrared sensors on them. That was the only explanation as to how they were able to drop grenades so close to people. Thankfully, my guys were ready and had plenty of cover. Their ears would be ringing for a few days, but that was a blessing compared to what Dallas got.

Fuck. I stopped my knife twirling and tightened my grip on the handle. Losing him was huge, a wound that the Steel Demons would feel for months, if not years. I barely thought about Python, but Dallas was just a good dude. It didn't feel fair. Why couldn't it have been Big G?

Reaper stopped Shadow and I a few feet away from the holding room where the Sons of Odin were being kept.

"Tell me exactly what happened," he instructed the big guy.

"I was overseeing the scouting team, as you ordered," Shadow reported. "As the smoke cleared, I saw three men approaching the front gate on bikes. They claimed they were not part of the attack, but happened upon it and stopped it. We stripped them of their weapons, cuffed them, and I came straight to you."

Reaper listened intently with his arms folded. After Shadow finished, he looked toward Hades as if waiting for some input from the dog. Whether he got it or not, he continued on to the holding room with me and Shadow right behind him.

"Well, let's meet our saviors, or see if they need to meet their maker. Gentlemen?" He pulled the door open and stepped aside, allowing Shadow and I inside first.

"Youngblood," T-Bone's familiar, gravelly voice greeted me. "Good to see you again, although this isn't the welcome we expected from the Steel Demons."

Reaper ignored him. "These the ones you met at the cantina?"

"Yeah." I studied all three of them, sitting with their arms and legs cuffed to metal chairs. "These are them."

"Where's that pretty little brunette you had with you?" T-Bone was in the mood to be a loudmouth apparently. "Gotta say I'm disappointed she's not in the welcoming committee—"

My knife was in my hand. And then it wasn't. No one saw a thing until the *thunk* alerted the whole room that my blade was half embedded in the wall directly behind our new guests.

And a small cut on T-Bone's cheek began to bleed.

"Sorry, I didn't catch that. You want to ask about our woman again?" I gestured between me and Reaper, who was trying his damn hardest not to smile.

All the bravado dropped out of the Sons right then. Their jaws clenched, throat muscles working with nervous swallows. It was one thing to give *me* shit, but disrespecting our president's property was not a road they wanted to go down. In all likelihood, they'd probably heard stories about Reaper's kills, including Python.

"Didn't mean nothing by it," T-Bone backpedaled. "She ain't my type, anyway. Youngblood, on the other hand..." He trailed off, eyes taking me in appreciatively from head to toe.

It didn't completely surprise me. I got that look from women, as well as men on occasion. What I didn't expect was T-Bone's two club brothers to slide narrow-eyed gazes over at him. It looked like jealousy.

"Enough," Reaper snapped, grabbing an empty chair and spinning backwards to sit in front of them. "Y'all are gonna tell me how you just *happened* upon our club while we were in the middle of an attack."

"Like I told your big friend there," T-Bone nodded at Shadow, "we weren't part of it. We stopped it. You're fucking welcome, by the way."

"How convenient," Reaper sneered. "How'd you do it? And for that matter, why?"

Hades growled at his side, showing his teeth off to the captives. Horus screeched on my shoulder, spreading his wings threateningly as he leaned forward. Shadow stood with his hands clasped in front of him, ever the loyal sentry. I swept my arms back by my sides, showing off the silver gleam of the 9mm under my cut.

Forget the good cop, bad cop routine from the movies. We were all fucking bad.

T-Bone didn't look scared, though. He just dropped all the cockiness and decided to give it to us straight.

"I saw you, Reaper," he began ominously. "At the remains of our clubhouse."

"Did you now?"

"I saw the little memorials you made with the personal objects. You paid respect to my fallen brothers and I thought, that's a man I can ally with. We're all that's left." He jerked his chin to indicate the three of them tied up. "And we need all the help we can get to rebuild."

"Why'd you confront me with my uncle's hand?" I demanded. "Did that have anything to do with your place burning down?"

T-Bone leveled his gaze at me, a predatory smile growing on his face. "Oh, it has *everything* to do with it."

"Don't leave us in suspense now," Reaper growled.

"Governor Youngblood reached out to our main employer, Governor Vance—"

"Of what territory?"

"Four Corners," T-Bone snarled. "Ain't a big terri-tory, but it's essential. Blink and you'll miss it."

"And what do you do for this governor?"

"The usual shit," T-Bone rumbled. "Patrol and protection. Inspection and oversight of trade. Do you want me to get to the point, or not?"

"So you're a good lap dog to politicians," I sneered. "Sure, go on."

"It's not like that." Dyno, the road captain, spoke up for the first time. "Vance doesn't do those power games. His trade is fair, he doesn't keep slaves, and no one goes hungry in Four Corners. But everyone wants a piece of the good thing he's got, so he employed us. Paid fucking well, I might add."

"So he loaned you to Uncle Jerry because...?"

"He gave us the choice," T-Bone picked up again. "It was a temporary contract with a fat payout. We'd been itching to ride somewhere new, break up the routine, so we said why the fuck not?"

"Did Vance know Gunner's uncle?" Reaper asked.

"Not well, I don't think. They'd never done business before, to my knowledge. It sounded like Vance was open to a trade agreement if our contract went well."

"I see," Reaper mused. "Go on."

"So we ride to Colorado—"

"Jerriton," I mumbled.

"Whatever. We get there, and this guy is living like a king. He's like Tony Montana, or some shit."

"Tell me about it." I rubbed my forehead.

"He had a lot to say about you," T-Bone's gaze narrowed at me. "It was pretty clearly a delusion, but he was convinced his golden nephew would fill his shoes one day. The heir to the Youngblood legacy."

"And you probably saw by my reaction to his severed hand, that I want no part in that shit."

"Let's hurry this shit up," Reaper sighed. "How did y'all go from working for him, to cutting his hand off and getting your place torched?"

"Right. The job itself went without a hitch. We escorted a general's troops up from the south—"

"New Mexico?" I barked. "They call it New Ireland, now?"

"Fuck, if you don't quit interrupting me. Yes, New Ireland."

I slapped my palms together and looked pointedly at Reaper. I fucking *knew* it. Uncle Jerry thought he was getting a cut of that land, but Tash would fuck him over, just like he did everyone else. Under the guise of being allies, Tash had invaded my uncle instead.

"Go on," Reaper implored T-Bone.

"Yeah, we finished the job. Went to collect our pay." He sucked his lip between his teeth. "Fucker wouldn't let us leave."

"Wouldn't *let* you?" I repeated. "How does an MC worth its salt *let* someone else control where they're going?"

"Your uncle took us prisoner," Dyno spat. "Those troops we escorted barricaded him in that mansion. And he ordered *his* people not to let us out of our wing. We'd be shot on sight if we were let out."

Reaper and I exchanged another long, narrowed glance. It felt like sheer, dumb luck that Uncle Jerry let me walk away when he did. Maybe because I came alone, and one biker wasn't enough of a personal guard detail. That, or some small part of him still cared about his family enough to let me make my own decisions. I'd never know now. But if I had gone up there at a different time, maybe with more guys to back me up, we might have met the same fate as the Sons of Odin.

"What did my uncle want from you?" I asked when the Sons fell silent.

"Who the fuck knows?" T-Bone groaned. "Our muscle, our connections to Four Corners' wealth, probably. All we knew was, we wouldn't make it home until we fought and clawed our way out."

"How did you get out?" Reaper leaned forward in his chair.

T-Bone gave a smug little grin at the question. "We had ears in the trees and eyes in the sky."

Horus clicked his beak. Hades' ears pricked forward. Us three humans all looked at each other, knowing what that meant without needing to say anything.

"Anyway, we took out our guards and slipped out in the dead of night," Dyno said. "Found your uncle's bedchamber, removed that lying tongue of his, and took our parting gifts," he added with a sneer. "We made it home to the clubhouse after two days. The next day, us three rode out to the Four Corners capitol to report the fuckery to Vance. After that, we rode home to a pile of smoking ashes."

"Our president, VP…" T-Bone choked up, the muscles at his throat working hard as he swallowed. "All our men, their women, kids. Fucking boarded up inside." He sucked in a ragged breath through clenched teeth. "I'm just hoping they died quickly."

Silence fell over the room. Reaper watched the three of them struggle to keep it together. Our loss of one man was a heavy weight in all of us. I couldn't imagine if we lost the entire club.

"I meant what I said the other day," I told T-Bone. "You did the world a favor by taking care of my uncle. But he was a minnow, and General Tash is a shark. I imagine you took out some of those troops you escorted when you escaped?"

T-Bone nodded, his gaze down at his shoes. "Grudge here picked off a couple of squadron leaders. He's good at the silent assassin stuff."

He jerked his head at the man with the long hair and beard, who'd been completely silent. Come to think of it, he didn't say anything at the cantina either.

"That'll do it," Reaper said softly. "Any slight against the general and you're living on borrowed time."

"He was probably hoping to use them after getting my uncle to surrender," I pointed out.

Reaper nodded his agreement. "We'd been working with Tash, until we fulfilled our usefulness a couple months ago. He turned one of our own against us and tried to take us out. We escaped, but it's been a shitshow of trying to stay ahead of him ever since. We lost one good man in the attack today."

"My condolences." T-Bone actually sounded sincere. He sighed tiredly. "We were hard up trying to figure out what the fuck to do. After meeting Youngblood here, we decided to swallow our pride and see if y'all would offer refuge to some homeless strays." He let out a bitter laugh. "Just our luck that we'd roll up to find fucking drones bombing your place."

"How'd you stop them?" Reaper's knuckles were white on the edge of his chair. Finally, the question we'd all been waiting for.

"Found a few small teams of well-camouflaged asswipes. First waves were close, only about a hundred yards from your wall. They triggered the launchers that tossed the tear gas over. Must've buried those things ahead of time in the dead of night."

"Shit," Reaper and I breathed in unison.

Our night vision was our biggest weakness, and that fucked us. Horus was a daytime predator, so while we saw every blade of grass moving when the sun was up, there was no way we could catch everything at night.

"Second waves were about a quarter mile out," T-Bone continued. "They controlled the drones. Pretty fancy setup, too. And so well-concealed, we almost missed 'em."

"But you didn't." Reaper peered at him shrewdly. "How?"

"Like I said, scythe-man," T-Bone smirked, noting his patch. "Ears in the trees. Eyes in the sky."

"Long story short," Dyno cut in. "We killed them, destroyed the controllers, saved the day. Want to stop treating us like the bad guys now?"

Reaper tented his fingers in thought for a few moments, then stood from the chair. "Take off the restraints, but they're staying in here for the time being." As Shadow walked up to unlock their cuffs, the president turned to me. "Bring these guys some food and water, then put people on their door. Twenty-four hour shifts."

"You got it, Reap."

As I turned to leave, a snarl and a curse made me pause.

"Fucking Demons," Dyno hissed, rubbing at his wrists, now free of restraints. "We save your fucking asses, tell you our whole story, and you *still* treat us like prisoners?"

"Easy, Dyno." T-Bone leaned back in his chair, his posture relaxed. "We had to decide if trusting them was worth the risk. Let them make the same decision."

"Listen to your sergeant," Reaper warned.

With that, he followed me out the door, with Shadow bringing up the rear.

MARIPOSA

"This is fucking humiliating," Jandro moaned.

"You want me to get a wheelbarrow?" Shadow huffed, bouncing Jandro higher in the piggyback position he carried him in.

"No, that's even worse! Mari, why won't you let me walk?"

"'Cause I shot you up with local anesthesia everywhere, and I don't know the extent of your nerve damage," I explained, not for the first time. "If you stumble and fall, you could end up worse for wear."

"I'd much rather stumble around like a *borracho*. Shadow sucks as a ride."

"I'm happy to drop you on your ass if Mariposa says I can."

"No," I huffed. "Your fucking ego is not giving me extra work to do tonight."

"But you *love* taking care of me," Jandro goaded.

I ground my teeth, still fighting the residual anger at his stupid act of bravery. "Don't push your luck."

I pushed open his front door and held it open for Shadow to follow through. The large man carefully lowered his friend to the couch. Freyja had already jumped up beside Jandro, waiting for him to settle so she could find a place to curl.

"Stop!" I yelled, letting the front door close. "Don't move."

Jandro froze, propped on his forearm as he was about to lie down. "What now?"

"Lie on your stomach, not your back." I gestured for him to roll over. "Nothing should press on your burn, aside from the bandages. Plus, it's gonna hurt like a bitch when the anesthesia wears off."

He flopped onto his stomach with a heavy groan. "How long do I gotta lay like this? I'm not a stomach sleeper."

"Until you're mostly healed. At least a few weeks."

"A few *weeks*?! What if I suffocate when I'm facedown?"

"Figure out how *not* to!" I pinched my forehead, turning to Shadow. "You see what I have to deal with?"

He actually cracked a smirk. "Welcome to my world."

"Want to trade places?"

After such a long, awful night, on top of Jandro going from human shield to whiny baby, I couldn't resist some lighthearted banter. Imagine my pleasant surprise to find Shadow receptive to it, not a twitch of discomfort on his face.

"Sorry, medic," he returned. "He's all yours."

I released a dramatic, disappointed sigh. "Well then,

maybe you can help me dispose of his body, if it comes to that."

Shadow's mouth twitched as if fighting laughter. I wished he would just let it out. I would've loved to hear that sound, just a single moment of uncontrolled joy from him.

"That, I can probably help with," he played along.

"I'm hurt," Jandro moaned, watching our exchange. "My roommate and my woman, plotting against me before my very eyes!"

"So do what your medic says without bitching." I sat down next to him, leaning over to kiss his least-damaged shoulder. "And we won't have a problem," I added in a sweet voice.

He let out a wordless moan into the couch cushions, while I peppered his face and shoulders with kisses to let him know I was kidding.

"Hey." He lifted his head abruptly. "Has anyone told Andrea what happened?"

Something tight and uncomfortable squeezed around my heart. "I've been fixing you up all day."

We both looked to Shadow, who gave a small shake of his head. "I was with Gunner and Reaper, talking to the Sons of Odin."

"Someone should check on her." Jandro's hands closed around the edge of the couch cushion. "Fuck. I don't know if *anyone* knows about Dallas yet—"

"I'll tell her." I stopped his movement with a hand on his arm. "She needs to be the first one to know."

"You don't need to carry that burden, *bonita*," Jandro said softly. "Find Reaper and get him to tell her."

I shook my head. "He's got enough on his plate. Besides, I checked Dallas's body myself. She should hear it directly from me, before someone else has a chance to give her wrong information."

"Why you always gotta be right?" Jandro sighed. "Shadow, go with her."

"No, that's okay—"

"Babe, don't fight me on this." All the humor was gone from Jandro's voice. "We still don't know for sure how safe it is. I'd feel a lot better if Shadow was with you."

I looked at Shadow's dark, looming figure still standing in the middle of the room. "Do you mind?"

"Not at all," he said quickly, then hesitated. "I'll stay back a bit when we reach her house. I don't think Andrea likes me."

"Why?" I demanded with genuine disbelief.

Jandro disguised a laugh with a cough.

Shadow's eyes slid to him before returning to me. "I think it's because I scare her children. I, uh, accidentally made her son cry once."

Jandro looked like he was dying to tell the story, but my mood for fun and humor had vanished. I was about to tell someone the worst news they would likely ever receive.

"Let's get this over with." I started for the door.

"Hey." Jandro grabbed my hand at the last moment, tapping his lips as he pulled me back to him. "*Beso*."

I lowered onto the floor next to the couch to kiss him deeply, all the tension and anger draining out of my body. I savored the kiss of my living, breathing man—

holding onto the warmth pulsing from his mouth to mine and shutting everything else out.

At the end of all this, I still had my man, and Andrea didn't have hers.

"Te amo," I murmured, my lips refusing to lose contact with his.

"Te amo, mi Mariposita," he whispered. "Hurry back to me."

Now the last thing I wanted to do was leave, but I forced myself up, and headed for the door where Shadow waited.

Andrea lived only four houses down, at the end of the block. We began our walk together in silence as cool, quiet darkness settled over the day that had been so chaotic.

"Thanks for coming with me." I hugged my arms around myself, even though it wasn't that cold. A memory of the man walking alongside me, his arms around me in a hug and my head in his chest, flashed through my mind.

"It's no problem," Shadow answered. His gaze was fixed straight ahead when I glanced at him, long strides keeping pace with my hurried steps. "How, um, how's your tattoo?"

"It's fine. You know, itchy."

Neither one of us seemed able to hold a conversation to distract us from the one about to happen. Andrea's house loomed up in front of us a long, tense minute later, and yet all too soon.

We stood at the bottom of her driveway, where Dallas's lifted truck was parked.

"You okay to stay back here?" I asked Shadow.

"Yeah," he swallowed. "If you don't mind. I don't...I don't want to make anything worse for her."

"That's awfully considerate of you." I forced a smile and exhaled quickly. "Okay. Wish me luck."

"I'll be right here," he promised.

I walked up the driveway, each of my feet feeling like lead. As I raised my fist to knock, I silently prayed that she already knew, that I wouldn't be the one to shatter her whole world.

She opened the door right after my knock, looking confused and worried, but that was all.

"Mari! What the blazes is going on? We got the order to stay inside and hide. Is it over now? Where are my children?" Her dark hair, streaked with a few gray strands, was held up by a red bandanna. Bright blue eyes, lined with a few crow's feet, peered at me for answers. Answers I didn't know if I'd be able to give.

"There--there was an attack," I stammered out. "From the air. Drones dropping grenades. The kids are safe. They're at the clubhouse with, uh, Martha, I think."

"Oh, thank God!" She pressed a palm to her chest and leaned against the doorway. "They're at the club-house, Elise!" she yelled into the house.

"Told ya our boys would keep the babies safe!" Another woman walked up to the door, someone else's wife I didn't know as well. "Is the coast clear? Can we come out?"

"Andrea," I started, fighting the closure of my

throat, the desperation to not hurt her. "I came to tell you about Dallas."

The smile dropped from her face as she straightened up. "Did my silly old man get himself hurt?" She tried to laugh, but it came out hollow.

"I'm—I'm *so* sorry..."

She stepped closer to me, grabbing my shoulders, though I barely felt it. "Tell me the truth, hon. Is he hurt bad?"

I tasted blood from biting the inside of my cheek so hard. "He...he didn't make it. There was nothing I could do. It happened so fast. I'm sorry, Andrea."

She didn't make a sound, but her friend behind her gasped. "Oh no. Andy..."

"My husband's dead?" she demanded.

I nodded, my whole face sore from trying so hard to keep it together. "It was instant, painless." Like that made the situation any better. "He saved the kids from getting hit."

That last bit of information seemed to be the trigger. Andrea released a choked cry, her knees buckling underneath her. I moved in to support her, but her friend was already there.

"Oh, Andy. I'm so sorry, honey..." Her friend's tears fell freely, soaking Andrea's red bandanna as she held the new widow's head to her shoulder.

Dry, heaving sobs wracked Andrea's whole body. Pained moans escaped her, like she was dying herself. Her body slumped against her friend, all strength gone.

"Come sit down, honey," her friend sniffed, dragging

her to the couch. "Oh my god, I can't believe he's gone..."

I reached forward and pulled the front door closed, then stepped numbly down the driveway. My purpose was fulfilled and I was no longer needed.

It occurred to me that I'd never had to do that before. Sure, patients had died in my care, but it was on war-torn battlefields. I had to report the deaths to generals and lieutenants, but never loved ones.

Deaths were tragic, but common enough in my field that I became desensitized. I knew since the beginning that my skills could only go so far, and I never expected to perform miracles.

But Dallas...I never wanted so badly to wave a magic wand and make him reappear, alive and well. He would never be a nameless corpse in a mass grave. I only knew him briefly, but he was *someone* to me. And someone more to Andrea, his kids, and the men I loved.

It hurt. I hated that any of us had to lose him.

I met Shadow at the end of the driveway, barely aware that I had walked at all.

"How'd it go?" he asked.

I didn't want to freak him out by being emotional, but I couldn't hold it in anymore. All my resolve was gone in speaking those few sentences to Andrea.

A sob escaped, painful and ugly as it dragged out of my chest. I tried to tell him I was sorry, but another one came out. And then the tears blurred my vision.

"Mari—?" Shadow moved as though to touch my shoulders, then stopped himself. "Shit. I'm sorry. Can I—"

I didn't give him a chance to finish talking. I just squeezed my eyes shut against the tears, as my forehead pressed into his chest. The sobs heaved through my lungs as I cocooned my arms between my body and his.

Not a moment later, his arms wrapped around my back and held me tightly.

TWENTY-FIVE

MARIPOSA

Every Steel Demon wore somber expressions, their hands clasped in front of them. The only sounds floating over the desert were Andrea's soft sniffs and cries. Noelle and Tessa stood on either side of her—each of them rubbing her back and arms. Tessa gently bounced her sleeping daughter strapped to her chest.

Dallas looked like he was sleeping. I knew nothing about preparing a body for burial, but I cleaned him as best I could, and dressed him in his favorite leathers. He was laid on a tarp on the ground, next to the hole dug that morning. His hands were folded on top of his broad chest, like I'd often seen him when he laid on the patio couches during the parties.

But this time his head wasn't in Andrea's lap, her gentle fingers massaging over his scalp, nor were his kids climbing all over him like a jungle gym. He was going into that hole in the ground. And he wasn't coming back.

I held onto Reaper's elbow, listening with my head bowed, as Gunner stepped up to recite a prayer from his worn-out Bible. His grandmother's, he told me right before the funeral began.

I found myself latching onto innocuous details like that. Jandro stood on my other side, solemn face to the horizon. On the other side of him, Shadow's dark eye kept looking skyward. I realized he was watching Horus circling above us.

The passage Gunner read told of sacrifice and faith, of the peace brought upon Dallas's soul now that he was in his final resting place.

Next to me, Reaper's muscles clenched.

When Gunner finished, Reaper gently removed my hand from his arm. He slowly went to stand in the middle of the semicircle his club made around Dallas's body.

"You all probably know I wouldn't have prepared anything to say, even though I felt I should." His voice was rougher than usual. He barely got any sleep the night before, just fitful tossing, turning, and getting up to smoke on the balcony.

"The truth is," he let out an exhausted breath, "there's nothing I can say that'll make this any better." His eyes lifted to address his club. "Dallas shouldn't have died. He's gone because I failed to protect us. Don't!" He raised a hand to silence the arguments ready to burst from twenty open mouths. "I ain't gonna make this a pity party about me. It's about *him*, and what he left behind."

Reaper lowered his hand, resting it on his hip. "Dallas is someone we should all strive to embody. He was a true Steel Demon, living by the code we uphold," he paused, "and dying by it." He turned to look at the body in question. "He ran straight into the path of danger, of death, to protect what mattered most." His eyes lifted to Dallas's two children, clinging to Andrea's legs. "His future. His legacy."

Reaper rubbed the back of his neck, almost sheepishly. "I've asked every one of you, when initiated into this club, if you'd be willing to do what Dallas did. And every one of you has told me yes. You *meant* it. That's why you wear the patch and ride next to me. I take your oaths seriously. But—"

His jaw clamped down, and I clasped my fingers together hard, fighting the need to run over, to hold him to me and let him release his grief. I understood now that it had to wait for a private moment. In front of his club, he had to be the strong, infallible president.

"But it doesn't make it any fucking easier when it actually happens," he forced out through clenched teeth.

I blinked back tears and released a shaky exhale. Jandro rubbed his palm into my lower back.

"I'm not changing your oaths." Reaper's eyes scanned the men standing before him. "I'm not saying this fucking hurts too much to happen again, because it will. I'll do everything in my power to prevent losing another brother, but I only have so much control. We *know* this is a risk of the life we lead. So I want you to ask yourselves honestly," he lifted his chin. "Do you still want to wear the Steel Demon on your back, knowing you could be the next one in the ground?"

———

THE WAKE FOLLOWING Dallas's burial was just as somber, if not more so, only with alcohol. Everyone poured a bit of their first drink out for their fallen brother, but no one seemed able to muster up the good cheer to celebrate his life. His loss brought a dark cloud over a sunny, warm day.

I wiped at the sweat trickling down my neck, eyeing the empty pool. But it didn't feel right to strip out of my floor-length black dress. I piled my hair up in a bun and my upper back was bare, save for the thick layer of sunscreen over my tattoo. I wanted to make sure it was visible today, even though it was still healing, to show my support for Reaper in case any of the other guys started having doubts about their oaths.

As everyone milled around the patio, I stayed by his side, touching him in small ways. His face remained stony as he chatted with his men, but his thumb stroked over my ring every time he held my hand. When I wasn't looking at him, I watched the sun move slowly over the sky, counting the moments until we were alone and he could let his guard down.

Toward the end of the day, as people finished paying their respects and began to head home, he tugged me toward Andrea.

"I'll need your help with this," he murmured, brushing a kiss across my forehead.

"What do you need me to do?" I whispered.

"Just be with me," he sighed and squeezed my left hand, caressing over the ring again until he kneeled in front of Dallas's widow. Releasing his hand, I took a seat next to her on the couch.

"Andrea."

Her tears had stopped hours before, but her face was still puffy. Eyes vacant. Her fingers were limp as Reaper took them in his hands.

"You'll always have a home with us, if that's what you want," he said gently. "You don't have to decide now, but you and your children will always have our protection. Just say the word and the Demons are yours."

I rubbed my palm along her back. Understandably, she didn't react to Reaper or me.

"My sister can stay with you," he offered. "My dog is here to guard you at any time. If any of the men try to…to crowd you before you're ready, just let one of us know."

Andrea lifted her hands out of Reaper's grip, and leaned away from my embrace. "Thank you, Reaper," she said flatly. "If you don't mind, I'd like to go home now."

———

"SHE FUCKING HATES ME." Reaper slammed his heavy glass tumbler on the kitchen counter and poured a generous amount of whiskey into it. "As she should."

I walked up behind him, and he stilled at my light

touch on his waist. Turning my head, I laid my cheek on the center of his back as I hugged him from behind.

"She's heartbroken," I murmured. "The love of her life is gone. She's going to see him every time she looks at her children. Sure, she probably blames you for some of it, but that's part of her grieving."

Reaper turned to face me, his body stiff, but he didn't remove my arms from around him.

"Have you ever lost someone you loved? Someone you thought would always be there?" His voice was still rough from lack of sleep and chain smoking, which made the question sound like a harsh accusation.

"You know I have," I retorted. "My dad. And then my mom. I don't even have the closure of knowing if they're really dead or not."

"Closure," he snorted, like the word amused him. "A whole fuck-ton of good that does to make you feel better."

I stepped away, letting my hands fall to my sides. He clearly wasn't about to let his guard down tonight, to spill out his grief and sorrow in my arms as we fell asleep together. He was wounded by grief, by ego, and by the pressure he put on himself to protect and lead.

Those wounds were not something I could heal right then.

"You know what's fucked up?" He took a deep swallow of whiskey. "I never told Andrea I was sorry. I wanted to, but," he turned back around, pouring more into his glass, "I fucking hate those words. They're just so hollow. They don't *mean* anything."

"But you mean them." I placed a hand on his arm, watching the internal conflict he struggled with.

"More than anything," he whispered, head bowing low. "Daren at least knew what was coming. He made that choice himself. But Dallas…it's all wrong. He should still be here."

Reaper gently removed my hand from his arm. "You should spend the night with one of the other guys, sugar. I'm not going to be great company for a while."

He was right, but the statement still stung. "I don't want you to be alone."

"I won't be. Hades'll be with me."

The dog raised his head from the floor at the mention of his name. He looked calm and regal, paws stretched out in front of him as he observed us.

"I'll be with Jandro," I told Reaper. "I need to keep an eye on his burn, anyway."

"Okay." For a moment, he looked like he didn't want me to leave. Longing and love softened his features as he leaned in for a kiss.

"Do me a favor?" I murmured against his lips.

"Anything." His arm on my waist tightened slightly.

I pulled back to see his whole face clearly.

"Let your brother in," I whispered. "Let Daren talk to you. He communicates only with Noelle because you shut him out."

I slid out of his embrace before he could ask any more, not that I'd be able to tell him anything that Noelle hadn't said.

Before leaving I knelt down next to Hades,

scratching over his velvety fur. "Take care of him," I whispered. "He needs you now."

The dog, or god within, didn't respond with words. I didn't know what to expect, but it wasn't the weight of a warm hand on my shoulder. Even so, a sense of comfort washed over me, and I bowed my head in a silent thank you.

TWENTY-SIX

JANDRO

"What did he do?" I stared at Mari as she walked in, even though she didn't meet my eye.

I saw it in her posture, though. In the way her shoulders slumped forward, and the pinched tightness of her brow.

When she didn't answer me, Gunner backed me up. "What happened, baby girl?" He was sprawled on my couch, boots up on my footstool. I didn't have the energy to tell him to take his damn shoes off.

Mari dropped her supplies on the coffee table and sat down next to me. "Nothing, he's just," she sighed, peeling away the gauze on my back, "being Reaper."

"Dallas's death doesn't give him an excuse to be an asshole." I ground my teeth against the odd sensation of my injury.

It didn't hurt exactly, but I felt a weird pinching and pulling, like my muscles were too tight. Sometimes an area would seize up or suddenly go numb. Mari said it was because my nerves were damaged, and my brain was trying to communicate with what was no longer there.

"He wasn't being an asshole," she protested, inspecting my burn closely. "If I insisted on staying with him, it might have gotten to that point, though."

"Good thing you didn't," Gunner remarked.

I tossed a smile his way. "You're starting to get the hang of this group thing, huh, bird boy?"

"Yeah, whatever." He flung a hand at me, but an adoring smile crossed his lips as he watched our girl tend to me.

"How's it lookin' back there?" I could only turn my head so far to look at her. My neck muscles felt like they'd been shortened by several inches.

"Good," she muttered, dabbing something all over my back with a gloved hand. "Really good, actually. You're healing faster than I thought you would." Then, in a lower breath to herself, "I don't know why that surprises me anymore."

"When can I ride?" I dropped a kiss to her shoulder.

"Getting *way* ahead of yourself, *guapito*. I don't even want you out in the sun for at least two weeks."

"Two weeks?!"

"Do you know if anyone has a humidifier?" She started pressing fresh gauze onto my back. "Your skin needs to stay hydrated to heal."

"I got parts in the shop. I can make one."

She gave me a wide-eyed stare before laughing softly. "Of course you can."

"Maybe a better question is," I dragged my lips from her shoulder to her ear, "when can *you* ride?"

I felt the grin at the edge of her jaw. "Well, my seat still works, doesn't it?" Her fingers trailed up my thigh and I never felt so alive since coming back from the dead.

"Even if *that* burned off, I have another place for you to sit." My tongue darted out, dragging along her earlobe with my teeth.

"I don't know how you can be in the mood right now," she sighed, though her grin never faded.

"It's easy when I'm right next to you." I pressed a slow, smoldering kiss to her jaw. "And after the last couple of days, I think we could all use some feeling good."

"Am I included in that *we*?" Gunner rested his chin in his hand as he smiled at us.

"Yes," Mari and I said in unison. "And you're not just watching this time either," she added.

"That took convincing," I squeezed her knee with a chuckle.

She looked at me, face etched with concern. "I still don't want you to—"

"Put pressure on my back. Yeah, yeah, I know." An idea struck me right then. I stood her up, spun her around, and smacked her ass in Gunner's direction. "Gun can take you lying down. I'll be standing."

She gave me a coy look over her shoulder on her way to the bird boy. "Shadow's not home, is he?"

"Don't really give a fuck if he is." I followed like a predator, staying one step behind her as she lowered into

Gunner's lap. He grinned like he won the fucking lottery as she leaned toward him. "Hey, baby girl."

"Hi, handsome," she returned sweetly, before kissing him.

I don't know how he did it that one time with all of us, just watch her without touching her. That could never be me. I needed contact with my woman like I needed air to breathe.

While the two of them had fun, I did the work. Gunner kissed her, and I lifted her clothing up and out of the way until they littered my living room floor. My dick punched a hole in my jeans as he kissed every inch of newly exposed skin. Our girl sighed so sweetly, still reaching behind her to feel for me.

"Not going anywhere," I promised her, my mouth against her nape. "Just work on him for me."

Her attention returned to Gunner, getting him out of his clothes while I stepped back for a moment. I pulled apart my belt buckle, letting my jeans fall as I choked my dick in my fist.

I lasted for all of about five seconds watching. Her feet hit the floor—calves, thighs, and mouthwatering pussy on display, as she worked Gun's pants down to his knees. When she bent over to draw him into her mouth, I couldn't stand it any longer.

Her pussy called to my tongue like a magnet. I descended on her like a starving man, holding the back of her thighs in place with both hands.

She made those sexy little moans around Gunner's cock, while her sweet wetness coated my tongue. Gun was being noisy too, cursing and grunting as she took him down her throat. Hearing him was kind of hot too, I had to admit. Not that *he* did anything for me, but knowing our woman was so good at what she did. Mari was meant to be pleased by multiple men. I couldn't thank whatever higher powers enough that I got to be one of them.

"I need to be in you," Gunner groaned.

Mari's panting breaths and soft whimpers told me her mouth was free. "Jandro," she whined.

"Mm-mm." I smacked her cheek to the right side of my face. I wasn't done feasting.

"Please—ah!"

Her sweet begging got cut off by kissing sounds. I rolled my tongue through her flesh, sucking her decadent lips into my mouth. She was drenching my face, thighs quivering with her oncoming release. I loved this part so much. When she was so close to the edge, practically in tears from nearing the crest of her pleasure.

Reaper liked making her come fast and often. I liked to take my time and draw it out of her slowly. And now that he was too busy being a moody bastard to boss me around, I was gonna make her come my way.

"Jandroooo," she whimpered louder.

I pulled my face away, looking around her ass toward her head.

"Yes?"

Her beet-red face was on Gunner's chest, her whole torso draped over his legs. He just smiled down at her, so beautiful and frustrated. His hands petted her hair and stroked her back.

"Please let me come."

Her hand slid down in a desperate instinct to touch herself, but Gunner snatched it and held her forearm against her back.

"He'll take care of you, baby girl," he whispered soothingly, dropping a kiss to her forehead. "Just let him."

"Listen to your man." It pleased me more than words could say that Gunner went along with it. We discussed nothing beforehand, but he instinctively knew his role—to soothe her while I tortured her.

I took my time returning to my work, leaving a sizable bite mark on her ass before devouring her tender flesh again. Her clit begged for attention and I held out as long as I could before giving it. She couldn't even stand anymore, her legs draped on the couch on either side of Gunner, before I sucked that sweet pleasure button into my mouth.

Her release was instant and beautiful, sweeping her from head to toe in shivers and convulsions. I drank my fill of her orgasm, letting her ride my face through the aftershocks.

Gunner was enough of a good sport to wait until I pulled away before he seated her on his dick. She was still exhausted, just slumped against him while he moved beneath her.

"Sorry, I..." she trailed off breathlessly, head heavy on his shoulder.

"Baby girl." He cupped her face in his hands, forcing her to look at him. "Don't ever be sorry for feeling *that* good."

I hid a smile behind quickly wiping my face with a

hand towel. He really did get it. It took a hell of a time getting him here, but he really did fit in seamlessly with us. And most importantly, he treasured her.

Gunner held onto Mari's face, his eyes locked on hers as he kept rolling his hips beneath her—putting in the work while she caught her breath.

It didn't take long for her to take the lead, using his shoulders for leverage as she bounced on his stiff length.

"Hold on, hold on." He grabbed her waist, holding her poised above him before she could sink back down. "My turn for a breather," he said with a sheepish smile. "You just feel too good."

I didn't say a word, just came up behind her. I took her hips from his grip, and sank into her in one long stroke.

"Ohhh..."

Her moan was equal parts surprise and unabashed pleasure. She looked at me over her shoulder and that beautiful, sex-flushed face told me all I needed to know.

She loved fucking both of us.

I pounded her hard, holding nothing back as I watched that perfect ass bounce off me. The moment I started feeling close, I pulled away so Gunner could have her back.

Fuck, I could do this all day. Maybe I really did die because my idea of heaven was this right here.

Gun braced his arms around her back, holding her to his chest and moaning into her neck as her second orgasm squeezed around him. She barely came down, before he lifted her off again.

"Too good. Too fucking good," he moaned. "Feels like I'm fucking fourteen years old again."

"Don't let it get to you, man," I said, sliding in again. "We can't always be studs."

My cock felt as heavy and solid as iron. I was already getting close again too. Rather than pull out, I slowed down, drawing out my thrusts as my thumb rested just over Mari's ass.

"You like having both of our cocks, *bonita*?" I circled my thumb around the tight ring of muscles I had yet to touch, just to gauge her reaction.

"Mmm!" She had taken Gunner back in her mouth, bobbing on him greedily.

"Would you want us both at the same time?" I pressed directly on her ass now, just pressure without inserting.

She answered by clenching around my dick in another orgasm, one my stamina was powerless to resist.

"Fuckkk..." I drove into her with a crash, her pussy closing around me like it would never let go.

Gunner's fists closed in her hair and his head threw back in a hiss as he emptied himself into her mouth.

Now I had some sense of what Mari felt like after coming. I could barely stand, and I rested my forehead on her back.

She released Gunner from her mouth, head in his lap as she looked back at me with a woozy smile.

"Yes," she breathed.

"Yes, what?"

"Yes, I want you both at the same time." She hid her

face for a second, like there was anything left to be shy about. "It would be a first for me, though."

I made my way to the couch, a monumental effort after my soul had just left my body via my dick, and almost forgot to not roll onto my back.

"We'll work up to that," I panted, stroking her face. "Another time."

TWENTY-SEVEN

REAPER

"We have to move."

I placed my elbows on the table, my head in my hands. At my side, I felt Hades' nose nudge against my thigh. Across the conference room, I felt the weight of the eyes of my men as heavily as boulders.

On some level, I knew it would come to this. Hell, I probably knew it deep down from the first attack. Tash knew where we lived, where we stored our resources. And each attack was only escalating. We couldn't afford to be here for his next attempt.

The more I thought about it, the more I became certain that the Sons of Odin's clubhouse was a warning to us.

"Reaper."

"I heard you, Jandro," I snapped, dragging my fingers through my hair. "But where?"

He couldn't shrug because of that fucking burn on his back, so he lifted his hands, palms up. "We might have to do the nomadic thing for a while. We've done it before."

"Not with this many people," I argued. "Not with a zoo of animals and a newborn baby, for fuck's sake. We need a place to settle."

"And what's stopping Tash from finding that place, too?" he countered. "Reaper, our people are not safe anywhere. The safest place we'll be is on the road. Because then we can see the general coming."

"Everyone here understands the risks of rolling with an MC," I said. "Safety is never guaranteed. But we're not simple thugs on wheels anymore. We can't just drag everyone behind us constantly. We have a responsibility to those we're protecting. "

"Believe me, I know." Jandro raised a palm to placate me. "We have something *worth* protecting now. But settling can happen later. Who knows, maybe we can move back here after we're done with Tash. But not before then, it's too risky, man. The next attack could end you or me, or one of the kids. We don't want *any* more losses if we can help it."

But Death will come anyway.

Did I think that? Or did Hades say it to me?

My dog rested his chin on my knee, staring up at me with those big dark eyes. Wherever that thought came from, I felt deep in my bones that we hadn't encountered all of our losses yet. We could make all the right moves, but we were still gnats that the general swatted at. No true threat, just pests he had to clean out.

"I get what you're saying 'Dro," I rubbed my forehead, "but how are we supposed to coordinate an attack on Tash when we're constantly on the run?"

"Depends on where we ride and who we meet along the way." He lifted his chin, swiveling from side to side in his chair. "How'd the talk with the Odin guys go?"

"Fucking peachy. They're going to be three more mouths to feed from the sounds of it. Three more bodies fucking using up our resources."

"So you trust them?" he pressed. "You're letting them stay?"

"I haven't decided yet," I admitted.

He nodded in the direction of Shadow and Gunner. "What was y'all's take on 'em?"

"I don't see any reason to treat them like prisoners," Gunner shrugged. "It's not their fault Tash and my uncle fucked them over. We don't have to be all buddy-buddy, but us and the Sons are on the same side as far as I'm concerned."

"Shadow?"

"They've suffered a great loss at the hands of our mutual enemy." The usually silent man voiced his opinion without much prodding, which was noticed by everyone in the room. "Now we've lost a brother too, and risk losing everything as they did. I think they're the best allies we have right now."

I lifted my weary eyes to the room. Sleep hadn't come easily lately. "Any objections?"

No one said a word.

"Settled." I smacked my gavel on the table, but my heart wasn't in it. "I'll let 'em out after church. Now how the fuck do we plan a move?"

The discussion was primarily between me, Jandro, and Gunner, with the occasional comment from another one of the guys. Gunner knew the surrounding territories best, all their trade routes, conflict areas, and most attractive places to settle. An hour later, the conference table was covered in maps with a dozen of us leaning over it, and no agreement reached.

It all felt pointless, anyway. Even with the most recent maps only a few months old, borders could have been redrawn since then and areas of peace turned into war zones. We might as well just ride out to wherever the horizon took us. A tempting proposition, to be honest.

"Fuck this shit." I threw my hands up, storming out of the room after going around in circles.

We'd have time to squeeze in one more Fight Night before getting the hell out of dodge, but I wanted to spill blood right fucking then. I wanted to call Dallas back from the grave and shove my fist straight through his jaw. I wanted to yell all the grief in my lungs into his face, and tell him never to die on me again.

I almost went home. If I couldn't fight, I'd drink, smoke, and fuck my woman. But I almost forgot I had prisoners to release.

Turning in the hall, I found Hades already heading toward the Sons' room. He sat by the locked door, waiting for me with wide, expectant eyes.

"Still ain't saying shit to me, huh?" I withdrew the ring of keys from my pocket and unlocked the door.

He only licked his lips and grinned as we stepped into the room together.

T-Bone was doing push-ups on his knuckles in the middle of the floor. Grudge did squats nearby, carrying Dyno on his shoulders.

"President." The sergeant at arms climbed to his feet, panting slightly. "How good of you to visit. Did you bring cookies?"

I gestured an arm behind me, indicating the open door. "You're free to move about our compound as you see fit. The central clubhouse has a kitchen, the medic's office, gym, and conference rooms. There's an empty house on the corner two blocks down that you're all welcome to share." I reached a hand down to scratch Hades' head. "It probably goes without saying, but I'll say it anyway—don't trash the place and don't take more than you need from our stores. You're fucking guests here. We can rescind our hospitality at any time."

"And what a gracious host you are," T-Bone smirked. "You have my word that we won't be a nuisance."

"Sounds like we're still prisoners, with a slightly bigger cage," Dyno huffed, climbing down from Grudge's shoulders.

"Oh, believe me. You are free to go any time you wish," I snarled. "I'll even have my boys roll out a carpet for you. A proper fucking send-off."

"Easy." T-Bone halted Dyno from coming at me with a gentle tap on the man's chest. The touch lingered there, affectionate in a way I didn't miss, before returning his attention to me.

"Times are difficult now, even more than before," he

continued. "I understand why you're all still hesitant to trust us. So I'd like to put an offer on the table."

"Not interested," I snapped.

"Hear me out, Reaper." He took two cautious steps toward me before Hades released a low, warning growl.

"We don't know each other nearly enough to be making offers," I retorted. "I'm being generous enough, just opening my home to you."

"And we appreciate the hospitality, don't get me wrong." He paused, eyes flicking down to Hades before returning to me. "But word floating on the wind says y'all ain't staying here for much longer."

My blood turned to ice in my veins. My fingers clenched into fists at my sides. I just might get my goddamn fight in after all.

"How do you know that?" I took a step forward, seething that he had private intel from my church meeting not an hour earlier. "Who the fuck do you have spying on us? Church is sacred. You should fucking know that, *Sergeant.*"

"A little birdie told me," T-Bone sneered.

The next thing I saw was my fists curled into the worn leather of his cut next to his neck. Dyno shouted something and tried to come at me from the side, but Hades blocked his path. T-Bone's bald head slammed against the window on the wall behind him. I slammed him clear across the room and the rage in my blood still simmered, barely satiated.

"Now that was awfully quick," I hissed, inches away from his face. "Your welcome has been withdrawn. The three of you can kindly get the fuck out."

"Before you do that," T-Bone said in a rushed breath. "My offer was for the Steel Demons to stay in Four Corners. I guarantee you'll have the hospitality of the governor himself, for giving us refuge. It'll be safe for your women, kids, everyone."

"I don't want shit from you—"

"I listened to your meeting through my raven, Munin."

My grip on his cut loosened slightly from pure shock. "…What?"

"I can see and listen through my bird like I'm in his head. That's how I saw you all pay your respects for my people at our clubhouse." He sucked in a breath, shoving my hands away as I just stared at him dumbly. "You can't be that surprised, Reaper. I know your captain has the same ability with his falcon." He nodded down at Hades, who still had his teeth bared at Dyno. "And I'd bet both my nuts that dog is something other-worldly too."

"Why?" I fought to keep my focus on that anger, but it started to dissipate. "Why use your animal to fucking eavesdrop?"

"It's a standard cover-your-ass move when you've been locked up here for three days already," he retorted. "If y'all were planning on killing us, we would've liked a heads up."

As pissed as I was, I couldn't blame him for listening. After sweeping the area, we found the bodies dressed in General Tash's insignia and broken drone controllers. The Sons' story had checked out, and we hadn't exactly treated them with the best hospitality.

"Your raven," I repeated in a dumbfounded whisper, having never considered that gods could come to anyone other than me, Mari, or Gunner. "He told you his name?"

"Yes." T-Bone's voice was now low with reverence. "Munin was one of Odin's two ravens. The other was Hugin, who had chosen our president. We believe Hugin returned to the afterlife with him."

"My old lady," I breathed. "She has a cat called Freyja."

The thirst for violence was completely gone from my system now, replaced by sheer awe. I stepped back to give T-Bone some space.

"Freyja and Odin share the responsibility of taking slain warriors home," T-Bone said, the tension draining out of his body. "We believe our men are with Odin now. Maybe the man you've lost is with Freyja."

"But I also have Hades," I nodded to my dog. "Lord of the underworld of a different pantheon. And Gunner has Horus."

"Ah," T-Bone smiled. "You have quite the cultural mix under one banner."

"I still don't know what any of it means," I admitted. "I literally looked them all up in a book three days ago."

"That's the thing about gods," T-Bone chuckled. "You never really know what they're getting at, not until it clicks into place."

"Right. Still fuckin' waiting for that part."

He stroked his beard, watching me curiously, if even appreciatively, then folded his arms across his chest.

"I think the gods led us to find each other, Reaper. Don't you agree?"

"I dunno about all that." I headed back for the door, Hades at my side. "So you've got good timing and a special bird. Doesn't mean you're any more trustworthy than before. Not until I see the proof with my own eyes."

"So, you kicking us out of this place or not?" The demand came from Dyno, arms crossed as he leaned against a wall.

I paused in the open doorway, glancing down at Hades. Again, nothing. Not a word or even a feeling. My dog looked back at me, but apparently no one else was home.

"You can stay for now," I answered. "But trust goes both ways, all right? Listen in on me again, I'm slicing your bird into three parts, which I'll feed to the dog, cat, *and* the falcon."

————

THE HOUSE WAS dark when I got home, which meant Mari was still out tending to Jandro, or one of the other injuries from the attack. I flicked on a light, surprised to find Freyja sleeping in Hades' dog bed.

"Why aren't you with your human, rodent?" I knelt to rub her exposed belly, earning a palm full of teeth and claws for my efforts. "Suit yourself," I muttered, heading to the kitchen in search of alcohol.

Three full drams of whiskey later, I realized it was a bad idea to drink alone. But by the time I reached that point, I couldn't stop. Alone, with no one to watch me, my mind went down a road it hadn't in years. I learned to soften up around Mari, but this was beyond even that.

"Fuckin' Dallas," I slurred, dragging my fingers down my face. "Why the fuck…"

His blood was on my hands, a wrongful death that never should have happened. While at the same time, he was a hero. A martyr. Selfless and pure. He'd become a Steel Demon legend, one that our grandchildren would talk about. Everyone would remember him fondly, as a man who was loyal, protective, and warm.

"Dallas!" I barked to the empty kitchen. "Why the fuck did you have to die? It coulda been, I dunno, fuckin' Big G, an' that woulda been fine."

An idea went off like a lightbulb in the drunken haze of my brain, and I nearly missed the floor when I slid off the barstool. Moving clumsily from the kitchen to the living room, I looked around for Hades.

"Hey, dog!" I called out. "Hades, lord of the underworld, whoever the fuck. I needa talk to ya."

A disgruntled bark whipped my head around to the dog bed, where the massive Doberman and black cat cuddled together like old friends. I was too drunk and focused on my mission to notice how strange that was, and stumbled closer to the animals.

"Hades." I lowered myself to the floor, faithful whiskey bottle in hand. "We're friends, right? Partners and all that. Well, I need you to do me a solid." I took a swig from the bottle. "Bring Dallas back."

The dog actually narrowed his eyes at me.

"Come on," I urged. "You know he shouldn't have died. He's nothing like the ones you have me reap."

Hades had the balls to yawn, poisoning me with a face full of dog breath.

"Damn it, Hades!" I pounded the floor with my fist, my desperation turning to anger. "He was a good man, all right? He had kids that needed him, a wife he loved. He never even looked at another woman. He didn't deserve this."

The dog blinked, but otherwise remained expressionless.

"What kind of fucking god are you?" I seethed. "You're just sitting there mocking me! You have me reap for you, and I'm fine with that. But I ask you to spare one innocent man and I get nothing? I haven't heard anything from you in weeks!"

You do not make demands of me, *Reaper.*

The voice knocked me back. Pure fear gripped my heart in a cruel fist and refused to let go. I wasn't even a man anymore, but a lowly, undeserving animal. I felt smaller than when my fathers yelled at me as a boy.

I rule the dead. Hades' face remained unchanged, dark eyes staring at me with an eerie calm as his voice reverberated through all of my senses. *I do not control life and death. I owe you nothing. You are a tool, an instrument for my bidding. But you are human, and even you do not wield absolute power as my reaper.*

"Some fucking god you are," I muttered.

Hades barked, his teeth snapping within an inch of my face. His lips and ears pulled back, snarling at me like he never had before.

All that research and you still understand nothing.

"Then explain it to me!" I cried out. "What are you? What's the fucking point? What do you want from me?"

Another menacing snap of teeth caused me to flinch.

Death is neither right nor wrong. It simply is. *You cannot control or undo it. Once your species stopped dragging its knuckles, you became obsessed with death. How to prevent it, how to use it as a weapon. You obsessed so much about something you could never control, you gave it a face. A name. You gave it a story.*

I leaned back to rest my palms on the floor, still hopeless to reconcile my dog's face with the sound of this voice rattling through my ribs and teeth.

In an ironic turn of events, Hades yawned, *humans gave life to the concept of death.*

"So what, this is all in my head?" I stammered out. "You're just a figment of my imagination, even though Mari has heard you? Even though Gunner has flown through Horus?"

We are manifestations of the divinity within all humans. The dog licked his lips. *Humanity may have brought me to life, but I am very much real.*

Every answer only led to more questions, more *hows* and *whys*. They ran laps in my head, stringing together into gibberish. Mari's curiosity seeped into me, but it only made my head hurt. I wanted to undo everything and go back to never questioning my dog's abilities or what he was.

"My brother." I didn't know why those words were the ones to leave my mouth, but it made sense as soon as they hit the air. Thinking of him was the only spot of clarity in the garbled mess that was my mind. "Daren. Can I talk to him?"

You can, if you are open to receiving him.

The voice that answered was softer than Hades'. It was feminine and almost sweet. Instead of the sound vibrating my bones and organs, this felt like a warm caress on my skin.

Freyja stood and stretched, arching her back like a bow. Sliding her body against Hades, she settled between his front paws with a loud purr.

Your brother is with me. As is your fallen brother-in-arms.

"Why you?" I blurted out, quickly adding, "No offense." It occurred to me too late that these were *gods* and I should have probably groveled or offered one of Jandro's chickens or something.

But Freyja didn't seem offended. *Their deaths were sacrifices. Selfless acts of love.* Her sharp, feline eyes fixated on me. *Rest assured they are at peace.*

"Can I talk to Dallas too?"

No, I'm sorry. She stepped off the dog bed and walked toward me. A cat-goddess purring loudly and rubbing on my leg was the last thing I expected, but a small, almost minuscule, sense of ease washed over me from the contact. It was like a small piece of my grief lifted and evaporated into thin air. And not just the grief for Dallas, but the long-time festering guilt I held for Daren's death.

Dallas is not gifted like your brother, Freyja explained to me. *He cannot communicate from beyond. But his children, the products of his love, will feel his spirit. So will their mother, even after her heart mends and she falls in love again. Their memories of him, their joy in this present life, give him peace.*

My eyes couldn't stop moving from the cat to the dog, to the rafters in the ceiling, to the air in front of my face. The voices seemed to be coming from everywhere. I might have been well and truly losing it, but at least I wasn't the only one. It was time to face the music.

"So what am I supposed to do?"

Freyja answered first.

Protect your people, especially the children. Love your woman with your whole being. And when her heart opens to love another, do not refuse her.

I narrowed my eyes in confusion. So Noelle had to be right. Mari would have a fourth man, but who else would there be after Gunner? He was the last of the men I trusted with Mari's heart, let alone her body.

A low, rumbling growl pulled my attention back to Hades. He stared at me squarely, eyes bright and ears erect. I sucked in a breath, bracing myself. I knew what was coming.

When I give the order, you will not disobey. You will reap.

TWENTY-EIGHT

MARIPOSA

I released my breath while squeezing the trigger once, and then pulled again to squeeze it a second time.

"Nice double-tap, baby girl!" Gunner beamed at me.

"Did I get it?" I lowered the gun and squinted at my target.

"Pretty close. Your groupings are getting closer, see?" He came up behind me, resting his chin on my shoulder as he pointed out my shots.

"Hey, they are!"

"All it takes is practice." A kiss landed on my cheek, followed by the warmth of his arms around my waist, hugging me close. "You'll be nailing those bull's-eyes in no time."

"I have a good teacher." A smile formed on my lips as I turned my head, nuzzling against his mouth. It felt good to smile again, and my falcon boy turned out to be right about target practice releasing frustration.

Not that I could pinpoint the cause of my frustration. Reaper shutting me out again? Maybe.

Nearly losing Jandro to him being a hero? Possibly. Having to leave the first place in years that I called home? Likely. Myself, for not being able to save Dallas's life, however irrational it was? Even more likely.

"I heard you're sleeping with your teacher." Gunner nuzzled my neck, his grin teasing on my sensitive skin. "Bad girl."

"What can I say?" I leaned my head back on his shoulder, reaching up to grab handfuls of that gorgeous hair. "I like working for extra credit."

His warm laughter cut off abruptly. When I looked at his face to see why, his blue irises had just returned from rolling back in his head.

"We're about to have some company," he muttered, reluctantly untangling from me.

"Who?"

"The Sons." He became preoccupied with checking and reloading the magazines of our guns. "They're not close enough to hear us yet."

"What's your take on 'em?" I picked up my favorite handgun and began reloading it myself.

Gunner's face brightened as he watched me do it just as he had instructed me. "I dunno yet. I don't *dislike* those guys, just don't know 'em well enough to say. Offing my uncle definitely puts them in a pro column though."

"Are they going their own way when we leave? Or coming with us?"

He clicked his tongue. "Sounds like they're coming along. They don't exactly have anywhere to go."

Heavy footsteps crunched over the rocky ground as the three Sons of Odin approached.

"Mornin'," greeted T-Bone, accompanied by a caw from the raven on his shoulder.

Freyja, who'd been scratching one of the fence posts, arched her back and hissed in reply.

"Don't mind my cat," I grumbled, glaring at her like I would a petulant child. "Good morning."

"She's protective of you," T-Bone said with a small grin of understanding. "And I'm a stranger. No offense taken."

"Can we help you boys?" Gunner's hand slid possessively around me, resting low on my hip. I bit my lip to hide my smile, the touch making my insides dance and flutter.

"Just going around being neighborly, making our introductions," T-Bone remarked. "You two know us already, so figured we'd check out the target practice."

"We haven't formally met the third of your trio." I lifted my chin at the quiet one hanging in the back. I'd yet to hear a word from him, or the Sons mention his name. He reminded me of Shadow.

"That's Grudge," T-Bone turned to acknowledge his silent friend. "He ain't much of a talker. Prefers to listen and observe."

The tall guy, Dyno, lifted his eyebrows slightly as if daring me to talk shit. To ridicule or write off his friend for being different.

But I just shrugged and looked past the two men in front to address him directly. "Fair enough. Nice to meet you, Grudge." Then I returned to loading my handgun.

The raven fluffed his feathers and let out a cackling set of caws that sounded like laughter. T-Bone and Dyno visibly relaxed.

"So," T-Bone eyed the arsenal of weapons laid out before us. "What's the Steel Demons weapon of choice?"

"We like our rifles here." Gunner leaned on a fence post, relaxed and in his element. "Handguns while riding, 9mm usually. Sometimes automatics. Me and a couple of the guys are into knife-throwing, too."

"You put scopes on these bad boys?" Dyno broke off from his pack, meandering over to admire Gunner's collection with a closer look.

"Nah," my blonde demon answered with a smirk. "Me and Shadow especially don't need 'em. We train all the guys to shoot without scopes, because you're more likely to use them as a handicap. Without em, you'll learn to be more accurate using the eyes God gave you."

Grudge followed Dyno to admire the guns and nerd out with Gunner, while T-Bone bumped into me with his elbow.

"Mind if I share your target, little lady?" He pulled a matte-black handgun from his holster and set it down next to mine, followed by a series of magazines of all different sizes.

"Suit yourself." I felt Gunner's eyes on me from several feet away. If T-Bone so much as looked at me wrong, I knew my man's weapon would be drawn faster than any of us could blink.

And that was *if* I wasn't faster while right next to the big sergeant at arms.

"You can stop thinking about shooting me. I'm a fucking gentleman," he chuckled, slapping his first magazine into his gun. "Besides," he lifted his weapon, tattooed arms extended straight in front of him, "pretty as you are, you're not my type."

He fired off a series of rounds, each trigger squeeze relaxed and controlled. I saw his first bullet hit the golf-ball sized red center of my target, but none after that. The center hole just got bigger as each subsequent shot chipped away at the cardboard. I'd only ever seen Gunner shoot that accurately.

"Nice work," I said, keeping my voice light. "And by not your type, you mean…?"

He popped the release on his mag, shooting me a playful grin. "I like dick almost as much as you do, Mrs. President."

Heat flooded my face, having nothing to do with the desert sun. I had suspected that T-Bone swung that way. More out of a gut feeling than anything he actually did. Neither he, nor the other two Sons, looked at me the way men usually did. Even with the protection of my men around, it was a relief not to be the object of yet another heavy stare.

T-Bone looked down to load another mag, his playful expression falling, turning distant and somber.

"I loved my president, too," he murmured, before raising his weapon and firing off another dozen rounds.

"I'm sorry," I whispered when his gunfire ceased. "I can't imagine going through what you did."

"Y'all might go through it just the same if the Demons don't get their asses in gear." His mouth closed abruptly, lifting a quizzical eyebrow at me. "Sorry, I dunno how your club handles women knowing their business."

"Reaper and the guys tell me everything." I double-checked my own weapon and raised it to take aim. "I'm the medic. I clean them up after business is handled, so I kind of need to know everything."

I squeezed my trigger to release my shots, going slower than T-Bone's rapid fire and checking my aim in between each round.

"Looks like you're becoming quite capable of handling business yourself," he remarked. My grouping made a small pattern just above his bullseye on the target.

"That's my girl!" Gunner hollered from further down the range. He and the two others took turns with long-distance targets and shotguns.

"I'm getting there," I smirked at T-Bone.

REAPER WAS STILL PASSED out on the couch when I returned home, the empty whiskey bottle on its side on the floor next to him. Hades lifted his head from the dog bed, releasing a soft whine as I came over to stroke his head.

"No change, huh boy?" I whispered, allowing him to lick my hand.

Freyja immediately hopped up next to the dog, kneading a soft place on the bed with her paws, before snuggling up to his side.

"Aren't you two the cozy couple?" I remarked as I made my way over to the facedown man stretched out on the couch.

"Sugar?" he groaned as I lifted his head, turning his cheek gently to lay on my lap. He rolled over to face upward with his eyes still closed, but hummed as my fingers dragged over his scalp.

"How bad is it?" I asked.

"Mmph." His brow pinched as he rubbed his forehead. "Seven out of ten. Been worse."

"I'll get you some Tylenol and water."

"No, stay." His arm went around my waist to hold me before I could stand up. "I love you, Mari."

My chest fluttered and I leaned back into the couch. My ring caught the sunlight through the windows, twinkling like a star as my fingers dove through Reaper's dark hair.

"I love you, Rory." My hands moved down to massage his neck.

He moaned at my touch, eyes slitting open. "What have I done this time to make you say my dipshit birth name?"

My fingers stopped moving, contemplating for a moment. "Nothing, really. I guess I'm just worried about you."

"Worried why?"

"I've never seen you hungover like this, for one. I don't like that you didn't want me around after Dallas's memorial. But," I placed a finger on his lips to ensure he'd let me keep talking, "I get it. You're in a tough position with losing Dallas, as his president and friend, plus moving, the attack, and dealing with the Sons. I'm not angry, love. I just want you to be okay." My fingers returned to kneading his shoulders and neck. "You carry such a burden all the time, but you don't have to do it alone."

He let out a deep sigh that deflated his whole chest. "I know, babe. I told you to leave because my head wasn't in a good place after the funeral. I didn't want to hurt you by saying something fucking stupid again."

A surprised breath escaped from my chest. Reaper tilted his head up to look at me, eyes green and clear, while mine filled with tears. I thought I knew before, but now I was certain.

It wouldn't be him. This man would never, ever break my heart.

"Sugar, what's wrong?"

"Nothing." I smiled and wiped my eyes before he could reach them. "You're just the best and I love you."

"I'm not the best." He took my hand and kissed my wrist, his fingers playing with the band of my ring. "That's why you have other men, to love you when I'm a fucking dick."

"I love you even when you are a dick," I laughed.

"And that's why you have my ring." He kissed the underside of the band, then laid my palm flat over his heart as he looked up at me. "I called you my wife to Shadow during the attack, when I didn't know where you were. It just slipped out in a panic, but it's true, Mari. We might not be bound together by any law or god, but you're *mine*. You'll always be mine."

"I bet we know of some gods that'll approve," I

chuckled, raising my gaze to the dog bed. Hades was curled around Freyja, both fast asleep.

"Ain't that right." Reaper wrapped a hand around mine on his chest, his thumb stroking over my palm. "I have a lot to tell you about what Shadow and I found." He pinched the bridge of his nose, eyes squeezing shut. "Soon as my head stops fucking pounding."

"Let the medic take care of that." I leaned down to kiss his forehead, and blinked droplets of tears onto his skin.

I blinked again, the tears rolling freely down my cheeks now. Reaper sat up, a protective hand cupping the back of my neck to pull me into him.

"Something else bothering you, my love?" he asked tenderly.

"I just…" A ragged breath sawed out of me, taking all of my strength with it. I leaned heavily against my husband, melting into his calming heartbeat and gentle strokes of my hair. "I just miss Dallas."

His arms squeezed around my back, lips raining soothing kisses on my face and hair.

"I do too."

TWENTY-NINE

MARIPOSA

"Remember what I said." Scooting off the bed, I gave Jandro a light swat to his ass.

"You'll pin me down under a bike and have your way with me?" he murmured, facedown in his pillows.

"No," I laughed. "No rolling onto your back allowed."

"Si, mami," he answered sleepily, before I crept out of the room to let him rest.

His healing was going well, and I was hoping he might not need skin grafts after all. The damage still limited his range of movement, however, and he wasn't likely to sit with his arms forward on a bike for a few weeks. Thankfully, Reaper decided to hold off on moving until his VP was in riding shape. It would give us time to figure out the logistics of uprooting so many people, and allow us to say goodbye to our home.

I headed downstairs, following Freyja as she scurried down fearlessly. She went straight for the sliding glass door to the backyard, paws up and eyes wide on Jandro's chickens.

"You be nice to them," I told her, sliding up the lock. "They're not for you to hunt."

I cracked the door open and she squeezed through the gap to dart outside. But she bypassed the chickens completely, running straight to the workout area.

"Damn it, cat." I muttered under my breath, my face heating up. "You are absolutely shameless."

Shadow was doing a set of bench presses when Freyja jumped on his thigh. He paused for a moment when he felt her, then carried on with his set like normal. His labored breaths and soft grunts of effort made my pulse quicken. The worst part was knowing that he had truly no idea how hot it was.

Displeased at being ignored, Freyja decided to walk up his thigh and settle on his stomach. She proceeded to knead him, paws moving rhythmically up and down as she purred up a storm. I could hear it all the way from inside the house.

Shadow finally set the bar on the catches and rolled up, holding her gently against his torso.

"Hello again, kitten." He cradled her like a baby in the crook of his arm, scratching her cheeks and chin as her eyes closed in bliss.

His shirt was off, chest muscles flexing as he petted her. With his long hair tied back, I got an unobstructed look at his face for the first time. A long, deep scar cut through his eye, stretching from his forehead to his cheek. My throat closed up uncomfortably. It was a miracle he still had that eye at all.

That scar didn't match the rest of the ones on his body. Whoever made it had taken out something personal on him, wanted to hurt him with more than just a surface level cut. Someone wanted to maim and disfigure him. But by all accounts, Shadow seemed perfectly capable of seeing with both eyes.

I could never imagine wanting to hurt the large man playing with my kitten. He was now curling his fingers into her belly, laughing softly as her claws and teeth dug into him. The evidence was written into every inch of his skin that this man had been hurt deeply, and for many years. Perhaps more than anyone else I ever met, he needed to be loved.

And that scar on his face did nothing to slow the fluttering of nerves that happened now, and whenever he was nearby. If anything, it only amplified my body's response to him.

I turned away from the sliding door, busying myself in the kitchen before he saw me. A few minutes later, I was entranced by a packet of Mexican hot chocolate mix when he came inside, still holding Freyja.

His shirt was back on, hair loose and pulled forward over the scar, the iris of his pale eye peering at me through the dark strands.

"Hi, Mariposa." He greeted me first, no longer trying to hide while I sought him out to say hello or good morning.

He set the cat down gently on the floor, where she proceeded to wind around his ankles.

"Hi, Shadow." Despite his dark, serious demeanor, I

always felt like smiling around him. "Congratulations, I think you have a new cat."

He let out a dry laugh, watching Freyja rub all over his feet like a shameless hussy. "She's not mine. I still haven't figured out why she likes me."

I bit the inside of my cheek. *I can think of a few reasons.*

"You, ah, ready for this move?" My fingers crinkled up the hot chocolate packet, like the sugary brick was the key to breaking the tension between us.

"I think so. Excuse me, can I get past you?"

He closed the distance between us in one long stride, and my senses filled up with the warm, earthy scent of him.

"Oh yeah, sure! Sorry." I crossed the kitchen in a leap, like a gazelle.

"It's okay." He pulled open the cabinet that had been right above my head and brought down a tall glass. I openly stared as he filled it with water from the faucet and drank deeply.

Yeah, I'm thirsty too.

"I'll have to leave most of my books behind in the move," he said, oblivious to my ogling. "But my tattoo equipment should all fit on my bike. I'll just need someone's truck to hold my solar charger and generator so my machine can have juice."

"Are you doing a lot of tattoos before we leave?"

"I have designs in the works for a couple of the guys, but no, not many." He set his empty water glass in the sink. "Why?"

"If you have time, I," my shoulder crept up bash-fully, "think I decided on my next one."

"Oh yeah?" A dark eyebrow lifted, as did the corner of his mouth, just slightly. "What did you decide on?"

"Something that portrays that I'm a medic," I said. "To you know, signify this time in my life if there's ever an end to this war, or the Collapse altogether."

Or, if my body is found before it all ends, someone will know what I did.

Shadow nodded. "What kind of design did you have in mind?"

"I was thinking just the word *Medic* with a red cross on my arm, like the armband the combat medics used to wear in the old wars."

Shadow tilted his head in thought, lips pursing in a way that was almost cute. The thought of kissing him sent my insides fluttering. How would he respond to an affectionate touch? Something more intimate than a hug. I wasn't even thinking of any part of him under his clothes, appealing as those areas were. No, I wondered about kissing that scar on his face, the one part of him he adamantly didn't want me to see.

"Can I show you something?" he asked, quickly adding, "If you don't mind."

I imagined pushing his hair away, letting my fingers trail over the hidden side of his face. "Of course you can."

He turned and left the kitchen, carefully stepping over Freyja sprawled out on the floor. She looked at me and then at him as if to say, *why aren't you pouncing on him? Do I have to do all the work?*

He returned moments later, flipping through a book, before he turned it around and held it out to me. "Have you ever seen this?"

I took it from him, studying the symbol on the open page. "I don't think so. What is it?" The image was of a staff with a snake wrapped around it. My first thought was that it would look right at home on a motorcycle jacket.

"It's called the Rod of Asclepius," Shadow said. "It's associated with the Greek god of healing and medicine. And it was a medical symbol before the onset of the Collapse." He took the book back from me and closed it, seeming embarrassed all of a sudden. "I just thought you might like to see it. You don't have to—"

"Shadow, wait." My hand caught his forearm as he turned to put the book away. "I *do* like it. It's a cool symbol with a lot of history." I smiled at him. "And I bet it would look better on my arm than a blocky red cross."

"I—I thought so, too." He hesitated, glancing down at my hand on his arm. "But it's up to you. It was just an idea I had when you said a medic tattoo."

"You have good ideas." I allowed my hand to drop from his arm. "I'm glad you showed me. Let's do the Rod of Asclepius instead."

"You're sure?"

"Positive." I wanted to hug him again to reassure him and show my excitement, but I settled for smiling and clasping my hands behind my back. "When can we do it?"

"Um, well." He reached up to rub the back of his

neck, his massive bicep flexing. "I can draft a few designs this afternoon. You can pick your favorite tomorrow, and we can get started right after that, if that works for you."

"That works perfectly," I grinned. The urge to hug him was so intense now, my fingers tightened almost painfully around each other behind my back.

If it was anyone else, I wouldn't have hesitated. But I didn't want to push my luck, nor his precarious comfort zone with me.

"Great, good." He lifted a booted foot to gently remove Freyja, who clung to him like velcro again.

Somehow that silly cat eased the tension between us, while shamelessly demonstrating exactly how I wouldn't mind touching him.

Again.

I shoved down the stubborn memory, so vivid, but in a closed-off part of my mind like a distant dream. It never should have happened, and everyone treated it like it never did. But there was no forgetting how the space inside me stretched when it filled with him, nor the heat and texture of those scars under my palms. Scars I itched to feel and explore again.

"Tomorrow, then," I practically skipped out of the kitchen, restraining my own hands behind my back. "I'll be over in the morning to change Jandro's bandage."

"Okay." He licked his lips, flexed arm falling to his side. "It'll be fun to draw. I'll come up with something you'll like."

"I know you will." I forced myself to turn toward the door, despite wishing I could lean my head on his chest again, and this time press a palm to his face. "See you then, Shadow."

"See you, Mariposa."

Epilogue

REAPER

I rolled to my side and found her there. Beautiful and looking like an angel in her sleep. Jandro had scooted near the bottom of the bed, using Mari's thighs as a pillow. Apparently that helped him to sleep while lying on his stomach.

On the other side of me, Gunner slept near the edge of the bed, his long arm hanging down to the floor.

Taking care not to disturb any of them, I scooted off, grabbed my smokes and headed for the balcony. Hades and Freyja waited there for me, their black fur turned silver by the moonlight. My hands were already shaking as I pushed open the doors, and stepped out into the cool, night air.

Of course the moon was full. It never looked so eerie and cold before.

I stuck a cigarette in my mouth and lit it with a trembling hand.

I *had* done this before, and not too long ago, even

though it felt like an eternity. But I never meant it. This time I had to.

No matter how badly I wanted to dive back into bed and pull my woman close.

"What's it like?" I asked.

Freyja wound herself around my ankles, her purr floating up to me.

It's like a dream, she answered. *But it's just as real as you or me. The hardest part for humans is trusting that it's real.*

"Can he—can he hear me right now?" I stammered.

Yes, he always has been able to.

My throat tightened, all the incidents of me cursing what he did running through my head. Every single time, both privately, and to Noelle and Mari, he knew. Never more did I yearn to walk away from this, but I kept my feet rooted to the ground. If he already knew the full gamut of my emotional state, then I had nothing left to hide.

I had to face what I spent a year shoving down. The demon that haunted me the most was the one thing I swore, then failed, to do—protect my family.

And I just wanted another chance to talk to someone I missed so much.

"I don't know what to do," I confessed.

Just begin speaking to him as if he were here, Freyja said. *Because he is here.*

I took a final long drag on my cigarette before tossing it away.

"Okay, Daren," I began. "We're long overdue for a conversation. So let's talk."

___

TO BE CONTINUED IN HELPLESS - STEEL DEMONS MC BOOK 5

PRE-ORDER HELPLESS HERE!

Acknowledgments

Here we are again! A super special thank you to Izzy, Danielle, Telisha, and Janet, who help my books become the best they possibly can be, before being sent out into the world. Your feedback, support, and friendship, are priceless!

Major thanks and fist-pumping to my hype team: Kathryn, Helle, Brandy, and Aleera. Nothing gets me pumped for a book release like hearing from you ladies, whose work I admire and friendships I'm so lucky to have.

PS: I just made up that hype team thing, but too late now, y'all are in it!

An equally humongous thank you to my hardworking ARC team! Your dedication and honesty play a huge part in the success of these books. I appreciate every single one of you!

And last but never, ever least, thank *you*, reader, for joining me on another leg of the Steel Demons ride. We're almost to the halfway point of the series, can you believe it? Thanks for sticking it out with me this far, and hold on tight because there's a lot more to come!

If you'd like to hang out with me regularly, join my reader group, Crystal's Coven. We're a friendly bunch, and I'm always posting teasers and new excerpts there before anywhere else online.

See you in the next book!

-Crystal

About the Author

Crystal Ash is a USA Today Bestselling Author from California. She loves writing steamy, heart-wrenching romance with tortured heroes, especially if they're in a reverse harem. Crystal's other loves include animals, mythology, and well-crafted alcohol, most of which can also be found in her stories.

When she's not writing, she's probably drinking craft beer with her husband or trying to coax her feral cat into accepting affection.

crystalashbooks.com

facebook.com/Crystal.Ash.Romance

instagram.com/crystalashbooks

amazon.com/author/crystalash

bookbub.com/profile/crystal-ash